T0158011

THE FUNDAMENTAL
THINGS

THE FUNDAMENTAL THINGS

Phillip Dibble

authorHOUSE®

AuthorHouse™
1663 Liberty Drive
Bloomington, IN 47403
www.authorhouse.com
Phone: 1-800-839-8640

© 2010, 2011 by Phillip Dibble. All rights reserved.

No part of this book may be reproduced, stored in a retrieval system, or transmitted by any means without the written permission of the author.

First published by AuthorHouse   07/05/2011

ISBN: 978-1-4634-1564-8 (sc)
ISBN: 978-1-4634-1565-5 (hc)
ISBN: 978-1-4634-1563-1 (ebk)

Library of Congress Control Number: 2011909118

Printed in the United States of America

Any people depicted in stock imagery provided by Thinkstock are models, and such images are being used for illustrative purposes only.
Certain stock imagery © Thinkstock.

This book is printed on acid-free paper.

Because of the dynamic nature of the Internet, any web addresses or links contained in this book may have changed since publication and may no longer be valid. The views expressed in this work are solely those of the author and do not necessarily reflect the views of the publisher, and the publisher hereby disclaims any responsibility for them.

PROLOGUE

Madrid December 1936

The crunching reverberations of marching boots came and went, drowned out by the cheers of the Madrilenos as Rick Blaine led the men of the Lincoln Brigade in the parade. Rick's mood was excitement and tension as he ran his eyes over the crowd and the rubble of war-torn Madrid. Flags, banners and posters were everywhere. The crowds cheered and clapped as the non-descript marchers zigzagged around the piles of rubble while doing their best to keep in step. A banner overhead caught in the wind and swayed as it announced, "Viva Espana." Groups of cheering Madrilenos began singing, "Bandera Rosa." As the marchers turned onto The Gran Via Rick saw a huge cloth banner at least six stories high that appeared to have written on it a story or a poem.

I've been in Madrid one week and now I'm going to war, "Rick mused. "Not only that, I'm leading a battalion of men I hardly know marching down a boulevard I've never been on before." He shook his head. His men of the Lincoln Battalion were such a concoction, a mixture of political zealots, some adventurers, while others were simply starry-eyed idealists. This was not a union head knocking; they were no longer just demonstrators protesting a lockout or a wage cut. This was different, for too many of these men would never see sunrise in their native land, some would not see sunset here. Why Spain? They believed, to a man, that the heart of world liberalism beat here in Madrid, and should it's beat be stilled here, it would die everywhere. Did he believe this? Not anymore. He was a leader here, a military man. He sniffed in self-derision. What did he really know of combat leadership? Ethiopia and the Italians. He sniffed again. The Italians. Their buffoon leader, the square-jawed Duce, his antagonist the Emperor Haile Selassie, The Lion of Judah. Were all the leaders of the world like these two, done over and over again with mirrors? Was he any different, ready to espouse meaningless victories?

Now he was here and so were the Italians. His own passions were simpler, the men of the Lincoln Brigade, the people, and his own yet to be uttered idealism. Yet, he felt kinship with no more than half of his men, the rest were too radical in their politics, too consumed with ideology. Frankly, in his mind they were rabble-rousers.

Rick wondered what his father would think of him now. Goddamn commie? But he would admire the leadership position. Yeah he would do that. Perhaps it would close some of the distance between them. Probably not.

The sudden sound of aircraft ended his reverie; apparently the rebels were about to rain on the parade. Down they thundered, the pilots of the German Condor Legion, with their Junkers, Stukas, and Heinkels while Herr Goering awaited the results of his experiment. Terror through air power, death and destruction had entered the emerging depersonalized technology of the twentieth century. Goering had something to prove to Herr Hitler who was not yet interested in committing his new Wehrmacht in someone else's dispute, preferring to concentrate on his plan to occupy the Rhineland.

Rick yelled for his unit to disperse, but they had already scattered in all directions. The street was suddenly a cloud of dust and debris, a cloud-filled cauldron, as the first bomb hit. The explosions tore his ears; people appeared from the cloud, screaming as they ran. Six more bombs struck the area, but none found its mark in the already dispersed brigade. Some of the civilians suffered minor injuries, and wandered around in stunned disbelief, staring first at their wounds, then the sky, then back to their wounds.

The crowds again screamed as the planes, having turned about, came back to strafe the rutted avenues. Machine guns, mounted on the roofs, stuttered their cacophony at the diving aircraft. Oblivious to anything but their objective, the planes came in low and fired their bursts, hitting people, shop windows and street lamps. Rick ducked into a storefront, a toy store. Another explosion knocked him into the store where he collided with a glass case full of Jack-in-the-Boxes. He stumbled over a teddy bear as he stepped back then brushed the dust from his uniform. He walked out amid the screams from the crowd as the planes turned to attack again. His chest tightened and his belly ached as he resought shelter. Despite the defending guns the Condors came in low firing their bursts, the firestorm exploding shop windows and peoples' bodies. Rick whirled around and began running through the rubble. He saw a Lincoln with his face half-gone crash to the ground and he began looking for more of his men. He stooped the retrieve what he thought was a rag doll but it was a child's hand around a rag doll. Depravity! He clenched his fists and shook them at the sky.

The planes abruptly left, the parade was over, and Rick began to rally his new battle mates. He collared a militiaman who calmly saluted him and said, "Orders Captain Blaine?"

"Yes, order them to reassemble at the Brigade's temporary bivouac at University City next day at 0900 hours. And I want a tally of any killed or wounded." He saluted the sergeant and ducked into a smoky bar where a few scruffy looking men stared at him. "Si senor?" The bartender offered.

"Una brandy," said Rick. He sat down, lit up a Chesterfield and waited for his heart rate to settle down. His mind floated again, back to his past and the beginnings of this new chapter in his life.

CHAPTER ONE

Little Rick

Three-year-old Ricky Blaine held out his arms to the man looming above him. The air was redolent with the contents of his bulging diaper. The man's face bore a permanent scowl, but it was his daddy's face and Ricky wanted to be lifted up and hugged. Instead the big man turned away, saying, "Helene, what's the matter with this kid? Why does he need to be held all of the time? You're making a sissy out him.

Ricky's mother smiled nervously and said, "Richard, he never cries. Can't you just hold him once in a while just to let him know you love him?" She picked up the little boy and hugged him.

"Helene you will hug the manhood out of that boy." With that, his father left the nursery and walked down the stairs to his den. Before closing the door he called back, "Mark my words."

Rick grew up always facing this disapproval; he was skinny, awkward and walked like an ape with shoulders slouched and his feet pointing outward. His parents enrolled him in a lab school associated with Princeton University because Helene liked the small, academic, protective environment while his father liked the name "Princeton." Father had gone to Princeton and never forgot it. When he inherited the mantle of Chairman of the board of Blaine Manufacturing he had his office done in orange and black, and strategically placed Princeton memorabilia.

By the time Rick was seven the, bigger more athletic boys were taunting and teasing him. Often they would push him down to the ground and sit on him. Rick would stare up at their belligerent faces and wonder why they always chose him. The teachers ignored these actions convinced that boys will be boys.

One rainy recess, one of the bullies, Billy Hooper, pushed him down, turned him over and wiped his face in the mud. Ricky did not fight back, and when the bell rang he slunk back into the classroom. All of the kids began to laugh at his muddy face and clothes while the teacher looked at him and said, "Ricky Blaine, whatever have you been doing? Get yourself into the boy's room and clean yourself up."

Rick obediently turned around and started towards the rest rooms when Hooper tripped him, causing him to fall into the desks. When Ricky regained his balance he turned and suddenly hit Billy Hooper in the face as hard as he could. He felt Billy's nose fold under his fist, then Billy fell over onto the floor screaming, his face and twisted nose a carmine mass of blood and snot.

The teacher grabbed Ricky by the shoulder and dragged him towards the door. "What in heaven's name are you doing," she screamed. "Why did you hit Billy? That was the meanest thing I've ever witnessed." She started to shake him. With that he retaliated by kicking her in the shins, then he pushed her and she shrieked as she sprawled in a heap on the floor and began to cry.

Later in the principal's office he sat quietly while his father spoke to the principal in another room. His mother sat next to Ricky, wringing her hands in despair. He heard his father's voice echoing loudly behind the closed door. "We're pulling him out of this damn sissy factory and sending him to a real school." With that, the door opened and a red-faced Richard Blaine emerged. He picked up Ricky with both hands and carried him out of the building, Helene in hot, tearful pursuit. His father said nothing to Rick, just deposited him in the back seat of the company limousine and told the chauffeur to drive them home. Richard Blaine hid his satisfied smile from his son and wife.

The next week Ricky was enrolled in a private Catholic boarding school for boys where he remained until the ninth grade. He saw his father at Christmas, Easter vacation, and the one week in the summer that the elder Blaine appeared at their summer home in Bar Harbor, Maine. His mother visited frequently, always obsequious towards the priests, and never inquiring about his behavior.

"Ricky, I'm sure they like you here, they never mention any trouble you've caused. Such a good boy." With that she would kiss him and leave.

Rick remained a loner and preferred it that way. He maintained a rich fantasy life in which he was the all-powerful emperor, controlling every person, every act.

When he had finished his freshman year at St. John's, his father transferred him to a private co-ed high school. He asked his father, "Why am I changing schools? I haven't had a problem here and I like it."

His father replied, "It's time you learned about boy-girl things. I won't have you growing up uninformed. Besides, these Jesuits are dangerous. And, you will live at home now.

Rick became an apt student and a successful athlete. He lost his awkward walk, and was no longer bullied. In fact the boys seemed to like him. He wondered if anyone from Princeton had mentioned the infamous altercation.

He hoped his relationship with father would change but until that day he would practice his indifference and offer himself to no one. Like his hero Nietzsche, he believed that which did not destroy him would make him stronger. Still, some of his nights were spent in the fantasy in which he lived in a loving family, laughing as they frolicked in all that life could offer the economically blessed. He blamed his mother as he loved her believing she should be capable of changing this monolithic man into something more pliant, more loving and open. Yet he knew that she had tried and failed. Instead she turned all her affection to him and her own secret garden. Ah yes, the garden, a poisoned garden whose products were the sweet oblivion that Lady Macbeth sought. Her private mailbox was filled daily with the seeds for her garden, the merchants only too willing to prolong her journeys to the Lethe. These were the memories of his non-childhood that lead him into a young adulthood of distrust and a recognition that he was totally and solely responsible for any personal realization.

He graduated from high school with honors and entered the University of Chicago, majoring in Philosophy and Business: Philosophy for himself and Business for his father. He had few close friends so he was surprised when, at the end of his sixth semester, George Wilson came up to him and asked, "Blaine, how'd you like to go to Europe with me and some other guys? We could have a skidoo time."

"What other guys," Rick asked.

"Torrance, Ballance, and Duell."

"Those are swell guys. How do you know they want me to go?"

"Cause I asked them."

Rick was guardedly elated, this was a great bunch of guys. But why did they want him to go along?

The trip was great and Europe was their oyster. They met a group of American girls on the ship who joined them for the summer. One was Gretchen Van Dyke, a pretty, although vacuous flapper type. "Hey Blaine, Gretchen thinks you're the cat's pajamas."

Rick blushed but he thought she was swell, too. But then his experience with girls was limited. By the time the summer was over, Rick thought he was in love with Gretchen and asked her to be his girl. She laughed, but she agreed. "OK Rick, I'm your girl."

Gretchen was not naïve; the Blaine fortune beckoned and she felt Rick wasn't a bad sort. She allowed him to kiss her and they petted, but her virginity was her future and there was no yielding there. Rick respected that; unaware that Gretchen had "been around" with at least two boys. These ambitious girls moved in tight formations behind their beautiful but empty, undamaged faces and a phalanx of expectations; their goals were soft living and hard cash.

On the return from Europe, Rick was a frequent visitor at the Van Dyke's home. Mr. Van Dyke was a moderately successful broker with Morgan Guarantee, and himself a trust fund recipient. Rick found him easy to talk to and admired his easy grace but he was unaware of the brilliant campaign being waged; a campaign designed to surround and capture one Rick Blaine. When Rick proposed to Gretchen she coyly accepted. The couple was feted at numerous engagement parties, which gave Gretchen an opportunity to flash her ten-carat diamond ring, a Blaine family heirloom.

Rick graduated at the end of the seventh semester because of his outstanding and aggressive scholarship. His father had always assumed that Rick would join him at the Blaine factory and Rick did not disappoint him. Richard Blaine said proudly, "You're a Blaine and someday this business will be yours if you keep your nose clean. I might have hoped for a classier dame than Gretchen, but what the hell, she's got a great body, a fine baby-making machine. Have you had any of it yet?" He laughed, assuming that he knew the answer. Rick was angry and did not reply.

At this point his life was made up of work, tennis, and time at Gretchen's house. They saw less and less of Balance and Duell; Rick did not like their leftist leanings and their talk about communism being the political solution in America. Politics bored Gretchen; in fact, most things seemed to bore Gretchen. More and more frequently Rick would leave her house after a date and feel empty; this despite her urging body and deep kisses that excited him. She was beautiful and sometimes even witty, and very sexy. Still there was something wrong, things that niggled Rick whenever they were alone. He realized that it was all in the conversations they had: she prattled on about the parties, restaurants, her plans for their wedding of weddings and where they would honeymoon. "Would you prefer Paris or London?" She asked, "I prefer London just because of the language, French is far too complicated." Rick finally realized that she lacked curiosity, no lust for the other road. Maybe things would be different after they were married . . .

One morning he came to the office early, his dad's car was already in the parking lot. As Rick approached his father's office he heard the unmistakable sounds of love making coming from behind the door. Grunts, moans, pounding noises, then silence. Did they hear him? He hurried out through the double doors that separated the inner office suite and entered the stairwell. He was angry, humiliated, and finally decided that a confrontation with the old bastard was necessary. He would wait an hour, let his temper cool and then proceed.

At ten o'clock Rick stormed unannounced into his father's office. "What the hell are you doing to my mother?"

His father did not look up at him as he replied, "What's your problem now, boy? How do you see yourself having a right to interfere in our affairs?"

"Affairs are the word all right! You've been screwing around with a girl one-third your age and now I suppose you want to marry her. You're destroying my mother! Screwing a woman in your office, for Christ's sake. Why not do it in the parking lot?

His father chortled, "It's none of your fucking business what I do. As for your mother what's left for destruction? She's done a dandy job doing that herself." Rick recognized that he held no cards against this man, in fact, his father held them all. "If I were you, son, I'd just pay attention to your own vacuous life and do something more with it." Rick left the plant in disgust, impotent before his father's icy wrath.

He drove to Gretchen's parent's country estate. He parked, and as he walked across the broad expanse of lawn he spied Gretchen's teen-age sister Jordan lying in a hammock reading a book. Jordan looked up at him, "Hi, Rick. What's the latest with you? You look like you just lost a pal or two." Jordan was the girl that Gretchen should have been but would never be. Tall and slim, her blonde hair in braids, she looked like a Viking's fantasy. Her blue-gray eyes danced with a playful sensuality that belied her age.

Rick would have loved to tell her about the dispute with his father but elected not to go there. "Not much, Jordan, just a hard day at the tennis courts.

She laughed, "Can't imagine you having a bad day playing tennis. You're unbeatable." Jordan had a huge crush on Rick. She rolled onto her side and said in a seductive tone, "Why don't you forget about boring Gretchen and stay here with me?"

Rick felt his patricidal anger ebbing; he loved joshing with Jordan. "Depends on what you're reading today."

She held up her book and Rick read the dust cover. "Lady Chatterley's Lover" by DH Lawrence. "Shame, Jordan, that's a banned book. Why do you want to read trash when there are so many really good books around?" He felt a surge of big brotherly feelings.

Jordan laughed and said, "Because I'm not supposed to, Ricky. C'mon, don't you get it?"

Rick nodded his head. "You're right, Jordan. No reason why you can't read anything you want to." Rick had issues with those who would meddle with other people's freedom.

"You need to read it Rick, it's about a woman who is the dark side of Gretchen."

"Dark side?"

"Gretchen laughs at your sweetness, Rick. She's a nasty gold-digger, just like the rest of her friends. For an intelligent man you are a naïve callow youth. Plus, I would never do what she does to you behind your back."

"Jordan, what do you mean by that?" Rick's feeling of paranoia heightened.

"Ask your buddy Gregg Duell. I think he knows my sister really well. Watch your back, little Ricky Blaine," warned Jordan. She rolled off the hammock and ran crying into the house.

Rick took a deep inhale from his cigarette feeling his heart pounding with a sudden sense of dread. However the dread was soon replaced by a feeling of release, even repose. He tossed the butt away and walked to his car and drove away. He realized that in most of their conversations, Gretchen prattled on about the parties, restaurants, the wedding of weddings and where they would travel. Would he prefer Paris or London? She had said, "I prefer London just because of the language, French is far too complicated." Rick finally realized that she lacked curiosity and his conversation with Jordan sealed the decision he had just been delaying.

Two days later he called Gretchen, then Mr. Van Dyke and told them he had changed his mind, mumbled an apology, and hung up the phone. After an aimless week in a hotel in the city he booked passage on the *Queen Elizabeth* for Europe and solitude. At the George Cinq in Paris he received a wire from Jordan informing him that Gretchen and Duell were engaged. Rick realized that he felt nothing, then wondered if she had given his ring back to his mother,

CHAPTER TWO

Rebirth

Rick returned to America after a two-month sojourn in Germany and France feeling empty and chronically angry. His mother had met him at the pier when the ship docked. Rick had said, "My God mother, what's happened to you? You've changed so much I hardly know you."

"How about you Rick. You're so skinny and you look so sad." She hugged him tightly and then began to cry. "It's been so hard without you. Since your dad sued for divorce everything is such a mess."

"It's ok, mother. I'm basically fine. How are you getting along? Do you hear anything from dad?"

She sighed and said, "I haven't seen him since you left, but the union is threatening a big strike at the plant and the papers talk about violence. You know your dad; he won't give an inch to the unions. Just like him, isn't it?" They walked to the waiting limousine and headed for the Blaine house. Rick had resolved that he would try to settle his feud with dad as soon as possible. When he tried to arrange a meeting with him, his dad had refused to speak with him.

He got a phone call from Gregg Duell inviting him to a party at his apartment in Manhattan. His parents were a couple of swells, rich and idle. (He had met them just prior the collegiate trip to Europe.) "Balance will be there along with some other guys you don't know. You'll like them."

Rick took the train into Manhattan then cabbed to 300 Central Park West, home of the Eldorado apartments. He walked through the archway through intricate glass doors into the classical entrance lobby. There he was greeted by wood paneling and marbled floor, as well as muralled walls.

The door to 701 was open and the sound of a piano was welcoming. There were a dozen people standing around in the luxuriously appointed room sipping wine and cocktails. Greg Duell walked up and shook his hand, saying, "Hi Blaine . . . welcome to poverty towers. "Rick smiled in spite of himself. "Have a drink, Rick and I'll introduce you to our crowd."

The "crowd' turned about to be mostly young, wealthy, radicalized young men who were talking like Red sympathizers. At first Rick was uncomfortable but his U Chicago experience turned on a different mindset for him. These guys were serious about the poor and downtrodden. The Great Depression had destroyed the economic lives of millions, people were begging for jobs, money and food. The ex-soldiers from the Great War, demanding their promised bonuses, rallied in Washington, DC and had been ousted by the army without any monies being distributed. Many of these men were politicized by this action and were joining various groups, Anarchists, Socialists, and Communists. The anger led to the election of Franklin Roosevelt, the left-leaning consummate politician. The young men in this apartment, wealthy all, chose to support the downtrodden with actions of their own. Rick respected this and was surprised to feel a swell of pride in being asked to be a part of it all. Fuck Blaine Auto! His father could blow and Rick would be happy.

After considerable discussion Rick, Ballance, Duell and a guy Rick didn't know, Mel Melnik were selected to organize the union movement in the auto industry. Rick was elated, he knew the industry, and he knew the inequities in the system. The meeting was over at two AM with plans to meet as separate groups. Gregg Duell urged all the groups to practice silence on these activities. The all were aware of the consequences of leaks.

Rick was attached to the 'Solidarity' cell, made up of mostly University of Chicago alums, guys who had been involved in campus politics and intentionally active in the CP after graduation. Gregg Duell continued in his role as cell leader, or Commissar as his friends laughingly called him. It was, however, not funny to Duell. At a strike planning session he addressed the worker group in his strident, pompous fashion. "Comrades in arms, tonight we have an action to begin." Cheers filled the overflowing hall but Duell raised both arms, seeking quiet. "Thanks friends but things are not that simple. Our worker comrades still don't see capitalism as the enemy so they've been unwilling to take any action against it. That is until we told 'em otherwise." Again, spontaneous cheering. "Wait up now,"

Duell yelled into the microphone. "Wait now, it's not time for cheers. Here's what we've got." Duell then described the strike in action in the same detail that Rick had read in the contents of the manila envelope he had received by messenger several days before. When Duell finished the hall was pandemonium, cheers, backslapping and pumped fist were the rule.

Duell pushed his way through the demonstrators towards Rick. "All right, Blaine. The drill is over, time to move. This action now belongs to you." Rick nodded nervously, his face flushed with tension and he felt he had to hide his hands so no one would see them shaking. Ballance pushed forward, saying, "Yeah Blaine, the stage is yours, you're our top banana now."

"What a pompous jackass," thought Rick. Out loud he said, "Jeez, this isn't Broadway. My role's just to provide a stage for all of this. Forget the theater, guys. I just hope my dad never gets wind of this. He'll call out the damn army."

Duell sneered, "Then it's up to you to see that he doesn't find out." Rick hung around for a while listening to and watching the others posture and pose, then turned and left the building.

Rick sat behind the wheel of his car, his mind a tumult of self-doubt. He jerked the wheel back and forth in his frustration, and then pounded it. Goddamn, his father's omnipotence over him left him disadvantaged even when he knew nothing about the up-coming action. Calmer now he started the car and drove off, speeding down the narrow street. He came upon a small crowd of people in the street standing amongst piles of boxes and furniture that blocked his passage. He stopped his car and rolled down the window, "What's happening?"

"Sorry buddy, we just got evicted from our flats." The man's face was grim as he stared at Rick and the shiny new LaSalle. "Now we got no place to go." Rick got out of his car and looked around.

"What'll you do?"

"Got any suggestions?"

Rick pulled out his wallet and gave the man a twenty-dollar bill. "The man smiled and said, "Thanks buddy, this'll help."

"Sorry to hear about your problems," said Rick and got back into his car. As he maneuvered past the obstacles he heard someone mutter, "Thanks for nothing, you rich prick."

Rick thought about the comments he'd heard, like the "The paranoia of the proletariat." Yet he knew that they had real gripes and knew that his family and other richies sat astride these people. Many of them had given up their kids to the Orphan Trains, trains that took the children from the teeming cities and took them to the vast Midwest. There they were put on display like cattle, ready to be taken in by farmers and others, many of whom would treat them like slaves.

Returning home he raced to his room and began again to study the plan. He read and reread it, taking notes, well into the early morning. In the final analysis his role was simple; he needed to see that two things happened. The first was to be sure his father found out nothing, the second was to prevent him from coming to the plant before the action began. How would he manage this? Take him out to breakfast? The old man never ate out at breakfast; he ate at home in a stately dining room served by a maid with food prepared by a cook. Rick chuckled; kill the cook? He turned on the radio and again Father Coughlin began spewing his hate message. Rick listened, hypnotized by the delivery.

"This is Father Charles Coughlin broadcasting from station WHBI, Newark, New Jersey. As many of you know, I've been blacklisted by the major networks and have had to retreat like a nigger slave to these independent stations. And it won't be long before the commie loving FDR and his Jew friends in the banking world will shove us out of here. We need to withdraw from the likes of them and stay home and fix the problems here. International Jewry and Zionism are natural enemies of the proud United States. Huey Long has it right; it's all about the PEOPLE! We need bank reform; we need money to go to the POOR! Not the relief suckin' poor but the real poor, the people whose jobs have been blown away by the cash famine. What about the two faces of Satan, Wall Street and Communism? Our finest colleges are turning RED! I'll have more to say bout this later in the program." His voice grew more strident as he continued, "The Russian revolution was launched by these ratty little Jews running through Russia, and now they are here! Only the voice of the PEOPLE and the Church can block their schemes. Remember," his voice now thundering, "The Jews and the Reds are out to put you in chains. The Reds are forcing UNIONS on you, God only knows what after that . . ." Rick twisted the dial in disgust. "Damn, the man makes his points with hatred towards his enemies, calls the Jews the Antichrists, and yet can call himself a Catholic and a man of God."

Rick lay pondering the priest's message, especially the one about the colleges being red. U Chicago sure was, and he still wondered about his own conversion to it. He was aware that his pulse was racing and his brow was sweaty, He lit a cigarette and lay back down on the bed. He joined the party because he hated the depression and the militant response of the establishment when the workers tried to improve their lot. His dad had called the men at his plant, 'fleas,' parasites on wealthy dogs, gnawing away at the productive people. Rick's dilemma was, did he join the party because his dad was against it or because he thought the country would be better off with the Reds in control? He thought for a while then decided that he knew the answer.

CHAPTER THREE

The Radicals

Two days later there was another planning session, this time they met in an old warehouse in Harlem. Despite the location there were no blacks in attendance. Rick thought about addressing this issue but thought better of it. These guys were the pros and supposedly knew what the drill was. Duell continued in his role as commissar and after a quick welcome he introduced a tall, well dressed man with a thick dark moustache that Rick thought looked familiar. Dark hair, curly, high forehead, sensitive eyes and a sensual mouth He began to speak in an accented English.

"Good evening ladies and gentlemen. My name is William Weinstone and please call me Will. I am an officer in the CPUS and I am presently responsible for the organization of a new organization that we will call the United Auto Workers. We made an attempt in the past to organize such a union and it failed miserably. It failed in spite of the fact of underpayment underrepresentation and overwork on the part of the thousands of autoworkers like to give you a just a brief history of my work in this area. I have been to Moscow and I've talked to world leaders in the party. The impression is that American labor movement needs help. We don't have to go to Moscow for help, we can get all the help we want right here in the United States of America. I would like to have you all stand now, stand together raise your right hands make a fist and yell, Solidarity! Solidarity! Solidarity! That's what it takes to form a union that will be able to represent the people the industry yes even the country. I have been fighting the good fight for the party since 1921. I have been into the deep South have attended and been involved in the trial of the Scottsboro boys.

I don't know if you know about the Scottsboro boys yet but they represent the maltreatment of the underclass of our society, the Negro American.

I would like to add at this time that my whole name is William Wolf Weinstone. I want you to pay special attention to the name Wolf. We talk of the Wolf as a lone wolf but actually they are very social animals and yes, they travel in packs. I want you to think of yourselves as wolves, superior animals that travel in packs and work together to accomplish a mission. Our mission? Take down the plutocrats that run these companies. Our aim is not destruction; our aim is direction that moves in favor of the worker.

So ladies and gentlemen it is my fervent wish and my primary drive to direct my energy combined with yours that we might bring this change about. With change comes social improvement and social improvement comes from what's the word? Solidarity!"

The group stood as one wildly cheering this new leader of the movement that would direct the new changes in the automobile industry. Rick was excited at the thought of his father. "My dad is one of those people who exploits the workers in his plan. Wouldn't it be wonderful to bring him down while bringing up his workers that he has dominated, starved, and exploited all these years?

Dual came up to him, smiling, and said, "What did you think of Will?"

Rick replied, "Now there's a real man. I can see why the party chose him. He's a man with real leadership skills. We oughta collect his ideas and practice them to a T."

Duell said, "That's the spirit Rick. I knew that you would be willing to contribute your unusual intellect and insights to the goals of this group. I wonder if your dad would be proud of you knowing that you are working for the best interest of the people here and the people in the automobile industry rather than just making more money for himself. By the way, Rick did he include you in the will?"

Rick smiled and said, "That's funny Duell. I'll remember your comment and maybe sometimes in the near future I can share it with my dad. But as you know I don't share a whole hell of a lot with my dad or anyone else for that matter." Rick walked away thinking to himself. What a smartass jackass.

The meeting broke up into smaller groups each involved with a specific area of the new action. The new action was to consist of a sit down closed-door action by the workers. The workers would remain in the plants and refuse to work and to refuse entry to administration. Rick was enthused about this because he felt that the best way for the workers to gain their aims and their ends would be not locked out but locked in.

The meeting lasted until after midnight and Rick left the warehouse with a spring in his step. Now something was going to happen for the little guys! He had parked two blocks from the warehouse because the streets had been crowded and parking places were nonexistent. As he turned the corner it was quite dark and the streets were empty. He saw his car sitting at the curb and noticed what looked like a hole in his windshield. It was a hole indeed and as he walked up to the car the driver's window gaped, He opened the unlocked door and slid into. The goddamn dashboard was torn open and his radio missing. Viva la proletariat!

CHAPTER FOUR

Union Busters

They stood in the small warehouse outside the gates of the big GM plant. Walter Rothstein, a veteran strike planner, had driven in from New York City, along with four burly organizers who looked like they worked for Dutch Schultz. They wore denim trousers and bulky jackets which hid God knows what. Jack Torrance the night foreman, a tall, skinny fortyish man with an under slung jaw and bad teeth stood nervously near the small door that opened towards the plant gate. His gaunt face was white as he continually mopped his forehead. Rick and Balance chain-smoked while Duell stood calm and aloof from the rest. Finally, Torrance spoke. "Are you guys sure of this? Lots of my boys have kids, you know . . ."

Duell swung around and said, "When will you workers realize that the owners have you hanging by your pricks? You're willing to let your kids starve because you're afraid? Christ sake, man, get some balls!" He turned away. Rick agreed with Gregg's outburst but felt sorry for Torrance and the other workers, knowing they had the most to lose. He elected to keep quiet as they walked into the factory where the engines whined and moaned, the workers strained and lifted, pounding parts and screwing them together as the skeletons of Chevrolets clattered down the assembly line. The night supervisor, a bulldog of a man who worked for management, walked up and down the line yelling instructions at the sweating workers. It was late November but it felt like mid-July given the heat from the machines. Jack Torrance walked directly towards the super and

Jack raised a clenched fist, and nodded at the worker closest to the main line switch. When he dropped his fist the worker threw the switch to 'off.' Instantly all of the noise ceased.

Torrance cried out, "OK boys, we've done it! Let's shut the Goddamn place down!" The super started towards the switch but Torrance grabbed his arm, "Sorry Butch, but this is a strike and you're our hostage." Butch tried to pull away but the stronger Torrance held him fast. "Forget it Butch, we've had enough of your bullshit," and thumped him aside the head with a large monkey wrench. The super dropped his knees as blood gushed from his head wound, then collapsed. The men cheered with a nervous gusto. Torrance said, "OK fellows, this plant is ours to hold as long as we've got the guts to hold it!" The men cheered again, this time with enthusiasm.

Some workers rushed to secure the plant, moving unfinished car bodies to block the doors, then welded them together while others positioned metal sheets against all the windows to stave off gunfire. They set up stations for wetting down clothing against tear gas were set up and paint sprayers were at the ready as defensive weapons. Torrance yelled out, "Blow the fuckin' whistle, let 'em know we're in here."

Meanwhile, outside the plant, Rick and the organizing team sent telegrams to distant newspapers while phoning the local ones. It didn't take long for the press, the police, the National Guard and the supervisory staff to rally outside the sealed plant. Workers opened the third floor windows and hooted and jeered at the crowd below. "Hey boss, look at us. Who's in charge now? Fuck the bosses, fuck the bosses!" That and other chants went on for half an hour, and then the men closed the windows. (The sighting of rifles in the hands of the plant cops played a role in that decision.)

The organizers decided it was time to sneak away, and they dispersed through the crowds without notice. They met at a truck stop down the highway and began formulating the next step; a staticy radio behind the lunch counter suddenly blared the news of the sit-down. "This is a Red plot," the announcer yelled, "These commies are demanding a 40 hour week, no piece work. Blasted commies!" The conspirators shared a chuckle at this but were careful not to be over conspicuous among the people in the cafe. The radio suddenly let out an electronic squeal and stopped.

Duell began to speak in a low voice, "Guys, we've done it. Now we wait them out."

"What about the plant cops and their rifles," said Rick.

Duell's mouth twisted as he replied, "If the cause is important a few casualties will make it more so." He gave Rick a kick under the table, then stood up and said, "Blaine and I have some things to discuss. You guys can leave and we'll meet here again at five this afternoon." The others stood up more than ready to go. Duell gestured Blaine back to the men's room. "Damn it Blaine, you give too much away with your puking and muling about casualties. It's their responsibility to accept them."

Rick stared him down, saying, "So long as it's not Duell's ass it's OK?"

Duell turned around and said, "Be back here at five," and left the toilet.

While this exchange was taking place, things were accelerating back at the plant. Ballance had been in charge of the worker's cadres and had done a thorough job. In the next two days committees for food, police, toilets, and up to date bulletins began to act and the workers fell into line, proud to be working for the general good. Violations of the rules were dealt with on the spot. At night those not on guard slept on the auto cushions. There was even a mail system but every letter passed through a censor committee. Boredom was not an issue; plays, writing classes, even dances were organized. Food was shipped in via city buses, all union drivers. Support, both verbal and financial, poured in from all over the east coast. "Solidarity!"

Rick knew it would be only a matter of time before the Company struck back, he had listened to his father talk of the necessity for rapid retaliation against the commies who threatened the livelihood of all serious Americans. And strike back they did. While the unions added members by the hundreds after the news of the success of the strike spread, Management ordered their goons to storm the plant. Yelling "goons! Commies! Reds!" they began close quarter assaults on the workers, clubbing and bloodying heads. They threw tear gas canisters through the open doors and broken windows. In the meantime Rick and his cadre were at the truck stop drinking coffee and planning the next move, a move to seal the plant, making it all but invasion-proof. Following the meeting the organizers set out for the strike bound plant.

Back at the plant the workers' wives were supporting their husbands by dressing their wounds and washing the teargas from their faces. Others stood in front of their men daring the goons to attack them. The workers set up water and foamite "cannons," and prepared to fight to the death.

Some of the men had smuggled in pistols and rifles, despite warnings to the contrary by the strike organizers. National Guard troops stood with fixed bayonets to prevent further supplying of the bastioned strikers and mounted guns and howitzers around the secured perimeters. Additional deputized militia joined the Guard troops, prepared to assault the plant buildings.

Returning to the plant Rick was aghast at what they found when they on arrival. Military people, police, sandbagged howitzers and machine guns were everywhere. The stink of tear gas made Rick and everyone in the area hold handkerchiefs to their faces.

When Rick walked inside, a worker wearing greasy coveralls and a stubbly beard came up to him and said, "It's just like the Alamo, Mr. Blaine. We got us a war, and by damn we're goin' to win it." Rick patted him on the back. "Look at the women," said the worker as he joined in the cheering. A large crowd of women wearing red berets herded their children through the crowd while they carried clubs, pokers, and bats, causing the workers in the plant to cheer wildly. Duell grabbed a bullhorn and began to address the crowds. "Solidarity!" He thundered.

The crowd began to chant, "Solidarity, solidarity, solidarity!" Ballance, Duell and the other organizers came forward and Duell passed the bullhorn to them. Each of them hollered, "Solidarity!" Rick stood apart so he would not be seen with them because of his father's status as a manufacturer. Rick just stood in the crowd feeling pride and embarrassment.

A rending sound announced the opening of the barricaded gates and the workers, bearded, faces lined with fatigue, swarmed out. Confetti flew from the second floor of the building and the wives and children hugged their heroes. "The Union makes us strong!" they chanted.

Balance and Duell walked through the jubilant crowd, Duell grabbed Rick by the elbow and they walked to their waiting car. "Nice job, Blaine, your organization talents have been noticed by the higher-ups. Remember that you're being watched. I've already put in a helpful word for you from our cell committee.

Rick nodded assent but thought, "These guys are really into this for themselves." Being noticed by the party bosses was not a part of his reasons for supporting the strike. He just wanted the same breaks for everyone, not tiny breakthroughs for the workers and promotions for the party leaders and commissars. Was he cursed to spend his life in an ever-descending spiral of disillusionment that swept away any ideals he might hold?

We are betraying these men and it makes no difference to these guys. He felt sudden surge of rage and knotted his fists, saying, "You know Duell, are you really in this for the Union or is it for you as a egotistical self-promoting narcissist?"

"What the hell does that mean, Blaine?"

"That means that when the action is over at Blaine, I'm through with you assholes. I'll find my own way." He turned and walked to his own car.

CHAPTER FIVE

Outrage

Rick toyed with the revolver he had removed from his desk drawer. He didn't know why he was holding it or what he was going to do with it. Despite his black mood self-destruction was not on the menu. He was thinking about his father and what he could do to change things. He had no desire to spend time in Sing-Sing for patricide.

The plans for striking Blaine Manufacturing continued, but Rick kept away from Balance and Duell. He preferred working with Rothstein, he was clever, dedicated, and had checked his ego somewhere else. A month later the plans were complete and the strike was on. Blaine senior had given Rick more fuel for his hostility against his dad. He had overheard the sounds of lovemaking in his father's office and walked in on his half dressed dad and an unclad secretary. Rick left them without a word.

In a reconciliation attempt Rick had resolved that he would try to resolve the hostilities with his with dad as soon as possible. When he tried to arrange a meeting with him, his dad had refused to speak with him. What followed was to ruin life as he had known it.

The strike had started the week before and dad's response was quick and brutal. Hired goons and the police carrying truncheons were everywhere. As he sat pondering his alternatives a group of demonstrators appeared, shouting and jeering as the scabs entered the plant's gates. Someone with a bullhorn shouted a command. A volley of gunshots rang out, changing the shouting to screams of wounded and terrified men.

Rick sprang to his feet, took the elevator down to the main floor and ran out the main entrance of the Ad building. He saw several bloodied, inert bodies on the sidewalk. Others were sprawled on the grass holding their heads in their hands as uniformed and plainclothes goons beat them with long truncheons. He winced at the sound of the sodden thwacks and crunches as they clubbed the men with repetitive blows. One man rolled over on his back, already dead, with the yellow brain ooze filling both nostrils.

Enraged, Rick ripped the truncheon from one of the goons and clubbed him across the face. The man's head snapped and he slumped to the ground. Another turned to him with a gun in his hand; Rick felt his heightened rage as he seized the weapon by the barrel and with his other hand clubbed the man in the groin. He then dropped his club and began shooting and several men dropped to their knees in silent supplication.

Rick felt a wave of nausea as he turned and ran into the building with no one in pursuit. He dashed out the rear officer's exit, jumped into his car and careened out the private exit used only by his father. He tried to think of someone who would ask no questions, shelter him, and find a way for him to escape the country. He only knew that he had to do it soon.

CHAPTER SIX

Exile

Rick knew that his only option for a quick exit was to call the cell offices and ask for assistance. "The Cell." A euphemism for the commie group he had abandoned a month ago. He rang the number and a familiar voice answered. "Yes?" Rick scrabbled through his brain for name recognition, came up with it and he wanted to hang up. "Duell?"

"Who the hell is this?"

"Blaine. I'm in big trouble. I just killed a couple of scabs at my dad's plant. I gotta get out of the country for awhile."

"Killed a couple . . . gee that's too bad, Blaine. Only two? Isn't it too bad that you've found us distasteful for so long and suddenly you need us right away?" Duell's voice was thick with sarcasm.

Rick was ready to hang up, but realized he lacked choice. "You're right, I do need something and I need it now." His mouth was dry and he had major pain in his gut.

"Where are you now?" said Duell."

"I'm in a phone booth at the Waldorf."

"OK Rick. Walk around the block then go back to the bar and have a drink and a smoke. In an hour a man carrying a briefcase and an umbrella will come up and sit next to you. He'll leave the case by your feet and leave. Go outside and take a cab to Grand Central. When you get there, read the message in the case and do what it says. And remember this Blaine, you owe us."

Rick followed the directions, leaving the Waldorf and walked down Park Avenue. Despite his tension wrought hyperacidity he lit a cigarette feeling every eye was on him. He was aware that he was checking his watch so often that he began to relax, even chuckle. The hands on his watch crawled painfully towards the top of the hour. Finally he skulked back to the Waldorf and into the bar. He ordered a Scotch rocks and lit another fag. Looking towards the lobby door he saw a short, slim man wearing a black hat and suit, carrying a briefcase entering the bar. The bar was dimly lit and the man's hat was pulled low Rick could not make out his face. He hung his umbrella on a coat hook and sat down next to Rick and mumbled something unintelligible then turned his head and ordered a rye and rock candy. The bartender brought the drink and black hat paid then got up and disappeared.

Rick felt the briefcase pressing against his leg grabbed the handle and left the bar. He was mopped his face while his heart pounded. "Hell, this is sure new to me," he said to himself. He left the hotel and hailed a cab. "Grand Central, driver."

After a few minutes of nervous reflection he shrugged and looked out the window. On arrival Rick walked into Grand Central, looking up at the clock that read three o'clock. He sat down and opened the briefcase. Airplane tickets, a passport, and a two-page letter of instructions plus a leather portfolio that was marked 'do not open'. How the hell did they do that so fast?

The letter instructed him to take another cab to Flatbush Avenue and the Floyd Bennett Field. There he would board a DC-3 scheduled for Miami. He hailed third cab of the afternoon, "Floyd Bennett Field and make it snappy, I have to catch a plane."

"Yessir, but this is early rush hour so hang on to your hat." The driver urged the big Checker cab into gear and roared away from the curb. "Don't know how you arranged that flight from Bennett. Where did you say yer going?"

"Miami," replied Rick.

"You're just in time. The Coast Guard's gonna own it in a few months. They need a base pretty bad. Seaplanes. New airport coming in Queens." By the time they arrived at Floyd Bennett Field, Rick was as tense as he had ever been.

The building was a wide, red brick structure with two tall white pillars that announced the entrance. Rick had never flown before and was scared to death. His pulse raced, he could feel the sweat running down his sides and his gut ached. He craved a cigarette, took out his pack and lit one.

A cop came close and Rick's heart sank. The cop smiled at him and gave Rick a small salute and turned away.

Fortunately the check-in was fast and Rick walked out the departure doors to the plane. A large hangar with the sign, 'City of New York Department of Docks Floyd Bennett Field.' Rick climbed the ramp up into the airplane where a uniformed flight attendant greeted him and escorted him to his seat. There were about 12 other passengers already seated and in a few minutes they were airborne. Rick buckled his seat belt and soon was asleep, head against the window.

The pilot's voice awakened him. "Ladies and gentlemen we're 15 minutes from our landing in Miami. The flight attendants and I thank you for flyin' with us today. We all hope to see you again on our fabulous DC-3, the safest plane in the air."

Rick hurried from the ramp and into the small terminal building. Harried looking people scurried in all directions and the crowds made him feel less noticeable. His next destination was Dinner Key in Coconut Grove and the Pan American clipper terminal.

The Pan American terminal was a pleasant surprise. A flat two-story rectangle of white stucco; there was a frieze of winged globes and rising suns, with eagles at the corners. Rick entered the building that was dominated by a giant revolving world globe in the center of the lobby. Rick walked to the ticket counter marked 'Brazilian Clipper' and presented his tickets. The young bleached blonde female agent smiled approvingly at him as she processed his reservation. "Do you wish to check a bag Mr. Blaine?"

Rick had packed a small folding bag that he intended to carry on with his briefcase so he answered, "No."

The agent accepted his answer with a "Traveling light, eh Mr. Blaine?"

Rick managed a narrow grin and responded, "Yeah."

"When the service is called, you go out the door marked 'to planes.' Our limousine will take you to the dock where you'll board the Clipper. I hope you enjoy your flight to Rio." She cocked her head in a flirtatious gesture and then called, "Next please."

Rick walked up to the second floor promenade and looked out at the dock area. The Sikorsky S-42 was a beautiful sight as it bobbed lightly at its mooring. Larger than he had anticipated, it had a full-length metal hull and the overwing had four huge engines across its span. The wing was braced to the fuselage. Two pontoons kept the wings from dipping into the water along with two side extensions at the base of the hull. Finally he noticed the twin tail assembly. He sat down and lit a cigarette. His initial fears were replaced by a sense of anticipation as he read the brochure describing the plane. Four engines, a range of 1120 miles, cruising at 150 mph at 5000 feet. A voice over a speaker system announced the boarding of the Clipper; the rock in his chest lifted and a sense of release arrived. He was taken by limo to the dock along with five other passengers. The blue liveried driver was about 25, tall, Florida blonde, and very handsome. "Gigolo," thought Rick. He escorted them to a narrow dock that led to the plane's door that was just underneath the words, 'Pan American Airways System.' At the bottom of the three steps, a beautiful young woman in a blue stewardess uniform greeted Rick and checked his documents. "Mr. Blaine, welcome aboard The Clipper. We are so glad you're with us." Her smile heated his heart

He smelled fresh paint and new fabrics as she escorted him through a large compartment painted blue, and with a russet colored carpet. Completing the picture were blue chairs and windows with venetian blinds. The walls were curved giving the impression of a dwelling rather than a plane. The stewardess led him aft through a series of carpeted lounges to his own private compartment. Rick was reminded of his stateroom on the Queen Mary a lifetime ago. The woman left him with a smile and he sat down in a beige chair.

The roar of the four great engines sprung to life interrupting his reverie. The big ship settled in the water like a sprinter waiting for the gun, then the scenery outside sped past him as the plane accelerated. He suddenly felt release as the plane seemed to surge free of the water. He could now see the hangers and the terminal below him. The plane was free and so was he. The pressures of the past three days lifted like a fog melting in the sun.

He took a shower in his tiny stall, shaved and quickly dressed. He needed a scotch and another cigarette so he left his room and went out into the lounge. A large divan beckoned and he sat. A steward came up to him and said, "Something to drink, sir?"

"Scotch, neat, please." Rick sat, smoked and enjoyed his drink. Dinner was announced, but Rick did not want to dine at his assigned table for four. He was just too apprehensive that someone would comment on the shootings or that he might reveal something he'd regret. Instead he amused himself by looking out the window at the view since the plane, although capable of 12,000 feet, flew mainly 300 feet above the water. He wondered why he felt nothing about the men he had shot.

The long flight from Miami ended in Rio de Janeiro. The aircraft had lumbered slowly around the eastern bend of the South American continent. The journey had seen too many cities and countries pass into memory. The days had passed in a blur and Rick was mentally depleted.

The next leg of his journey was a surprise to Rick. The instructions were to travel to the German district along the harbor of Rio. When he left the terminal to try to find a cab, a dark skinned mustachioed man stepped in front of him with a placard that read, 'Richard Blaine.' The bottom of the placard indicated that he represented 'DLH.' What the hell was 'DLH?' "Sorry I no speak good English, but I you driver to the seaplane docks."

Rick shook his extended hand and said, "I must apologize for speaking no Portuguese." The driver smiled but said nothing. They walked to a Cadillac limousine that looked like it belonged to some Chicago bootlegger. It was a shiny black with wheel protectors to prevent an easy gunshot from piercing the oversized tires. The upholstery was dove grey and there was a glass shield between the front and back seats. Rick smiled when he saw the speaking tube. Rick said to himself. "This thing must weigh 3 tons. Probably goes like hell, too."

He sat back and looked out at the Rio cityscape. He dozed, but was awakened when the driver's voice came through the tube. "We are here." The driver opened the door and grabbed Rick's extended bag but Rick denied him the briefcase. Rick saw a two-engine seaplane bobbing at anchor across the docking. He saw a man in a white suit and white Panama hat approaching him from a small building on the dock. "Mr. Blaine, I am your guide to the island of Fernando de Noronha. This little plane is your new home for a time. My name is Klaus." No last name?

Rick looked at the man carefully. Acne scarred face, sharp chin, flat face with eyes shadowed by the brim of the hat. About six feet tall. The friendly tone of his voice seemed icy to Rick. His accent? German. "What now," he said to himself. The man led the way down a swaying boarding dock to the plane. He climbed up the three steps and ducked, then turned to grab Rick's bags. Rick scrambled aboard the six-place plane; the pilot and co-pilot occupied the first seats. Neither of them turned to face him. The plane's engines thundered to life as it made a wide turn, and then churned down the bay and into the sky.

"Herr Blaine, you will be impressed with our new 'Dornier.' It is the latest in our aero-technology and it is just the beginning. The Fuehrer has great plans for our aviation program. You will see this by the time you reach Berlin." Rick nodded but said nothing to Klaus. The engine's roar was giving him a headache and he wanted a cigarette and a long sleep. "Is this your first time in Brazil?"

"Yes. I've been to Europe but went by ship. I was in Berlin in '28. Great city." Klaus smiled in agreement while nodding his head vigorously.

A puzzled Rick asked, "Why doesn't your clipper land and take off from Rio?"

"That is a question you not entitled to ask," said Klaus stiffly. "But just wait, you'll see a new and different Berlin, an evolved Germany. The sky is the limit for the Reich." Klaus flushed and his eyes sparkled. New sweat beaded his forehead as he unleashed his excitement. He finally settled back in his seat and said, "Ja!"

Rick had seen this arrogance in 1928 and wondered how much worse it had become.

He opened his briefcase and rechecked his instructions. This flight would terminate at Fernando de Noronha. From there he would be a passenger on a DLH Dornier Flying boat. The Germans used this plane to carry mail from South America back to Germany. Occasionally passengers were taken on. Rick wondered how the 'Cell' had been able to arrange this passage with the Nazi government. There must be a transection of purposes that somehow brought these opposing factions together. Was that purpose good for America? The briefcase contained a leaden envelope with no apparent way to open it without obvious evidence of tampering. He shook his head in bewilderment. The politics of the world were still unfolding for him and he had few insights into the subtle machinations of how it was managed. Nevertheless it seemed that he was meant to learn.

The pilot turned to Klaus and said something that Rick could not hear over the engine noise. Klaus said, "We're soon to land. Look out the window."

Rick looked and saw a group of islands, mostly treeless, lying below, jewels of brown and green in a turquoise sea. He decided they must be volcanic. Then he saw a large flying boat, four motored, lying at anchor off the shore. "Ist das der 'Dornier,'" asked Rick. In the distance some kind of tender ship rode at anchor in the open sea.

Klaus smiled at his German and said, "Ja, das ist der 'Dornier.' Eine schonste anblick, nicht war? We are proud of our superiority in transatlantic flight."

Rick said, "You're not saying that plane can fly the Atlantic, are you?" He was incredulous.

"Later you will learn," Klaus said, in the most arrogant tone he had yet assumed.

The landing was smooth as the plane coasted up to the dock. A gangplank was extended, and they exited, carefully maneuvering the swaying gangplank and onto the dock. Two uniformed men greeted them. Both wore black tunics with wings pinned to the left side indicating that they were fliers. Rick was really impressed with their caps, black officer's caps with silver eagles on them. Both men were well built. They wore black flying trousers bloused into their black boots.

One flier smiled at Rick and said, "Welcome to der Dernier Wal. We hope you enjoy this unique form of travel to the Third Reich."

Rick mused to himself, "So now everything is in place and the Third Reich is king of the seas."

"Come Herr Blaine, come aboard our little treasure." The party walked down the dock to the *Dornier Super Wal.* Four motors mounted on the wing, which was placed over the fuselage. Black swastikas were emblazoned on the twin vertical fins of the tail assembly. They boarded in a similar fashion as the Brazilian Clipper but no pretty airhostess greeted them. Inside Rick saw only two compartments, both spacious, dark gray carpeting with black leather seats built along the walls. A man who turned out to be the steward studied Rick carefully. He wore a black jump suit with the German eagle emblazoned on the left side of his chest. He smirked but said nothing. Rick thought, "Definitely not a gigolo."

Rick heard a great deal of thumping against the fuselage, then realized they were loading the plane with mail, and God knew what else. Herr Klaus was nowhere to be seen. There were no other passengers coming aboard but several porters toted in boxes and sacks with swastikas on them and put them in the rear compartment. The steward called to him, "Herr Blaine, would you like something to drink? Alzo, I know you smoke and it is allowed."

"I don't suppose you have scotch," said Rick hopefully.

"We have many drinks including scotch, mein herr. Soda, ice, or plain?"

"Plain, please."

The compartment began to rumble and shake as the engines idled then came to full throttle.

Rick felt the plane turn, the engines smooth, and they leapfrogged down the lagoon. Rick fully expected the plane to leave the water in the same fashion as the Clipper. He looked out the window and saw the ship he had seen from the air. It had a large crane extended off the mid-portion and a long cable hung from it like a noose. "Now watch this, Herr Blaine." A large wide mat that looked like a trampoline bobbed in the water underneath the cable. Rick realized that this was actually a platform. The plane taxied onto the mat and the engines grew silent.

"What is this?" asked Rick.

"Just wait, my friend. Please sit and buckle your belt, there will be a jerk." The jerk came sooner than Rick expected and but for the belt he would have tumbled to the floor. He watched as the deck of the ship came into view and he could read her name, *Schwabenland.* "Rick could see the clipper setting down between two girders which ran out to the foredeck. "What the hell is this," he thought. The plane settled down on the deck and all was quiet for a time. Then the engines roared to life in full throttle.

"Now Herr Blaine, hang on. The engines came to life; the roar shook the entire plane. Rick was pushed back in his seat as the plane was catapulted into the air. The engines thundered, the plane hesitated and suddenly took flight. Rick relaxed and he smiled hesitantly at the steward. "It felt like we were thrown into the air. What happened?"

The steward laughed through a wide grin, showing steel-capped teeth. "Zat, Herr Blaine, was our new catapult system in action. There is no place on earth we cannot take our planes."

Rick smiled but thought, "You mean there's no place on earth that's safe from you guys."

"What's your name," Rick asked."

"Val Mussberg I am called, but it changes from time to time. You call me Val."

Rick said, "So Val, when do we eat again." Val nodded and disappeared into the galley. After a dinner of a good German beer, a big ham sandwich and boiled potatoes he lit a Camel and wondered at the technological advantages the Germans seemed to possess. Perhaps it was all in their minds, this superiority. The thought being father to the deed also entered his mind. He wished that he could become a bit more laconic in his life; the constant dithering that he saw in his actions did not serve him well.

Val shook Rick awake, saying, "Look, Herr Blaine. It is time you know where you are. Below lies Gambia and the city of Bathurst. When we land you and I will say goodbye."

"Val, that will make me very sad," said Rick, sarcasm in his voice. "I have a question for you; why am I the only passenger?"

"Blaine, this is a mail service for the German government. You are considered mail on this trip." His tone matched Rick's sarcasm. "We occasionally carry human sacks of mail." His steely smile was tight. The plane had been cruising at 500 meters so the descent was brief. They landed smoothly, and then taxied to a docking area. A man in a Nazi uniform opened the cabin door. He ignored Rick, heading quickly back to the cargo section. "You may debark now, Blaine. A driver will take you to the airport. Auf Wiedersehen." With that he went forward to the flight deck, closing the door behind him.

Rick maneuvered the boarding dock with ease; climbing up to the dock was a pleasure. The heat and humidity was not, He broke into a profuse sweat as his heart rate rose. "Damn weeds," he thought. Three men in Nazi uniforms, two of whom were pilots, greeted him with smiles and handshakes. "The car waits for you, Herr Blaine. Welcome to Gambia." A large black Mercedes drove up, one of the men opened back door and beckoned Rick to enter the car. The others got in and the car sped off.

"How was your flight, Blaine? What do you think of the Super Wal?"

"Impressive, but the catapult really was the thing. Just amazing."

"German technology, Herr Blaine."

The group was silent for the rest of the drive. In 15 minutes the airport appeared and the car pulled up next to a rickety sheet metal building that appeared to be the terminal. The four men were whisked through the building and out onto the tarmac. Most of the aircraft were non-descript but one stood out. One officer pointed to the plane. "Blaine, this is our famous JU-52. It is the mainstay of the Lufthansa fleet and the most advanced plane of its kind in the world." Again, German hubris expressed in glowing tones. The four men climbed the stairs to the open door and ducked into the cabin. The smell was new leather; the plane had been reconfigured as a luxury craft. Fine tables and thick oriental pile carpeting throughout, with two divans that looked like beds. "We now fly to the Azores, we refuel there and then to Berlin. Good luck there."

The plane droned on to the Azores, refueled, and took off for Berlin. Rick breathed a sigh of relief; his destination awaited and he would be on solid ground again.

CHAPTER SEVEN

Berlin and Beyond

The next portion of the briefcase letter advised Rick that he would meet his Berlin contact in the bar in the Lufthansa terminal. Could he be the tall man in a lumpy suit that had jostled him twice on the stairs from the tarmac? An old gray hat hid his eyes so that Rick could not read the man's face. As much of it as he could see lacked any sign of character—certainly a useful kind of face in his business. His contact would be in the bar drinking a large glass of beer, and there he was. Rick saw on the table three empty bottles forming a triangle, the first signal he was looking for.

Rick placed his luggage on an empty chair at the next table, went to the bar and, in English, loudly ordered tea. This was the second signal. English speakers weren't unusual these days because Berlin was crowded with foreigners who had come for the 1936 Olympic games.

Rick returned to his table and found his man had disappeared along with the briefcase. Sitting down, he noticed a slim manila envelope lying on his suitcases. This was the third signal, that Rick should leave the terminal and flag a cab. He added some sugar to his tea, and smoked. It seemed to him he was always smoking; tobacco had become such a vital ingredient in his life, probably because he had no other that satisfied him more. He fidgeted, adjusted his hat feeling ill at ease; being a fugitive was not his gestalt. He considered himself to be a man in command of himself, a fact important to him because he saw little else he could be to command. After finishing his tea, Rick waved down a porter who took his bags to the main entrance of the terminal.

A large diesel Mercedes cab clattered up, the porter stowed his bags in the trunk. Rick tipped him, climbed in and the old cab pulled away from the curb. The driver turned to him, and Rick recognized his contact man from the airport.

"Where to, Herr Blaine?" The voice was soft and modulated, but Rick couldn't place the accent.

"Aren't you supposed to be telling me that?"

"I will take you where you need to go."

So this was Berlin 1936. His previous trip to this old city had been with two college friends years ago. They had celebrated in the old music halls, heard Lotte Lenye singing the songs of Berthold Brecht, and visited the bars where you telephoned the table of a likely looking woman. (One had to be careful that the object of one's desire was truly female.) Most of all, he had loved the cabarets, smoky dives with men and women singing songs of desperation and insouciance, people who put life on the line and laughed at it. People like that . . . That Berlin was once a Mecca for the arts and the intellect until the decay started. The decay, the depravity became the reputation of the city. Homosexuals, bohemians, anarchists, and communists took control. Rick asked the driver, "How do you feel about the changes in the city?"

The driver replied angrily, "It upset me a lot but our government paid no heed, and things got worse. Inflation and the depression made us German Volk frustrated and angry."

Rick said, "Is that why you accepted Hitler's promises and brought him to power."

The driver replied, "Our pact with the devil put the country back on its feet. Now the Volk are proud, getting rich, and the national pride has been restored. The queers, anarchists, and Reds are in hiding. But our old liberalism and democracy still lie deep underground."

"From what I hear, that won't be an easy task." Rick said, but he felt uneasy after the driver's comments.

"You are more correct than you know."

"What's the plan for me? I do speak German, but I have no idea of what I'm doing here."

"I will put you in touch with some people who will help you decide your future; it will require some traveling, but you're young and really have nothing else to do." The man chuckled as if he had told a good joke. He told Rick he would take him to his next contact, then drop his luggage at a hotel, the Pension am Steinplatz, where Rick would return when he had finished his other business. "I urge you to commit the contents of the envelope to memory after which you must to destroy it. You must not let this information be found; it could be used as a weapon to destroy our movement."

Movement? Rick did not like the fact that he was considered part of something he had neither volunteered for or knew anything about despite his old party affiliations.

They drove to a club on the Kurfurstendam, the famous 'Kudam' a street that Rick remembered from his past. It was a place where one could find any political or moral element extant. The driver turned to him and said, "The man you seek will be wearing a bowler hat and carrying a copy of the Paris edition of the New York Herald."

Entering the place, he sat at the bar, ordered a Schenkenhager, and then lit a cigarette. The bartender glanced at the cigarette pack, and slowly walked from the bar to what appeared to be a kitchen. He returned immediately and sat on a stool, staring blankly at the empty tables. The place was a dump, butts all over the floor and the stink of old beer and cabbage.

A man wearing a bowler walked from the kitchen to the piano, placed a newspaper on the music stand, sat down and began to play. Rick recognized the song as a Rudy Vallee tune, something about Ann Boleyn. The man sang in an accented voice, "with her 'ead, tucked underneath 'er arm, she walks the bloody tower . . ."

Rick walked to the piano and saw the newspaper was the New York Herald, Paris edition. He asked, "Can I borrow your paper?" The man nodded his assent as he continued to sing. Rick walked to a booth and sat reading the front page. He called to the bartender for another drink that he brought to the booth at a desultory pace. He wore thick make-up on his face, and his lips were painted.

The piano player stopped playing, got up and walked over to the booth. "May I have my paper please?" His accent was either Austrian or Bavarian. Rick folded the pages and handed them to him. The man whispered quickly, "Walk to the Zoo." He then left the bar.

Rick downed his drink and walked to the door. He took a quick look back at the darkened room and stepped out into the comforting bustle of the Kudam. There he saw a street sign that read, "Zum Zoo." He walked in that direction.

Feeling sleepy from the drink, he turned into Kranzler's Café for a cup of Viennese coffee. He looked with disinterest at the street traffic when he saw the piano player standing on the curb turning his head from side to side. Rick saw large prominent eyes protruding beneath beetle brows. His high forehead, previously hidden by his bowler, was wrinkle free. His mouth was petulant and weak, and he seemed close to tears. He then disappeared in sea of pedestrians. When the street cleared, the man was gone.

Rick had little time for the gay types but he felt that they were encumbered enough without his bias burdening them more. Live and let live. All over the world men were being prevented from living their own private lives. "What the hell, I can't cry for all of them," he muttered as he paid his bill and left, entering again the flow of people. He walked rapidly now, making up for his dalliance. When he got to the Zoo he studied the faces around him. A pair of large, sad eyes caught his, and then jerked away. Rick almost missed him for he had again affected the bowler. The Bowler entered the small mammal building and Rick followed at a discrete ten paces. Bowler entered the bat room, which was dark except for the haunting blue lights defining the cages. There were only a handful of people in the room making it easy for Rick to spot Bowler at the Vampire Bat cage. Rick sidled over and Bowler discretely handed him a small envelope, turned away and walked from the room, Rick did not attempt to follow, but stayed to admire this most misunderstood of all the mammals. The bat(s eyes glowed red and Dracula came to mind; the bat outside the window, red eyes hypnotically urging its victims to open the window and their lives to his horror. Rick suddenly felt uncomfortable and left the room.

He walked to a Trinkhalle and ordered a Florida Boy and a bockwurst. He sat on the wall surrounding the large birdcage and munched his sausage. The storks stood staring out at the daylight gloom, looking like gray, mangy human caricatures, seemingly drained of blood and purpose. He tossed his refuse into a nearby container, returned to the wall and opened the brown envelope. The message was floridly hand written in German script, but he had little difficulty deciphering it. "Meet at the Dahlem Museum tomorrow morning." Rick tore the note into tiny pieces and deposited the pieces in several trash containers.

Later, he sat in his hotel room wondering what the hell he was doing here. The Gestapo didn't know of his record; no one did, at least, not yet.

He had not been identified as the man who killed the strikebreakers and his papers were otherwise perfect. Why Berlin? Apparently his friends in New York wanted him to see, first hand, the fascist philosophy in action. Thus far he had only seen the most orderly, well-run country in Europe. Everything worked and there seemed to be an air of expectancy and optimism, an air he had not seen in the states since the crash.

His New York person had told him what was happening in Ethiopia, the Italians and their military illusions. "They are the same philosophies that are heating up all the capitols of Europe."

Rick knew that Germany had not forgotten that the armistice had taken its East African territories away. Hitler was watching with fascination and irritation Mussolini's imminent invasion of Abyssinia. Hitler ranted and roared to his Generals about the issue. He laughed at, yet envied, the Italian buffoon's prancing and posturing over his neat little war, a war sure to bring victory to him and the Italians. Victory could mean world prestige and respect that The Romans were back!

His New York friends also told him that they would help him provide guns for the Emperor of Abyssinia. The "international movement" would look with favor upon any man opposing the fascists. New York persisted in believing that Rick was "political" despite his repeated refusals to support the Party.

Rick knew there was something occult about himself, something that appealed to the Reds. They knew about his idealism and toyed with it. He was unaware that the party had orchestrated the entire scenario of the strike that involved his father's plant. They knew his intervention was so predictable that it had been written into the entire fracas that day. He was considered to be an idealistic marionette. Write the play, pull the right strings, and Rick will dance. Now he was dancing in Berlin. Their plan was to find a way for this young idealist to get guns to the Emperor of Ethiopia and give the Kremlin their first inroad on the black continent. Rick fell asleep without benefit of dinner.

Next morning he hailed a taxi and headed for the Dahlem district and its museum. He saw uniforms everywhere; the Germans seemed to have a penchant for wearing them. The Sturmabteilung, the Schutz Staffel, the Stahlhelm, Bund Deutscher Madchen, the Hitler Youth, all well nourished, all with self-satisfied arrogant looks. Occasionally he saw a Jew, clothes marked with their yellow 6-pointed star. On several occasions he saw homosexuals with their distinct pink patches. He also saw jack-booted SS troopers with dogs herding people from trucks destined for a staging area at the Madchen, or so the driver told him. "These are Jewish criminals and provocateurs that are being relocated. Look at the pedestrians looking the other way. They're afraid they might recognize a Jew they know."

Once at the museum, he strolled inside, catching a glimpse of himself in the mirror. Close-set eyes, long nose, ample mouth, a little slack-jawed, he looked less like a man on the run than a Jewish doctor who had been up all night.

He went directly to the Egyptology exhibits, his favorites.

The exhibit featured a cast of the face of Nerfertiti being foisted off as the original. Real or fake, he was fascinated by the beauty of this ancient face. Looking up from the cast he saw again his bowler-hatted friend with the bulging eyes and the tremulous affect. Rick walked directly to him and said, "What the hell is this all about?" Bowler's shoulders sank, his face paled, then reddened.

They walked out into the gardens, the ubiquitous German garden with its flowers, no trespass signs for the grass, and "Herrschen Dein Hund" signs for the dogs. Rick grabbed the bowler by the coat and growled lowly, "What in hell is your name, you little creep. Tell me what's going on?"

Bowler looked at him and collapsed into his coat. "Ugarte. Ugarte is my name. Some call me Hugo. No one calls me Franz but that's my given name. I am here to help you get to Africa." His face filled with confidence as he straightened up into his clothes and said," I know you are a man in trouble, I sense people in trouble, they have an aura."

He continued on, "I'll get you out of here before the Gestapo gets both of us. I will provide documents that you need. And, they'll cost you money." He turned his head towards Rick almost seductively. "But I know that you have plenty of that. I also know that if you go back to the states they'll arrest you. Did you know that? Did you know that your friends told the police about you and your temper? They know that you and others were involved in the violence." He smiled voluptuously as if he enjoyed the thought of Rick's crimes, making them fellow conspirators against authority. Rick saw him as a loser, an outsider, with the sense that people were pointing at him and damning him on sight. This would be one of the few times he could face another man and feel equal.

Later that day Rick sat in his room at the Pension am Steinplatz. He had avoided the larger, commercial hotels to escape the possibility of being seen by any friend of his or his family's who might be in Berlin for the

Olympics. Plus, he wanted to be close to the dives of the Friedrichstrasse to take advantage of the services still available there. New passports, letters of transit, new hopes. He assumed that many Jews were arrested there, men and families seeking safe exit from their suddenly hostile fatherland. He wondered about the destination of the relocated Jews.

Apparently informers were everywhere. Once a bustling entertainment center with cabarets featuring nudity, transvestite theater and prostitution, most were closed now. They appeared to allow the rest to remain open as lures to attract the desperate minority under assault by the Nazis.

Ugarte awaited him at the Adlerflycht Café, just off the F'Strasse. He whispered, "Here are your new identity papers and a letter of transit. The cost would probably be high, but we know about your Swiss account. Thank heaven for the Swiss! Theirs is the only sanity left in Europe. I assume that your transit will be to Zurich.

You are not to check out of the pension. Anything you need should be in your briefcase. It will be at least 24 hours before the maids notice your absence, and another three or four before the police are called. Zurich would be safe for at least a week, if not longer."

Ugarte then put his arm around Rick and walked him to a booth where a small, thin man sat staring at his coffee. He had the aura of a two-bit racing tout with clothing to match. Rick found him immediately despicable without knowing why, but one becomes accustomed to sleaze in such men. They sat down, a waiter appeared, coffee complete was ordered. Ugarte called to the waiter, "A little cognac for me alzo." The waiter sneered and disappeared.

They waited wordlessly for the coffee. The waiter returned, and they sipped the creamy brew. The thin man offered a clammy hand to Rick, lisping, "They call me Herr Valentin. And you are Herr Fahrer." It was not a question, Rick(s name was now Fahrer, German for traveler. Did this man have a sense of humor? Probably not. "I have your materials. Or should I say your life preserver?" He snickered the last, looking at Rick with slivered eyes. Rick narrowed his own eyes at this piece of work, saying, "You love your work, don't you? Guys like you don't last an hour in the sunlight. If you have business to transact, then get on with it. I don't have the time or the inclination to be grist for your slimy mill."

Valentin suddenly smiled, the smile of a fallen angel. "Let's be friends. I don't like to do business with people I can't call friend. Don't you think friends are important these days?" Rick didn't respond, instead he lit a

Chesterfield and scrutinized Valentin's face. It was a face he wanted to remember in case he should see him in the middle of a road.

"I need ten thousand American dollars," Herr Valentin said as he waited for Rick's response.

Rick smiled, "You sure don't come cheap. I'll give you five, and if you don't think that's enough, then I'll say no deal."

Valentin was indignant. "This is not a bazaar on Friedrichstrasse. The risks are great but the demand is even greater. Have you heard what the Nazis do to undesirables? They are as efficient in that as they are when they help you at the border. Their orders are simple. Break them, get them to tell everything, then off to, ah, special prisons."

Rick realized that this was no time to get cheap. He had the money, the need to get out of here, and the risks now were too great to mess with this fool. "All right, Herr Valentin, the money is in this briefcase. Let me see the papers." Valentin rose, and removed a large envelope from the seat and handed them to Rick, who opened the envelope. The passport and visa seemed in order. Jacob Fahrer, citizen of the USA, parents immigrants from Dusseldorf to the states. Business, import-export. Entered Germany two weeks ago. Two weeks ago? Had the tout and his friends done something to Fahrer? An interesting way to obtain viable papers and passports. Valentin shrugged his shoulders, giving assent to Rick's unspoken musings. Rick opened his briefcase and took out four packets. "Don't count them here. Cut the paper and convince yourself it's all there. If you can't do that, there's no deal. I don't want every jackboot in Berlin on my ass." Valentin's forehead suddenly glistened as he looked at Rick with avaricious ambivalence. "These are my demands, Valentin."

Valentin took the bundles, slit them with a penknife, grunted mournfully, and put them between his legs. He turned to Ugarte, who smiled hungrily at him. Valentin handed him a similar envelope. Ugarte produced a switchblade from somewhere and opened his packet. He scanned the papers expertly, then smiled up at Rick. "Mr. Rick, we are traveling companions. I, too, do import-export, and I, too, will attend the fair at Zurich."

During this interchange, the waiter had turned on the radio, and they heard the Berliner Rundfunk announcing the morning news. Haile Selassie had arrived in Geneva, seeking aid from the League of Nations for his Ethiopia, invaded by the legions of Mussolini. It seemed to Rick another portent pointing him towards trouble. Is this what he wants?

He rose quickly and left the bar, he wanted away from these people but Ugarte pursued him. Rick hailed a cab, slammed the door in Ugarte's face, and said to the driver, "Zum Tempelhof."

Rick looked out as the taxi raced through the streets of Berlin. His thoughts were not available to him; he was sponging up visual impressions of a city in transition.

His reverie was interrupted as a cab pulled up next to his and he saw the diseased face of Ugarte smiling at him through the glass.

CHAPTER EIGHT

The Fat Man

The Lufthansa transport landed in the rain, a Zurich rain with stinging pelting clouds of ice and water. Rick deplaned and hurried to the terminal building where he joined the soaked, shivering assembly in the customs area. He lit up a Camel and looked around. In a corner he saw the unfortunate face of Ugarte lurking at the periphery of the crowd. He wondered about this man's life, and what he must have endured to become the creature he was today. His exhausted cigarette butt burned him back to the present. He shook it from his hand and joined the passport line. Rick checked through without a hitch, then strode to the exit and hailed a cab.

"Monsieur Rick!" Ugarte's voice. He turned to confront the little man, but stopped short when Ugarte brushed past him and opened the cab door. "Come in, Monsieur Rick. I know a place where we can stay and enjoy our holiday here." Rick glared at him, but reading concern, maybe terror, in Ugarte's eyes, he got into the cab.

Ugarte looked past Rick towards the terminal entrance. As the cab pulled into traffic Rick turned to see two men hurrying through the doors, looking left and right. They did not see the two fugitives as the cab had already pulled smoothly into the sea of vehicles. Rick had no doubt as to their occupation or purpose and turned to confront Ugarte. He had nestled his slight frame into the corner of the big Horsch cab and was smiling seductively up at Rick. His unfortunate life had disfigured his face, turning it into a portrait of abasement. It was a face that would not know repose again. "Where are we going?" Rick asked.

"To a friend's place."

"I didn't know you had any."

"I have many friends, for when a man is a free spirit, he encounters many of his kind in his flight. Do you not know this? You must read Nietzsche. He has defined us as human, all too human, but he has made the life of the truly free man a rich and exotic one. You, Monsieur Rick, are a free spirit but either do not know it or will not admit it. Better you acknowledge this now, for it could save you countless sadness in the future."

Rick said nothing, lit a cigarette and watched the traffic flow around him. A free spirit? Not to his knowledge. To be adrift was not necessarily freedom, it can be limbo. Maybe one man's freedom is another's prison.

They drove for 45 minutes, past the Seilbahn, and up the Bahnhofstrasse. Well-dressed and prosperous looking people abounded, the shops were high fashion clothiers and jewelers. The Horsch stopped in front of a juilliere whereupon Ugarte opened the door, beckoning to Rick to pay the driver.

Ugarte tried entering the store, but a uniformed guard blocked his entry. Rick watched as a heavy-set man eased up to the pair and extended his hand to Ugarte who turned and beckoned to Rick. Rick strode up to this unlikely duo, staring at the face of a man introduced as Ferrari. Not just a face, a huge round face, with saddle-bagged eyes of pale blue, heavy jowls that concealed a slightly prognathic jaw, a jaw of ferocity and tenacity, the head deeply set into huge shoulders with no neck visible. The suit jacket seemed a never-ending tapestry of wool, set off by legs that knew no separation. Suddenly the face burst into a radiant smile, kindness and warmth poured from the mounds of flesh. Only the eyes remained cold. "Mr. ah . . . Fahrer? A very great pleasure. What brings you to Zurich?" The smile remained, but the eyes scanned his brain for signs of truth or fiction.

Rick reached for his Camels; looked back at the blue scanners, replying, "Import export. I broker the product that my customers request. Does that interest you?" Rick took a deep, lung-swelling drag and blew it in the direction of those hypnotic eyes. Ferrari winced and moved his head to the side as he spoke. "I have frequent need for this type of service. Diamonds, gold, precious gems, ah yes, and the things that they buy." His face was transformed briefly by gluttony, then turned quickly and beckoned the two travelers to follow him. His movements were those of the very obese, the glide that belies the poundage it denies. His slippered feet fascinated Rick; their soft quickness made him wonder if the man danced.

Once inside his cluttered office, Ferrari closed the door and bade them sit. He sat behind his desk, a rosewood table desk almost hidden by piles of papers and jewelry boxes. "This is safe haven for any and all conversations. Please be kind enough to tell me your name. Ugarte's friends have already told me of your departure from that tomb of decadence, by this I mean Berlin. Ah, Berlin. Once the home of Brecht, Weill, and Lotte Lenya, now the home of the new Philistines with their Kultur and their cursed Walpurgisnachts. They know no kindness, and we all know that the world needs as much of that as it can get."

Rick stared at this man as if he were a prism, trying to discern which part of the spectrum was real and which one was devious facade. He shrugged internally, blazed his butt on his lips, and said, "Why should I tell you anything? What are you to me, and of what possible use could you be to me? What part of your silly scheming could possibly appeal to me? What . . . ?"

Ferrari stood up, his plump forefinger applied to his haughty lips. "There are many words to answer your whats. I know that many would not appeal to you. Not money, not power, not women, not even personal safety. One word will. Fascism. I know about your American misadventures. I know about the crowd that used you. Please don't wince, Mr. Fahrer. The Party is clever in its use and manipulation of people. They find a cause for you, and then consume you in that cause. Rumor has it that the strike they planned for your father's motor company succeeded, but it succeeded only for them. You are here now, and you can't go back. They remain, they survived. You are nothing, a Philip Nolan, a man without a country. You are on a ship called Europe, bound for nowhere. But you have money and youth, you have your talents and you have friends." With this last word he beamed triumphantly and walked towards Rick, extending both arms in some kind of conciliatory gesture.

Rick turned away, dealt himself another cigarette and said, "My name is Rick Blaine Your analysis of my past and apparently my future is accurate as well. One thing you don't know and the thing you should never forget is that today I belong to no one, no cause, and no country. I remain my own man, and I choose not to stick my neck out for anyone else's causes. There is injustice in the world, that's true, but one man cannot make a difference, and, even if he could, I am no longer that man." His own words made him feel desolate, apart from the world.

When he had completed his brief soliloquy, he slumped into a chair. Ferrari opened a leather box on his desk and produced a large cigar. Lighting it he said, "We shall go to Rome, then to Eritrea. From Eritrea we shall go to Khartoum. There we shall find, shall we say, 'merchants,' purveyors of weapons, a commodity badly needed by a certain client state of mine. The sides here are terribly unbalanced in favor of my client's antagonist, a small but angry state, Italy, the former Roman Empire. My client's state is Ethiopia, a state that has not known star status for centuries. It died with the renaissance and has known only humiliations since. World War I saw them on the side of the victors, but their role was mainly harassment of the already crumbled Austria-Hungarian Empire. The end of the war brought them nothing but crumbs, and the buffoon who now leads them isn't satisfied with crumbs. He seeks peacock feathers for the little Italian sparrow. His minions strut into battle with airplanes, tanks, armored cars, and a variety of, ah, poison gases.

"Poison gas? How can they get away with that?" Rick's tone was demanding.

Ferrari shrugged, his great jacket moving like a tent. "Let me tell you about the gas. It has proven efficacy, burning both the skin and the breathing passages, terrorizing its victims and forcing them into helpless retreat. It is enough to make one pause to reflect again on the paucity of kindness in this world. Has God become so ashamed of his little rock patch that he wants all to perish? Ah yes, and my clients? Their arsenal is sadly deficient; a few spotter aircraft without pilots skilled in the art of war, a few armored vehicles without spare parts, some ancient artillery, not enough guns, and no gases, no shiny little canisters." He paused, looking at Rick with curiosity, gauging the effect of his ruminations.

Rick seemed paralyzed, staring down at his Camel as if he saw a microcosm there in the ashes of his cigarette. He stared past Ferrari's questioning eyes as the fat man continued. "And the Abyssinians march as if death were victory. At Adowa 40 years ago they transfixed and terrorized the Italians with their courage. Their battle songs as they charged, their lion-maned chiefs leading the white robed rabble were the catalyst that drove the Italians to their humiliating defeat."

Rick asked, "What does that jut-jawed jackass want with this country anyway?"

"Il Duce needs several things from this. First, he needs to erase the curse of Adowa. When the Italians attacked Ethiopia in 1896, they suffered the worst defeat in the history of colonial Africa, a defeat that made them the laughing stock of the emerging 20th century Europe. Were you aware that the captured Italian troops were forced to parade before the Empress Taitu and sing 'Funiculi Funicula' and other Neapolitan favorites? Furthermore, the Duce needs a bold, sweeping victory to silence his domestic enemies, and to show the world that his Fascisti will not to be sneered at. Moreover, he wants to take Europe's admiring eyes off Germany, where Der Fuehrer has launched an economic miracle. Victory over Abyssinia is the Rosetta stone for these grandiose schemes." Ferrari suddenly seemed tired, his bloated face sagging as he plopped into his chair. "Let us desist for now and we shall continue our discourse later. Now we shall find you accommodations in a secure place."

Rick asked, "Why the secure place? Who are we hiding from?"

"Mr. Blaine, I do not know, and that alone requires us to be on guard. The enemies to be feared are the ones we don't know. We meet in Zurich because Switzerland is a neutral country. Italy will be more dangerous for those who scheme against the Duce."

Three days later, after a final briefing from Ferrari, the three men took separate flights to Rome. Rick felt a surge of excitement as the trimoter stumbled down the runway and lifted off into the air. His life was uncertain, yet his exhilaration knew no bounds. He thought of Gretchen and their time together. He wondered what she was doing, why she had cheated on him, her marriage to Gregg Duell, and if she ever thought of him. His thoughts, like his cigarette, turned to smoke as he began to doze.

CHAPTER NINE

Rome: Sam

Rome's Ciampino airport was soaked in sunlight, the first real sun Rick had seen since he arrived in Europe. He smiled to himself and thought about Long Island and the beaches of his more halcyon days. He hailed a taxi for his hotel, the Flora in the Pantheon district. There he would await instructions from Ferrari, who emphasized that it could be several days. He was warned not to talk politics with anyone, politics being a touchy subject in these times. The Italian brand of fascism wasn't as repressive as the German, but the secret police are everywhere.

The hotel clerk checked Rick's papers quickly while remarking, "My brother lives in New York, but planning to return. Here things are booming," he said in accurate but broken English, "Especially if you can get in on the African expansion." He was proud of Italy's new look, new money, new roads, the best in Europe, he boasted, as well as the new found punctuality of the railroads. "Mussolini has made all this possible, our money is good anywhere, there are penalties for cheating by cabbies, porters, and hotels, so tourists are glad to be here. The government wants them here and will protect them. Can you say that about New York?"

"There's much that can be said about New York," Rick replied and smiled at the clerk.

The clerk returned Rick's smile for he felt his brother has given him all he wanted to know about America. "No more will the ships of the world be filled with Italians fleeing their beloved homeland. We are back", he boasted. "There are many jobs now, and those who would wish to rise even faster can go to the African possessions and find ample work and rewards. To serve in the army is to be paid well and receive quick promotion. I was wounded in the first days of the Ethiopian liberation and I shall receive full pension until I die. I get full medical benefits, and so does my family. Do you have that in America?" He smiled slyly, already certain of the answer.

"I see you came from Germany. How are those dunderheads doing? We have many surprises for those Germans who come south to laugh and mock the Italians. Rome is Roman again, and, in Africa, our flag flies higher than theirs. They cannot hope to compete with us now." Rick shrugged, lit a Camel and turned to a noise from the street.

He saw a group of children, dressed like boy scouts, the Gioventu Fascista. Their banner read, "Believe, Obey, Fight." The thought of these boys being ready to fight and die depressed him. He suddenly felt very old and very tired.

Later, in his room, he bathed, and then lay on the bed dressed only in his shorts. Two cigarettes later, he checked the time. Almost three PM. He dressed and took the rickety elevator to the lobby. The clerk called to him and presented him with his soggiorno, his permit to be in Italy. Without it he could become a fugitive, a marked man. The clerk asked about his plans. "I think I'll go to the Pantheon."

"Oh, very good, very good", said the clerk. "We Italians are very proud of the unbroken lineage we celebrate with our Roman forefathers."

Rick grunted and walked past two carabinieri to the Pantheon. He noted how closely they walked together. Somewhere he had heard it is good luck for a young woman if she can walk between two carabinieri, since they are required to walk close together. As he neared the steps of the Pantheon, he saw hundreds of cats furtively walking about; none of them fat, but looking as though this was the main trattoria for kitties.

As he entered the building, he marveled at the dome with the large opening in the center. A short, fat man walked up to him smiling. "Hello USA! I'ma you guide! Here is sevena pagana gods! One dollar, I'ma you guide. Look about you. Very old. Sevena pagana gods! I'ma you guide. I take you around; show you the things, the sevena pagana gods, all here, all still here. Roma liva again! Hail Duce!"

Rick handed him an Italian bill and the self-appointed guide examined it carefully. Rick looked about the place. No one was there. Maybe just the sevena pagana gods. He chuckled out loud; the guide chuckled, too, and clapped him on the back. His demeanor became more solemn, he turned to Rick and said, "Victor Emanuel monument." He then walked quickly to the door. More damn walking, but what the hell. Rick walked to the Piazza Colonna and stood looking up at the Marcus Aurelius monument. He marveled at the white marble monument called "The Wedding Cake," probably the most flamboyantly garish monument in Rome. He found himself liking it, because he liked the Italians and their heart-on-sleeve nature.

He stared at the Palazzo Venezia and the famous balcony from which Mussolini gave his many public speeches. Il Duce was not speaking that day. Rick felt someone touch his elbow and turned to find Ugarte. His smile was a study in perdition. "Monsieur Rick! How fortuitous! Shall we go to the Cafe Greco?" Ugarte didn't wait for a reply, hailing a taxi. The two men then drove to the old Cafe Greco, a long-time sanctuary for Rome's literati. Rick wondered why Ugarte and Ferrari were so close. He himself wouldn't trust Ugarte with anything.

The cafe was crowded with people of all ages and stations. The artists' faces reflected their distaste for the bourgeois customers who provided them with a livelihood. Ugarte led Rick to a small table in the rear where they ordered cappuccino with Sambucca. Ugarte began to speak in his hushed voice, "I think that Ferrari has made the appropriate contacts. We have new identity papers. He wants you to be ready to sail with us to Ethiopia. The two of you will then travel to Asmara, ostensibly as merchant entrepreneurs. I will travel to Khartoum where certain contacts will be made, contacts that will provide us with the wherewithal to be of service to the Lion of Judah. Ferrari assures me that these services will make us all rich. I will be in and out of Asmara, depending on what services are required where. You, Rick, can be thankful for my language and negotiation skills." He grinned shyly, his face reddening. "We will then have the option of going to Addis Ababa where, if our services prove successful, we might establish ourselves in some way or another." For the next hour Ugarte expanded on the plan that Ferrari had drawn up. Rick, always impressed with Ferrari's competence did not share those impressions about Ugarte.

Rick stared at him and said, "Why in hell do I have to be involved with you? Neither of us need nor want the same thing. Your politics are like shifting sand, your morals those of the rodents the sand shifts over. I trust you not. I like you not."

Ugarte responded with a soprano whine, "Why do you despise me Rick? I want to help you. I too wish to help." Rick sneered at the little man, but said nothing. He lit a Camel and turned in the direction of the piano.

A chunky, smiling black man was standing at the piano, nodding his head at the compass. "Thank you, thank you," he said in American English. He sat and just let his fingers caress the ivories. Suddenly he struck a chord and began to sing, "Swanee." Rick could see that the man could be a real draw and that his audience was well acquainted with his talents. He sang in a soft, unique fashion, a high tenor, carrying the tune gently, yet assuredly, to its ending. Finishing the song, he smiled, looked around, then bowed his head and caressed the keys, urging the music from them.

Rick felt very homesick, the music and the man made him long for peace and rationality. Rick got up from the table and walked over to the piano. The man looked up at him with a smile that went straight to Rick's inner being. "Can I play a song for you?" Rick asked for "Poor Butterfly," which the pianist expertly performed.

Rick took some money from his pocket and put it in the glass atop the piano. "What's your name, and what are you doing here?" The man smiled a crooked smile and said, "It's Sam, and you know why I'm here. I ran out of public houses to play in and I needed the money. Can I play something else for you?" Rick asked him to play "Avalon" and returned to his table.

Ugarte was gone. Rick lit a cigarette and looked around. No one he knew, and no one was interested in him. He ordered a drink from the waiter and drifted along with Sam's music. About a half-hour passed before Sam stopped playing. Rick beckoned to him to join him. Sam came over and said, "The boss don't like me mixing with the customers. Kinda like home. Thanks for the tip." Rick found this openness quite appealing and asked, "You got any family?" Sam shook his head. Rick beckoned for him to sit, and suddenly Sam sat down. "Got any reason to stay here?" Sam shook his head, his expressive eyes filled with tears.

"Got no reason to stay anywhere. Got no reason to do anything. My woman was killed in a race riot in Trenton two years ago. I kinda went crazy and did some things I should'na done. I hid out on the docks for a week, and then some commie longshoreman took me in. He understood all about the race prejudice, said I should join his group and work to change things in the States. It didn't take me long to learn that he wanted me do some things that I didn't want to do. I met some other coloreds who told me about Ethiopia and how the blacks there beat the tar out of the Italians 40 years ago. There is an American Committee for Ethiopia that arranged for a lot of coloreds to go to Asmara and build a community there for us all. They even got their own faith, named after the Emperor Rasta Fari. They's called 'Rastafarians' and they think they can have an all black church based on this faith. I don't know much about that stuff. I just got on a ship I thought was heading for there and got away. 'cept the ship wasn't headin' for Liberia. It was headin' for Naples. What could I do? I snuck off the boat at Naples, met a Somali woman there. She was helpful, got me some papers. Someday I want to go to Somaliland and find that woman. She went back with some party women to work at a club. I guess there a couple Somalilands though, and I don't know which one is hers. I came on to Rome to find a job and here I am."

Rick lit up a Camel and smoked thoughtfully. He shook his head and chuckled. "I've heard things about that black cult. Didn't Marcus Garvey try to set that up in the Caribbean?" Sam shrugged his shoulders, but said nothing. Then Rick asked him, "Why don't you think about coming with me. I'm going to Eritrea to open a club and I could use someone with your talents."

Rick thought to himself, "My God, I haven't given this any thought at all. You could be the Duce's brother-in-law for all I know. A club in Eritrea? I have never thought of a club before in my life. Hey, not a bad idea. What a great front it would be for any kind of activity." Better be careful, though, this may not fly with Ferrari. His cigarette burning his lips interrupted his reverie. His painful lip reminded him of the day when his father slugged him in the mouth and split his lip. His lisp was a result of that blow. Dad had called him a "weak pathetic little fuck." Rick was eleven years old.

Sam looked back, then threw back his head and laughed quietly. "Isn't it funny! I meet you, a song later I'm travelin' with you to God knows where. All I can say is, you seem like just about the best travelin' companion I can think of right now!" They both sat back, Rick ordered another drink and lit another Camel. Sam looked disapprovingly at him and said, "You sure got a love affair goin' with those things."

Rick feigned anger as he said, "I didn't ask you to marry me."

Sam began to fidget in his chair, looked at Rick and asked, "Mr. Rick, you ever kill a man?"

Rick was non-plussed at first, thought for a few seconds and said, "Yeah Sam, I have and that's part of the reason I'm here. Does it make a difference to you?"

Sam's face opened up and he said, "Naw Mr. Rick, it don't make no difference at all."

Rick looked around the room and saw Ferrari moving rapidly towards them, his face inscrutable. He stopped at the table, looked at Sam, and said' "What is this? Where is Ugarte?"

Rick lit another Camel and growled garrulously, "Meet my new partner, Sam. Sam, this is Ferrari." Sam stood up and offered his hand. Ferrari looked at him with distrust but plopped his fat fingers into Sam's then took them away.

Ignoring Sam's presence he turned to Rick and hissed, "Are you out of your mind? Do you want to sabotage this entire operation? Do you want to rot in a Blackshirt prison? This man is unknown to us!"

Rick looked at Ferrari with distaste, saying, "Since when have you and me been such big buddies? I don't know you from a walrus. This man goes with me or I don't go. You got the obsequious Ugarte, I'll have the Good Sam."

"OK Rick you take him as your Boswell. If you must have a minstrel then so be it. I cannot argue over ancillary details at this time. I must tell you that we have only a few days here. Our papers will be ready tomorrow, and then the hard work begins. I have information that the Duce has authorized the minting of a million silver dollars for use in subverting the Ethiopian tribal leaders. I want us to track that shipment, and when it is delivered, I want that money to be mine, ah, ours!"

"What a plan! How ironic, that the Duce's money would be used to buy the weapons that would oppose him," said Rick.

"Ah yes Blaine, Silver to lead, lead to silver! Not kind, but fair. I love the balance that nefarious dealing allows. The scales of justice were meant to be tipped, so why not in our direction? Lest I forget to mention it, it is my intention that all of the silver eventually be ours."

The waiter crept up to the table and took their drink orders. Rick noted that Ferrari ordered Turkish coffee. His questions about this man's past would never be answered, but he felt a strong sense of curiosity towards him. What was it then? The mystery of an urbane man who knew so many things about our world, as well as a strange demimonde that few are aware of? What of his reliability? Rick's present ennui didn't allow him to care. He needed the pace that the fat man had set.

They left the cafe separately, agreeing to meet at another locale, the Basilica Ulpia, in the district of the Coliseum. There they would mingle with people too rich or too well connected to be interested in their little intrigue. There the singer Del Pelo would sing the folk songs of Italy, songs they all could exult in, for Italy was on the march and soon Rome would again be the capitol of the world.

Next day, Rick met Sam at the Foro Mussolini, the sports center constructed by Il Duce for his world-class athletes. Under the banner of "The Duce is always right," the Italian athletes trained for the 1936 Olympics. Il Duce anticipated culminating his year of triumph by presenting medals to his athletes and the blood of Abyssinia to his nation.

Ugarte met them at one of the several trattorias that surrounded the complex. Rick smoked while the other two ate. The purpose was for Ugarte, obviously elated, to present each of them with an envelope. "Letters of passage, travel, and passports. Ferrari conveniently relieved Monsieur Sam of his documents that allowed me the pleasure of preparing his new ones. Ferrari seems pleased with your joining us. He thinks a song now and then will keep Rick on his toes." He smiled conspiratorially at Rick.

Rick laughed and said, "Ugarte, you are a fish, but you somehow swim to the right place. What of the travel plans?"

Ugarte smiled again, his sweet, disarming smile. "We leave by car for Naples in two days. There we will casually observe the loading of the Maria Theresa silver on the ship "Ganges." Mr. Sam, Mr. Ferrari wants you to return with me that he might get to know you better." Ugarte looked at Sam expectantly.

Rick didn't like this arrangement, but since he had brought Sam into the deal, he felt he had little choice here. He shrugged his shoulders and lit up a Camel. "See you later Sam. Come over when you're done and we'll have some dinner." Sam smiled rather nervously as he searched Rick's eyes for approval. Rick nodded his head at the gentle man and turned to go.

Later in his room Rick paced nervously. The bell rang and He bolted to the door. There stood Sam and Rick invited him in. "What happened with Ferrari?

"Seems like a regular guy. Wanted to know why I am in Italy, axed me if the police here had anything on me, axed me if I had known you before.

He seemed a little hung-up on that, couldn't believe you'd just kinda adopt me on sight. I tole him about the rasties and how I had thought about going to Ethiopia. Don't know if he had ever heard about the rasties, but he shore listened hard. I think he be the kind of man who likes to know a lot of things. I think he uses people and facts to make his life easier. I did mention starting a sporting club to him. He was surprised then really laughed. By George, Sam, a capital idea. Capital indeed."

Rick laughed as he picked up a bottle of Scotch from the table and poured himself a drink. "Just wanted to get to know you better. I'll bet he has cables going in 10 directions checking on you. Oh well, if he is careful about that, he'll be careful about the things that will make our lives a little easier."

The docks at Naples were alive with action. Passenger ships, troop ships, battleships, the spectrum of maritime activity. They found pier seven where the "Ganges" lay, a spectacular, albeit a little tacky, a white vessel, the pride of the Italian troop carriers. Several armored vehicles, surrounded by police and military motorcycles, were being unloaded. Additionally there were large boxes, carried by pairs of military police up the gangplank. Ferrari's smile was that of an expectant father seeing his son and heir for the first time.

The four allies showed their documents to the guard at the passenger gangplank. Ferrari waddled up the swaying gangplank to the vessel, where a young ship's officer checked his papers again, then turned him over to a cabin boy. Ferrari told the others that it would be best to be scattered about the ship, meeting on deck later. Then he would pass out handwritten instructions and briefings that would be responded to in writing at the next meeting. If necessary, meetings in which talking was permitted would be arranged. Rick and Sam were seated at the same table, Ferrari sat at the captain's table. How the devil had he arranged that? Rick marveled at this peripatetic man and his mental energy. Few men would dare put together a project so ambitious in a country so far away, especially a country so backward and inaccessible as Ethiopia. How would the Maria Theresas be transferred into their hands? He couldn't wait to learn.

As he puffed his Camel, he fell into a reverie. Home. When would he see it again? Would he ever see it again? Isn't it strange that freedom is not always what you think it will be? Freedom has to exist within oneself, he mused, and if there is no freedom inside, geography is meaningless. How to translate all of this into something meaningful? Despite his youth, he felt aged and vulnerable, too many flanks open for wounding. Maybe he would find something or someone in the coming new chapter in his life. He foresaw the coming Armageddon, the splitting apart of the sad remnants of that world made briefly free by the heroism of the lost generation. His mood flew away as Sam came up beside him. "Troubles Mr. Richard?"

Rick smiled wanly. "Not anymore Sam. You made 'em go away. Wish you had your piano up here." Sam laughed and the two men stood in silent camaraderie as the ship pulled away from the dock while the dockside band played and the crowd cheered and waved little Italian flags. Rick could see several other troop ships with their decks crowded with soldiers waiting to pull away, their well-wishers waving goodbye.

"Italy," Rick mused. "What the hell are you doing, sending these kids to some primitive God-forsaken place to kill and be killed for the evanescent glory it could bring to one man's pomposity. How many ships have left friendly shores in pursuit of the same, and what human cargo did they return with?" He would have to change; he would come to realize that some of us must ultimately make a decision where and for what we will stand and die.

CHAPTER TEN

Ethiopia

The Italian troopship "Ganges" left the port of Naples at 7 PM. She was once "The President Wilson," a member of Americas' transatlantic service. Old but fast, they said. The old lady carried 1200 officers and men, plus guests. The officers and guests occupied the first and second-class cabins, the enlisted men the third class cabins and a part of the hold section. Overhearing the conversations, it was apparent that the soldiers had nothing but scorn for the Ethiopians whom they saw as savages in lion skins who carried spears, shields, and ancient flintlock muskets. Their morale could not have been higher despite the warnings about the heat and the hostile terrain. Why? The Italians almost mystic adoration for Il Duce.

Rick and Sam watched and listened as a dockside military band played martial music, choral groups sang patriotic songs, flags waved and people cheered wildly. A medal bedecked honor guard strutted up and down the pier and then stood at attention as the ship pulled away from the dock. The ship's whistle pierced the afternoon air, and they were off to Rick's first war. Rick turned to Sam and said, "Wonder if the Romans had bands playing when their legions left for war?"

"Sure glad I jest play the piano. These guys look serious."

The summer sun hung low over the Bay of Naples, transforming the turquoise water into a flaming jewel. The glowering mass of Mt. Vesuvius loomed to the south, an ominous umber-gray hulk providing stark contrast to gem-like beauty of the bay. The massive crenellated towers of the 13th century fortress Maschio Angioino rose up on the shore as the ship turned south towards Messina.

Rick said, "I wonder if we'll ever see Naples again."

Sam replied, "If we do, I'll bet it won't look the same. Nuthin' ever does."

"Let's get a drink, Sam. I'm thirsty already just thinking about trekking in the desert. I'm buying."

"Sounds jest right Mr. Richard, I could use one too."

"Gentlemen, good evening, is this not a scene from Paradise?" The suited bulk of Ferrari approached them from one of the hatchways.

"Maybe Paradise lost," said Rick.

Ferrari guffawed. "Blaine, you need a large dose of optimism." He grabbed Rick's arm and shook it briskly.

"Join us for a drink, Ferrari. Might slow you down a bit." As they walked down the stairs to the lounge, Rick wondered as to the whereabouts of that little rat, Ugarte. He almost said something to Ferrari but elected not to bring him up. Why spoil a good Martini?

In the small officer's lounge the air was dank with sea air, tobacco and body odor. The combination stung Rick's nose, making him sneeze. Ferrari bulled his way to a small table that was being vacated by three young Italian officers, all tipsy and laughing. Ferrari commandeered a slim young waitress and ordered three martinis. He then sat back and smiled at anyone whose eyes fell upon him. How a fat man in a three-piece suit could scramble around as he did and remain unwrinkled and grandly avuncular was a wonder to Rick. When the drinks came Ferrari stood up, extending his glass. "Gentlemen." By so doing he commanded the room to his attention. "To the Duce and his ultimate victory." The officers staggered to their feet, shouting, "Duce, Duce, Duce!!!"

Rick was flummoxed by the response but he stood with the others. Sam looked bewildered but was also standing. He whispered in Rick's ear, "Good sweet Jesus, these folks are really serious about this."

Rick replied, "Not just serious, fanatic." He lit a cigarette and sat down, but before Ferrari sat first. Tonight Ferrari sat at the captain's table regaling the assembled company with his anecdotes. The captain approved, for it took much of the entertainment burden from his shoulders. Ferrari talked about the Duce and the intelligence of his African campaign, about Hitler and his jealousy of Italy, of the League and its feeble attempts at sanctions against Italy. Howls of laughter came at one point; Ferrari himself wiped tears from his eyes, some riposte about the British diplomatic service and a play on the word, "Service."

Later that evening, the four conspirators met in the dilapidated card room, smoking cigars and sipping cognac. All were up to date concerning the Ethiopian arrival. Ferrari looked about, then, seeing no interest in their table, turned to the others and murmured, "The Captain has inadvertently blabbed the details concerning our grubstake." He continued, "When we arrive, the cargo will be unloaded as it was loaded, by soldiers and military police. It will be housed in the dock offices overnight, then taken by special convoy to Eritrea. On arrival there it will be taken to the embassy where the governor general will dole it out. Our plan is to secure it during its journey to Asmara. Enough for now. Part of the money will be replaced by lead filled coins with silvered exteriors. The bogus money arrived on the same ship."

Rick drew on his expensive cigar and marveled anew at this corpulent genius. He believed that Ferrari would snuff all of their' lives if taken to the wall, but what the hell, to be forewarned is everything. If he needed to worry, he would worry about Ugarte, He, too, loved money, but lacked resolve and versatility. He would cut and run at the slightest provocation, leaving the web to entrap the others. So long as the promise of gain remained, Ugarte was 100 per cent reliable. Some zealot! So what! Rick had his eyes and he had Sam. The big question plaguing Rick was how Ferrari would get the silver without anyone suspecting them. There would be a large number of soldiers on guard and they would be prepared for any funny business from the convoy. Or would they?

Next morning the four conspirators met for breakfast in the officer's mess. Ferrari had preceded them and was surrounded by bacon, scrambled eggs, toast, and a large mound of morning breads. "Welcome my friends, let's celebrate the morning. Look, Messina awaits." He gestured towards the great window that looked out upon the vista of Sicily. "This is an island of surprises, of many heritages: Greek, Roman, Arabic, French, Spanish, English and modern Italy. He smiled broadly as he returned to worship his plentitude.

"Sounds like a great place to visit," said Rick. "Wish my Italian was better."

Ferrari smiled and said, "It's not a difficult language and the rewards are many when you learn it." They all laughed at the implied carnality.

Loud music interrupted the conversation as trumpets, drums, guitars and violins thundered out *Giovinessa,* the Italian national anthem. The troops began singing with vigor, while the ship's whistle blasted three times. The docks of Messina lay before them as two battered tugboats chugged out to bring them alongside pier 33.

More soldiers and their officers boarded the ship while yet another band played martial music, then *Funiculi Funicula.* Ferrari knew the words in Italian and bellowed them out in a stentorian baritone. Rick was impressed a performance that revealed further nuances of the man. He wondered of the background of such a man as this; surely a renaissance man. Where and how did he acquire such varied information?

The troop loading was quite orderly, surprisingly so given the usual anarchistic conduct of the soldiers. The rusty tugs tooted their whistles and the ship was underway. Rick smoked and fought back his reveries, thoughts of halcyon days and nights, while he wondered if he would ever know them again.

Rick's woolgathering abruptly ended as they exited to the deck. An improvised orchestra, led by an accordion, began blasting more Italian street songs. The upper deck was suddenly crowded with young officers pushing their way to the rail. They began singing along with the men below. They tossed bars of candy, cigarettes, and even coins to them. It was festival for these men and boys, full of the assurance of their superiority.

The uniformed rabble grew quiet as a burly man wearing the uniform of a general officer appeared at the rail; below the music stopped and the men sprang to attention A young lieutenant, apparently the general's aide, began to speak through a bullhorn. "My fellow Italians." This greeted by a lusty roar from the men. "General Garbano would like to say a few words to all of you."

The general swelled his chest, threw his head back and with arms akimbo Mussolini style threw out his right arm in the fascist salute. "Duce, Duce, Duce," he barked loudly. The men responded with their own triple Duces. Suez Garbano continued, "Paisanos!" The men cheered wildly at this gesture of familiarity, then grew silent. "We are launching a great campaign to restore to Italy the power and splendor that was our ancient Roma! Once we allowed the savages of Abyssinia to trample that majesty in the dust. Today is the first day of our retaliation. Revenge is not always sweet but it is a dish most enjoyed cold. In Abyssinia we serve them semifreddi." Wilder cheering accompanied this pronouncement. Garbano raised his hand to silence them and continued. "These Abyssinian pigs, blacks in animal skins, carrying their spears and believing they can overwhelm our tanks, cannon, machine guns and repeating rifles. And today I bring you news of another secret weapon. From our airplanes we greet these howling mobs with small cylinders of death, death from an agent so powerful they will die in minutes. That's all I dare say about that item." Again the men cheered him, and the general and his men roared, "Duce Duce, Duce!"

Rick was again surprised at their total worship of the squat man with the jutted jaw. Rick asked Sam to join him in exploring the ship. "Sure is a messy ship, Rick. Look how the paint is peeling. Look, there's rust everywhere."

"Right, Sam. Sure doesn't look like a luxury liner anymore. It needs paint, swabbing, and deodorizing. Let's go below and check it out." They took the ship's ladder to the next lower level. The smell of the unwashed attacked them. The combination of heat, humidity, and dirty bodies produced a remarkably powerful malodorous mix. They saw a sea of bunks, mostly unoccupied. The smell and the heat had driven most of the men up to the decks. Rick was surprised to see many of them eating their lunches of pasta with big chunks of meat washed down with red wine. The lack of discipline surprised and amused him. "Gee Sam, they sure look happy. Who needs order?"

That evening Ferrari came to his cabin and invited Rick to stroll on deck with him. Once outside, Ferrari said to him, "Look my boy." He gestured out to sea. At first Rick saw nothing, then he spied a group of tiny flickering lights right at the horizon. He turned to Ferrari and said, "So what is that?"

Ferrari harrumphed and said, "Those are the running lights of British warships. Ominous yes, but impotent. They don't like the Italians and their militancy, so they follow all Italian shipping to and through the Suez. They will be discrete but they will be a presence." Ferrari reached into his breast pocket and pulled out a sheaf of papers. "I obtained these from the radio room. They are dispatches with weighty words about the League meetings in Geneva discussing the danger of Italian imperialism. These will be distributed to the senior officers aboard who will deal with them as if they were broadcasts from the moon. All of Europe fears another war so they practice denial of the Italian imperialism, say nothing of the looming German threat."

Rick wrinkled his brow and replied, "So this war is an outlaw operation but nothing will be done to prevent it. The league has issued a toothless warning and the fascists have ignored it. What is your plan, Ferrari? I ask you because I know you have one."

"You're a clever man, Rick, and I admire that. My plan is one you may enjoy because I know you hate the big dogs jumping the small ones. Let's begin,"

"How about beginning over a martini," Rick said.

"A well thought-out suggestion, my boy.

Rick led Ferrari back to the officer's lounge, preparing himself for the odoriferous blast of the multiple stinks. He spied a place next to a porthole that he saw could be opened. After opening it he sat down as Ferrari had already ordered their drinks. "We'll have Compari and soda, my boy. More to drink and less brain damage." Rick regretted his assent realizing that the fat man was right. They did have much to talk about. The striker brought drinks and Ferrari sucked in the air in a deep draught as he began.

"My boy, I have trusted few people in my life, too few perhaps. I have known you a short time, but I find you and your Moor as trustworthy as men come. I have never been wrong in this area before and I don't believe I will be now." He took another deep breath and continued. "Rick, I can make you . . . I can make us all rich as Croesus." Rick half-rose in his chair, angered by the "Sit and listen, my boy. This plan will benefit the Ethiopians as well. I'm sorry if I offended your ideals." Rick sat down and lit a cigarette while he battled his anger.

"Rick, the plan is simple and complex at the same time. Here it is, distilled for brevity. We have a delicious brew of combatants here, not just the Italians and the Abyssinians. The British are acutely interested. They fear the loss of the Suez Canal as well as their colonies. The French have investments they are unwilling to lose. The Germans consider the Italians their wards and are prepared to clean up any mess the Italians might create. The Arabs, the Jews of the desert, want all the parties out of the colonies. They want their sandbox to themselves. Secondary parties are involved in promoting the impotent League of Nations, your President Wilson's fairy tale. In summary, none of the parties trusts any of the others and will do anything to garrote them. We are independent operators who at least are willing to help the victims of all this avarice and treachery and that would be the Ethiopians. I intend to provide them with the wherewithal to survive the treacheries of the others. I need you to facilitate the process." The fat man leaned back as he sipped his iceless drink and stared at Rick. His was a contemplative stare, less expectant than analytic. It spoke of his belief in Rick's idealism and his, Ferrari's, belief that he could manipulate both the idealism and the burgeoning cynicism. He knew he had erred in talking money, but he had to bring it to the table and take a chance.

Rick stared at a Ferrari he had not seen before, cleared his throat, and said, "Thanks for the trust comments, Ferrari, they are good to hear. But you're asking me to do something that I've never done before and that is to trust a stranger. All men are strangers to me; all are guilty of something until proven innocent. But now I've decided to trust you, hard as it is for me to do. Please continue with your plan. But before you do, remember that for me it's not about the money. We have issues here that transcend economics."

Ferrari smiled broadly and said, "Well spoken, Blaine. You've granted me your trust and I will strive to earn it as well as our respect along the way."

Rick growled back, "Just talk about your plan."

The fat man nodded and continued, "What I am about to relate is our second and even grander plan, a plan I think will fit your idealistic needs a bit better than the Maria Theresa scam. I have already worked out the details and made the contacts. The country of Djibouti lies just to the east of Ethiopia. It is a desolate place, not only barren but hotter than Hades. The people who inhabit the place are mostly bandits and smugglers and it's the smugglers that I contacted. Can't tell you how I gained the contact, that's a trade secret. Nevertheless they await our visit and the contraband they possess could swing the war towards the defenders of the faith. Comments or questions?"

"Yeah, who makes contact with these guys?"

"Why Rick; you, of course." Rick laughed and in the process was somehow changed, recharged. The fat man's brilliance made him realize that all that he said was doable made him feel ready for anything despite any consequences.

Ferrari continued on about their itinerary after arrival in Asmara. They would let some time pass before the operation. A band of Ethiopian irregulars would meet Rick and his party of irregulars and escort them to the transfer point just inside the border between the two countries. When he had finished, Ferrari slipped Rick a small folder of maps. Then they finished their drinks and went back on deck.

The convoy steamed down the mighty Suez Canal, ignoring the British gunboats that appeared and disappeared. Rick and his friends sat on deck watching it all. Sam spied a small roadster on the road paralleling the canal. A large Italian flag attached to the back fluttered in the breeze while the girl and her companions cheered and waved. She followed them until the sixth day when the convoy cleared the canal and entered the Red Sea. By this time the heat became unbearable and the little group of plotters gasped for any breath of air. The steel plates ship blazed with fiery waves of the reflected sun. Even Ferrari looked like a sweaty, beefy blob while Ugarte never left the area of a fan. Only Sam seemed to tolerate this inferno although he complained as much as the others.

Rick found refuge near the beer cooler in the officer's bar where he stood smoking. A tall ruddy-faced man in a wilted dress shirt and shorts walked up to him and introduced himself. "I've concluded that you are an American. So am I. Name is Herb Matthews, New York Times." The accent was heavily New York City. Rick wondered if this was another New York self-important snob. Yet his eyes were kind with a touch of desperation. The heat had him, too.

"Name's Blaine, Rick Blaine. What's the Times doing in this hellhole?"

"Damn good question. War and only war. If I knew then what I know now, I'd tell 'em to shove it, all of it. I've never been this hot. Must change my ways if hell is worse. What got you out here?"

Rick mopped his face and said, "Someone told me they needed a casino out here. Shoulda' opened a damn refrigeration business."

Matthews laughed. "Refrigeration? Wouldn't work. There's virtually no electricity in this country with the exception of Addis and Asmara. If you can curry a little favor with the Italians . . ."

"Yeah, I know what you mean. You'll have to meet my traveling troupe; I'm sure my friend Ferrari can arrange a little cooling device or two." He smiled and gestured towards the door. He and Matthews walked out to find Ferrari.

Ferrari gave Matthews a perfunctory handshake then started to turn away. Rick said, "Herb is a reporter with the New York Times here to cover the war"

Ferrari turned quickly, saying, "By George Matthews, it's a pleasure," and grasped his arm with a show of warmth. Rick took it all in and said to himself, "Another useful body added to the list."

At last the Massawa landmass popped up in the shimmering sunscape. God, anything to get off this stinking ship. President Wilson must be rolling in his grave, struggling to deny any kinship with this rusting, foul smelling wreck. The island loomed larger until finally The *Ganges* wallowed into the port of Massawa at three o'clock in the afternoon; its ship's whistle wailing amidst a cacophony of wails from the other vessels in the area. The waterfront was alive with transports unloading military cargo, hundreds of vehicles, armored cars, tanks, lorries, and thousands of young soldiers. There were many civilians, too, ready to start new lives in the Italian colonies, hoping to make fortunes. All would happen under the flag of Italy bringing glory and world envy to Italy. No more little swarthy men cringing into America with their hats in their hands, derided for their pigeon English. These were Italians speaking Italian, sweeping into a new Empire like the Legions of Imperial Rome.

The month of October made no difference in the temperature. Hot? Hellfire. The ship's crew scurried around like they moved in the most temperate of climates. Ugarte looked close to collapse, Sam 's face dripped sweaty tears, while Ferrari sagged onto the ship's rail. Matthews struggled to lower his ridiculous necktie. "Why the necktie, Herb?" Rick's tone was jocular. "You'd be better off without a shirt." Matthews laughed as he continued his struggle.

They stood at the rail monitoring the activity. They watched the cargo being unloaded, and they noted with specific interest the crates with the insignia of the Bank of Italy. Ferrari's fortune lay within, as well as Rick's answer to the despot that would terrorize the weak and enslave the dissenters. When had he come to feel this way? Introspection was a fear of his; the examination of his past might prove too damning for him. He had adopted the philosophy that he would never live in regret.

He thought anew of the senselessness of anarchy. Remembering Sacco and Venzetti and their fanatical dedication to their cause, their framing and their arrest and trial was regret enough for him. He who had been high born and high educated saw the waste of these two intelligent men, immigrants feared and vilified by the sons of immigrants in a nation of immigrants. Yet he felt he understood why his father had hated these men so, because he was just close enough to their situation that he remembered the hunger and the anger they displayed. Better these men be done with. The nation had to rise above the petty assassinations of Europe, rise above the encrusted class system and build a country where it was possible to rise by cooperating with, or ignoring the system. Now these Italian immigrants held the upper hand, they were now the classed society. All they needed to secure these is to aggress a group of tribal primitives with their lion skin dress-ups and their slave trade. They deemed these people lower than low, considered them God's hated creatures. He pondered the regret that he had not worked long enough in the system to change it, the curse of the cynical, young idealist who thinks he knows it all.

CHAPTER ELEVEN

Eritrea

"Let's go, everyone," said Ferrari as he waddled towards the gangplank looking for all the world like a mother duck. Rick saw the Italian troops starting down the aft gangplank, then heard them singing, '*Giovinessa*.

"Geez, I'm sure gettin' tired of that tune," said Sam. "They needs a good jazzman down there playing '*The Saints Go Marching In*."

Ugarte mumbled something unintelligible as he staggered onto the pier. An orderly confusion masquerading as chaos reigned; soldiers, crew, dock workers, stevedores, small bands of dark-skinned women milled as they laughed and called out to the debarking men in a strange tongue. They wore colorful but scanty costumes and their faces were heavily painted. "Whores," said Matthews, "The oldest profession representing one of the oldest civilizations in the world. Takes awhile but they will look better sooner than you think."

Rick laughed and said, "Yeah but how about the smell?"

"We Americans undervalue the exotic nature of the various scents of women. Such a shame; a level of enjoyment is lost. Actually I know nothing about this. Hearsay only." He winked at Rick who said nothing.

Ferrari broke the embarrassed silence and said, "Gentlemen, Napoleon is reported to have written to Josephine, "I will be home in four days, do not bathe. But we are part of a great moment in history; Napoleon is dead. The largest colonial army in history is now massed to take on the most unprepared country extant. Can we change the course of history?" His question went unanswered,

The military band announced the Italian army as battalion after battalion of Italian regulars marched towards the railroad station. "I just hope they don't sing Giovinessa again," Rick said to Sam. "Enough is enough."

"It's not so bad, Mr. Rick. Just think of all the other songs they could do."

"Rick, don't be so sour, said Matthews, "These kids are really expressing their bravado. Inside, lots of them are scared to death." He gestured towards Mussolini's sons. How many will never see their mommas and girl friends again? Mussolini is not their fault."

Rick's heart went out to the boys and in apology said, "Sorry guys must be the sun."

Ferrari had long since abandoned his jacket as he threw a sweat-soaked arm around Rick. "Let's catch a train, Rick. I have arranged an air-conditioned coach for us." Rick shook his head in wonderment; was this more of Ferrari's magic? Then he broke into his own version of a pigeon-Italian *Giovinessa.*

They passed by the fringes the red-light district and Rick was sickened by the smell. Sweat, musky; a spicy odor he could only interpret as sexual. Dirty bodies and cheap perfume? Hard to say. Sam was the first to speak, "God, Mr. Rick, I's ashamed to be colored. These people just don't wash their clothes or themselves."

Rick was taken by the presence of teams of mules, packed to capacity, stumbling along the wharf. The heat and the over-loading were making some of the animals stumble to their knees. The brayed piteously and some fell off the wharf into the sea. Rick thought of his own ability to withstand privation and wondered if he was ever going to adjust to this heat. The Italian stevedores were working furiously unloading the cargo from the host of ships lined up, stern first on the wharves. Large cranes lifted cargo from the holds while horse drawn carts and trucks shuttled through the masses. All of the men crowded aboard flat cars that took them across the causeway to the mainland. Rick said to Sam, "I don't know how anyone could walk around here for any distance. I thought I was going to vomit back there."

Sam nodded and said, "You and me and the Italian army."

An Italian Alpini captain came up to Ferrari and saluted smartly. "Senor Ferrari I regret to inform you that the Littorino cannot take us on our first leg to Asmara. We will take motor coaches to a Gebbi and stray the night. The train will be able to accommodate us the next morning." He saluted again and turned on his heel.

The convoy took form rapidly, and soon Rick and his compatriots were seated in a very hot and very old bus with no windows, and no air conditioning. Ferrari, for all his' weight, seemed quite cool and comfortable, while Ugarte sweated profusely and mopped his brow, his face a mask of sorrow. Ugarte always looked like he could burst into tears.

An Italian Major sat stiffly beside Ferrari, talking animatedly. "Ah this heat! My last post here was not so humid as this. But this time . . ." He rolled his eyes upward and crossed himself. "It will be hotter where I am going, but not as hot as I make it for someone!" He grinned at Rick who gave him a half-smile, cigarette dangling from the same dropped corner.

"And where would that be, Major?"

The officer looked about conspiratorially and whispered hoarsely, "Adowa. We revenge Adowa! Italy will march to Adowa and destroy the ignominy for all time!" Grinning with excitement, he asked Rick, "And what will you do in Eritrea? Are you a reporter?"

Rick said, "Sorta. I'm thinking of starting a club, you know, a spot where people can relax after a hard day fighting the Emperor. Maybe throw down a few lira at a table and forget the campaign for a few hours. Do you think the men would like that?"

The Major whistled softly, saying, "I think, speaking for myself, that maybe there will be . . . ah . . . women croupiers, eh?" Rick laughed, the man had a point, but he would wait for the chance to see what lay ahead.

Then the Major stood up and left the bus, waving a salute. Rick turned to Ferrari who said, "The more I analyze your idea, Rick the prouder I am of your Yankee Doodle ingenuity. A club. Why, even I in my grandest dreams couldn't have stroked a finer piece of genius!" He gave Rick a dramatic wink.

Rick was somewhat embarrassed by this. "I don't know a damn thing about running a club, but it seems simple if you have the right ingredients."

"The ingredients, dear Rick, are alcohol, money, and women. Sufficient intrigue right there, eh? But, we shall add another ingredient. Espionage. With the first three comes the fourth. The fourth will give us the information we need to keep apace of what might be rapidly changing events. Like Oscar Wilde, I find being in the know is a bore, but not knowing, a tragedy!" Ferrari chuckled at his little joke and rubbed his hands gleefully. "Besides, there will be kindness in our club, like your Statue of Liberty, we will take in the hungry and the thirsty, ply them with women, drink, and gaming, then their gratitude will bid them spill out the interesting news of the day." Rick felt great; Ferrari's elation was infectious. Ugarte mopped his brow with a flourish saying, "Oh yes! And there is more we can do! I am told that many Europeans are fleeing Abyssinia for the safety of Eritrea. There will be some who will be unable to seek documents from official sources, I say with no modesty that I possess, shall we say, talents in that direction." Rick ignored this obvious gesture of ego and asked Sam what he thought.

"Mr. Richard, right now I just don't know. I think I'd like a club, but I don't know about these other things, maybe I'll like them and maybe I won't. I'm not curious enough to do too much more that's illegal. Playing the piano and singing never got me nowhere bad."

Clapping him on the back, Rick lit up the last of his pack. "Makes me wonder if I shouldn't take up the piano."

The trip from the Red Sea port to Asmara would be tedious, and Rick thought about the wonders of flight. His brief fantasy ended when a tall black man boarded the bus. Ferrari stood up almost deferentially and grasped the man's hand. "Ras Tayfu! So happy that you could meet us in these less than noble conditions. Please greet my friends, Mr. Blaine, Mr. Ugarte, and Mr. Jefferson. Mr. Blaine is planning the opening of a casino in Asmara, and Mr. Jefferson is in charge of entertainment. Herr Ugarte is my liaison." Ferrari's obsequious behavior could mean but two things, power and money, and lots of both. Ferrari went on. "Gentlemen, a Ras is an Ethiopian general, and Ras Tayfu is a general's general! He is of Tigre, which is the province south of Eritrea, and a good friend of the Italians."

Rick stared, thinking that it wouldn't surprise him if a bolt from heaven killed them all. Chance of war? The war is already a fact.

The Major returned, saluting the Ras smartly. "The convoy is on its way. All will please sit and we shall depart." He ordered the driver to start the bus, and the parade was on.

The first 50 kilometers weren't terribly difficult except for the blowing sand and the fumes from the bus's diesel engine. It was too hot to smoke, so Rick slumped back in his seat wondering as he pretended to doze. "How does Ferrari know the Ras? What role did the Ras play in the money heist?" Then he knew. So simple. Ferrari had brought along boxes and crates of "equipment" which were' suddenly meant for the club. He had bribed the port authorities that he might bring in his possessions without duty. In the process they had not been examined for content! The content of those boxes bore the answer to Ferrari's little riddle and Rick was certain that it was going to be Christmas for the Ras.

A few hours after they had begun their climb up into the high plateaus of Eritrea, they came upon a squalid little fortress settlement baking in the desert sun. The convoy halted in front of a burnt brick walled Gebbi flying the Italian flag. Several native soldiers moved quickly to open the gates, and the convoy rolled into the courtyard. The bus partners staggered out into dust of mid-afternoon. Rick's nostrils crinkled against the acrid stench of human waste and garbage but Ugarte showed no olfactory repulsion as he hunched forward looking for all the world like a pudgy desert lizard. The major was smartly saluted, then greeted by an Alpini sergeant in his forest green uniform. The Major turned to the little party and invited them into his quarters, where they were served cool drinks. Rick produced a Camel; the Ras looked quickly at the package and helped himself. Rick lit both, took a long, hungry drag, and looked about. Simple room, whitewashed, clean, with IL Duce pugnaciously jutting his jaw at them from the wall.

Major Criti began an oration, "We are here, and we will prevail over these slave-keepers. Our mothers and wives have all united in an act of faith against Ras Tafari and his iniquitous mob. Every Italian woman has donated her wedding ring to this cause and wears a ring of steel in its place; a ring of steel for a mass of gold, gold and steel will bring victory to our Duce. We gave these perfidious savages every chance for peace, every explanation of our aims here in Africa, their failure to respond to our offers leaves us no choice but war, and war it must be! All glory to our Duce!"

Criti looked around without embarrassment, unaware that he may have been carried away by his zeal. By this time, the Ras had left the room. Rick nodded to Sam, they offered their apologies to the Major and went to their quarters.

Dinner was a huge banquet hosted by the Ras, and it included many spit-roasted lambs, and some wild game. The Italians had sufficient quantities of wine to add to the fiery honey liquor of their host. Both the Italian and the irregular troops shared in the bounty, and it took only a short time for all the men to become muddled and inattentive. Many toasts to victory were proposed and consumed, speeches were made, and braggadocio prevailed. Rick noted all of this as he limited his drinking. Ferrari seemed to be totally immersed in the festivities, but once his and Rick's eyes met, Rick knew the man was stone sober. As the intensity of the gala ebbed, individuals and groups drifted off to tend to their own needs. Sam left after a brief conversation with Rick. Soon Ferrari bade goodnight, leaving Rick, the Ras, and a few of his men still sitting.

The Ras smiled a toothy grin at Rick, "Ferrari tells me you intend to open a club. Have you done this before?" Rick shook his head and the Ras continued, "Will you have women? You must have women here, for the white men do not appreciate the pleasures of the Black continent until it is too late. Of course you will have women."

Rick shook his head, saying, "I'm not a pimp, Ras, I am a simple man who needs a livelihood."

The Ras said thickly, "if you wish to make a living here with a club, you must give the Italians what they need. They are lovers, not warriors, and they rank the glory of the flesh higher than the glory of victory in the field."

"Thanks for the tip," Rick said.

The Ras yawned, belched, and let his head fall onto his plate. As Rick stood up, the irregulars moved close to the Ras glaring at Rick. He turned and walked to his quarters. Sam was already asleep, so Rick lit a Camel and sat on the stoop. The night was black, the stars dimmed by clouds. He became aware of sounds and movement in the corrals and around the outer buildings and he knew exactly what to expect. Sudden there came a blinding, deafening explosion, screams and shouts followed, then darkness. Rick bolted to his feet and started to the door. Now, the clatter of horses' hooves, another explosion as a charge blew the gate of the Gebbi, and a horde of horsemen thundered through it. The Ras was saying good-bye.

Troops staggered from their barracks, stiff and drowsy from their excesses, as Major Criti stood in the center of a spotlight beam. "Turn on the electric lights!" he implored.

"They have destroyed the generator!"

"Where is the Ras?" he demanded.

"They're gone, all gone!" came the response. Rick grinned and realized that the pieces had come together. Ferrari! Where was Ferrari? Rick trotted over to his billet, and was surprised to find Ferrari standing in a small group observing the confusion. An incredulous look played over his face, but it was the look of a man practiced in the art of subterfuge. Rick asked him if he knew what had just happened, and Ferrari shook his head. Electric lights interrupted the torch play as Major Criti raced towards the vault building.

The metal door hung rakishly on his hinges; Criti pulled it aside, playing a large electric torch over the contents. The treasury boxes were tumbled and some gaped open, but the gaps were filled with silver coins. With a sob of relief, Criti turned to face the others. "They missed it, they missed all of it!" He ordered the detachment to run to the other buildings, as they did, Rick surreptitiously picked up a coin and stuck it in his pocket, then joined the others in the building-to-building search. The Ras and all of his irregulars had gone while eight Eritrean irregulars lay about the compound, each with their throat slit and both hands severed. As Major Criti assessed the scene he said darkly, "You cannot trust any of these blacks, ours or theirs, they care only for themselves, even Ras Tafari cannot trust them. They would sell his regime to the highest bidder, and sell it back to him again, should he offer more. Now we must secure the compound against the shiftis, for they know and exploit any weaknesses we have." The Major ordered that two armored cars be driven to the entrance to the Gebbi and sentries to patrol the outer walls.

Still in the courtyard, Rick took out the coin he had secured and looked carefully at it, then pulled out a small bag and withdrew two similar pieces. Looking from one to the other he shook his head. "They look and feel the same to me, but I can't believe the Ras would leave that money if his intent was theft. What other motive is there for his behavior?"'

Ferrari laughed a deep satisfying laugh. "Don't be a fool, Rick. The coins are real, at least the ones you have. Others of them are not, and you'd have to bite each one and melt it down to know the difference. I, too, was fooled when I had them made and shipped here. Believe me, they are excellent reproductions of the Maria Theresas. But real? Emphatically no! Is not reality only in the eyes of the beholder? I would like to believe that I am the master of the art of blending fantasy with reality; I find it the only way to remain sane." He chuckled and took out a cigar.

Rick asked. "If the Ras took the coins, they belong to him, not you. Correct?"

Ferrari slitted his eyes, threw out his considerable chin, and said, "The Ras is a clever man. Greedy, but clever. I simply let him steal the money, and I supplied the replacements. He needs money for guns. I shall provide him with the guns, he gives me my, ah, our, share of the dollars. His 'friends' will get the hybrid Maria Theresas and they will soon learn that they are fakes. Who do they blame? The Italians, of course. The Italians will lose valuable allies and Ras Tafari will win back their loyalty. Isn't that a happy ending?"

Rick laughed at the scheme, but felt the power of it. "You are a master, Ferrari. But is money the only thing you're getting out of this?"

Ferrari became pensive. His voice roughened, his eyes welled up in what must be an unusual display of unfeigned emotion. "Mussolini's black shirts destroyed the only thing that ever meant truth to me. She was the only perfect fantasy I shall ever know. The totality, the profundity of my grief prevents me from saying more." Sam and Ugarte were silent; the only sound was the pouring of more grappa.

Next morning the four struggled through the hordes of Italian fighting men towards a "Littorino" the swift Italian electric train. Matthews, who seemed to possess an encyclopedic knowledge of all things Ethiopian, told them about the train. "These babies are electrically operated and really fast. The other trains here take eight hours to Asmara; these make it in three. It's only 35 miles as the crow flies; there are lots of switchbacks, ups and downs on this route. Be glad you weren't here to work on it."

Rick mulled over Mathew's words. So the trip to Asmara was still going to be long and tedious, causing him to ponder the wonders of flight.

Rick found the heat already repressive, but Matthews' reassurance that it the train would be cool and dry cheered him. He found himself suddenly missing the urban ambiance of New York that had been his milieu for so many years. Club concepts began to dance in his mind. Gambling as such held some attraction for him; it was the gambling types that repelled him, greedy men and treacherous women, desperate people with grubby bills clutched in their hands hoping for that one big roll that would put them at the top of the heap. Gamblers had sexual responses to winning and losing, being on a roll was like having a sexual prowess never enjoyed before, the piles of chips rose like some phallic symbols erected to the gambling God. Losing was impotence, a rejection by a lover. He recalled a crapshooter (on one of his occasional trips to a casino) calling out to anyone who would listen to come see his good fortune, a man totally caught up in his exhibitionism. Rick thought about the money that would be made and what it could purchase. He lay back in his seat, content with his reveries.

The train pulled away from the station and soon reached maximum speed. The terrain immediately became mountainous and arid. Despite the heat, workers and soldiers labored at road and bridge building as the train sailed by. Rick wanted to sleep but the activity along the route was too interesting to miss. Matthews was sitting next to him and said, "Wait'll you see the tramway. The Italians built it to expedite transport from Massawa to Asmara. It's not done but it's close."

Rick asked, "How do you know all this? Been sleeping with a Mata Hari?"

"Don't I wish. I had several long chats with one of the engineers when we were at sea. He seemed to need to brag."

Rick realized that he hadn't had a smoke since they left the Gebbi and he lit up. The coolness of the car enhanced the pleasure. He offered one to Matthews but he declined, lighting up his pipe instead. Ferrari, looking fresh and dry, waddled up and said, "Excuse us, Matthews, we've got some work to do." He waved towards his seat and Matthews got up and squeezed past him. Ferrari wheezed into the too small seat and said, "Rick, we need to have a chat. We'll be in Asmara and we have to synchronize our stories. Let's start by designing just a base plan for your club."

"Fine, Ferrari, but tell me, how do we get our furnishings if we are going to build a casino?"

"I made arrangements in Rome for all of the equipment I think we'll need."

Rick half rose in his seat and thrust his finger in Ferrari's face. "Damn it Ferrari, your presumptions are beginning to irritate me. Your plans for my life may not be a match for mine . . . ."

Ferrari shot back, "And damn you Blaine, I'm truly sick of your American naiveté, your ideations of idealism that have no sense of preparation, of planning. You are an intelligent naïf, a man without regard for the future of others. Few citizens of other countries have the luxury of your American disregard for the need to form the future in their own image. Pay attention to this and grow up!"

Rick blanched, stunned by the outburst. He shakily lit a cigarette and looked out the window. His gaze fastened on an overseer who was whipping a black laborer. The scene changed but left its imprint. He said to himself, "Maybe Ferrari is right. I do have some growing up to do. Anger and disappointment are the only emotions that I know to this point." He turned to Ferrari and said, "Go on, I'm listening." He strained for calm but his heart pounded.

"I am truly sorry Rick, but I meant every word I said. Are you ready to hear me out?"

"Sure, Ferrari, I'll hear you out. Just don't push me too hard."

Ferrari's monologue was extensive and complex, and Rick took it all in. The ideas were great, the plan was waterproof. The casino was an assured success. When he had finished, Rick smiled at him. "Ferrari, I have listened and heard. All of it. Thanks for the therapy." Ferrari smiled, leaned his bulk back into his seat and closed his eyes. Rick found Matthews staring out the window at the landscape, a scene unchanged since before man first climbed down a tree and walked. Matthews looked up at Rick, "Ferrari chew your ass?"

"How can you tell?"

"Chagrin. Your innocent smile is no more. He got to you somehow."

"He told me off, that's what. An insightful man that Ferrari. I'd love to share it with you when I figure out what the hell happened. Hey, where's Sam?"

"He's in the observation car with Ugarte." Where did you find him, that Ugarte? There's a strange beast. Do you really trust him? Seems to me he would take off with any man who offered him more dough."

"Good observation, Herb. Funny you should tell me this. I just figured out what I've noticed about him. He has no odor, kinda like a non-person. It's bothered me since I met him in Berlin."

"You mean you've know these guys that short a time? God, you've got so much going with them; what makes you think they won't shiv you one night?"

"Herb, I ask my self that question at least once every midnight. I don't trust people I've known all my life, why should I worry about any other period of time? Matthews just shook his head and looked out the window while Rick went to find Sam.

Chapter Twelve

Clubbing

Rick found Sam and asked, "Where's Ugarte? Matthews said you were with him."

"He tole me he had business with one of the Italian guys. An officer, I guess. Mr. Matthews tole me you and Ferrari had a chat. Everythin' go OK?"

"We talked about the club in Eritrea, but not before he ripped me good. Made me think about a few things, including myself. He cast me in a new light," said Rick wryly. "We've got a good chance to make some money and do some good. But I told him I didn't want you mixed up in anything illegal or dangerous. You're the straight man here."

"Mr. Richard, if you're goin' for danger, I'm goin' for it too. I trust you and wanna look out for you like I know you gonna look out for me." The conductor's voice broke in and announced their arrival in Asmara. Rick looked out the window onto his first view of Asmara and it was a doozy.

He thought he would find found Asmara to be a clean, Mediterranean style city, with whitewashed buildings and tree lined streets. True, some of the buildings had been whitewashed, but very long ago. Dilapidated buildings of corrugated metal, half-crumbled stone block buildings, and unpainted board hovels spread for blocks. Dust clouds hovered over unpaved streets Pedestrians plodded and pushed through the haze choking on the smoke from the lumbering trucks, armored cars, and little tanks. Small shops with multicolored blankets on poles sprawled over the entrances. The convoy proceeded to the military headquarters, a large compound that breathed a benign bureaucracy. They were taken to a small building where Major Criti was waiting. He was gracious but firm in his demand that the civilians be questioned along with the soldiers, Rick felt a bit apprehensive about the interrogation. Although the relationship between Italy and Germany was tense, the two fascist powers cooperated in the extradition of criminals and political dissidents.

Ferrari was the first to be interviewed, floating away like a barge with Criti as the tugboat. A quarter hour later, they called for Sam, he turned and looked nervously at Rick, who smiled and winked at him. Sam went along with his escort and they disappeared behind the door. 10 minutes later, Ugarte got the call. Ashen-faced and tremulous, he staggered alongside his escort.

20 minutes later, Sam came out smiling. "It ain't bad, Rick. They just asked me about the Rastafarians and I tole 'em what I knew." He sat down next to Rick and touched his arm.

The soldier nodded curtly to Rick and he stood up wordlessly and went into the room. Major Criti smiled at him and bade him sit. Criti took out a cigarette, offering on to Rick. He lit both with an engraved silver lighter and sat behind his desk. "I'm sorry to detain you from your business, but we must know what transpired at the Gebbi. I'm sure that you were not involved with the raid but what do you know of the silver? Do you know why it is here and not on the packhorses of Ras Tayfu? Do you have any hypotheses as to his failure to steal any of the silver?"

Rick felt his tensions easing, and released a billowing smoke ring. "Major, you are correct in assuming I know little or nothing. I make it a policy not to get involved with things political or military. As to the silver, I have no idea why he left it." Criti looked at him with curiosity, almost pensively and began to write, totally engrossed in his effort. Finishing, he stood up and extended his hand. They shook, and then Criti walked with Rick to the door. Rick returned to the waiting area where Ugarte, Ferrari, and Sam sat waiting. Ferrari suggested that they seek out their hotel and meet at the bar for a drink.

A smartly dressed Italian civilian came up to them and said, "Your luggage is already at the hotel. Outside, two cabs are waiting". The four men then walked to the waiting vehicles. Ugarte and Sam took the first, Ferrari and Rick the second.

Driving through the congestion, Ferrari turned to Rick and whispered, "I'm sure you are wondering about my crates, Criti failed to notice their absence, and I don't wonder that he did. Such a nervous man! My crates are on the mules of Ras Tayfu with the silver of the Duce. My nouvelle coins are now in the possession of the Italian government."

Rick threw back his head and laughed away his fatigue. "Ferrari, you are a master! Where do you get your nerve? You've just robbed the Italian army and here you are, on the way to a hotel and dinner with their people. You're sure worth the price of the ticket!"

Ferrari guffawed as he blew out spume of cigar smoke. "By gad Rick, I know enough about you that it is important for me to attempt to stay at least one step ahead."

The cab pulled in front of the gaudy facade of the Victor Emmanuel Hotel. Liveried doormen swarmed to the cab, one hand on the door and one held out, palm up. Check-in was simple, the rooms sumptuous. Ferrari? Rick showered, poured a drink, lit a cigarette, and pondered the future.

He awoke several hours later, the sky already alive with the colors of sunset. Funny how he always thought of sunset as sunrise, the day beginning with the darkness. When had this begun? How had he become one of those living dead, faded and made indistinct by daylight, larger and brighter than life at eventide? Whatever bore the responsibility, he detested it.

He dialed Sam's room, and as he did, he heard alien clicks on the line. An audience? When Sam answered Rick was terse, saying only that they would meet in the bar. He then rang off. Who was listening in? Criti's boys, no doubt. Maybe Criti wasn't so gullible after all. Perhaps he had let them go to soften their awareness; after all, they were in a very large jail, with no immediate escape. One couldn't just start walking down the road. Very nice, he thought.

Sam awaited him in the lobby bar. A party was going on, most of the attendees were army officers, with a sprinkling of civilian males (government no doubt.) The female guests appeared to be women of an older and less complicated profession. They were black, white, and yellow, it seemed that every country was represented. Rick ordered a Compari, lit a cigarette, and whispered his warning to Sam who nodded without comment, turning to watch the action. Such action! Rick then remembered Sam's girlfriend, and wondered if Sam was looking for her.

"Sam, I wonder who is responsible for all these ladies being here, do you think Il Duce is their pimp?"

Sam rolled his eyes. "If he isn't, I would be, I've never seen so many lovelies in my life. You be right about them, though. They ain't just here for decoration. If I was in charge, I'd sure find out what these officers know."

Rick felt assured that at least some of these girls were spies, a brigade of Mata Haris waiting for some breach of security. Scanning the room he saw a garishly dressed man of middle age, swarthy, moustache, probably Greek or Turkish. His eyes were bulgy; his bald head ran with sweat. As Rick watched, a number of the "girls" sallied by him, some spoke briefly with him, others merely nodded. Some of the officers were becoming slightly drunk, and were weaving around the dance floor clutching a woman. At least one couple aimed for the darkened corridors.

Ferrari rolled into the room, apparently familiar with some of the officers, greeting them warmly. Spying Rick, he puffed up to him and winked. "Nice party. The girls are a brilliant touch, don't you think?" He winked again.

Rick replied, "Do you know that man over there?" He pointed at the Greek.

"Good Heavens yes," replied Ferrari. "That's Constantine Kosta. I knew him in Rome. He's a most influential man. Always seems to be able to persuade beautiful women to do his dirty work. He deals in flesh and blood. Women's flesh and men's blood. He is a dangerous scoundrel and a potential threat to our operation. We must consider the most felicitous way of dealing with him. I would prefer to kill him, but that would be the last resort. Perhaps he will become a temporary ally until we can neutralize his strength."

Although Ferrari's words chilled him, Rick agreed with him. "We need to be more than careful. I am assuming that you've already made allowances for the multiple problems this assortment poses."

"Yes I am. Please accommodate me and do the same." They spent the next several hours meeting many of the officers, thanks to the arrival of Major Criti who was a most genial host. It allowed for observation without be too obvious about it.

Rick and Sam had agreed that if there were an opportunity, Sam would play the piano and sing some soft American jazz. The opportunity arose, and Sam played several popular numbers. The crowd applauded wildly, crowding around the piano and cheering after every song. Sam finally rose from the piano drenched with sweat, bowed to the audience, and returned to sit with Rick and Ferrari, the applause and calls for encores gradually subsiding. Both men clapping patted Sam on the back.

Rick inquired as to Ugarte's whereabouts. Ferrari held a pudgy finger to his lips silencing the question.

"Time for bed," said Rick. Sam and he rose to leave, without waiting for Ferrari's reply. He, however, rose and padded out into the crowd. Rick watched over his shoulder as Ferrari and the Greek embraced

Rick and Sam walked down the corridor to their rooms. Rick was ready to say goodnight, but Sam was insistent that they talk about the Ferrari-Greek encounter. "Why didn't he tell us he knew him? What's Ferrari got goin here?"

Rick merely said, "We'll find out all of that in due time, Sam. Let's sleep on it tonight and find out what gives in the morning."

The law required that new business plans be approved by the Urban Council, a front for the Blackshirt-dominated city government. This provided the fascists with additional sources of personal income. Rick and Ferrari were to be the co-owners, with Rick as manager of the casino. Ferrari said, "My boy, I just can't be tied down to Asmara." He winked conspiratorially. "I do trust you, and Ugarte will insure that trust. I have decided that Ugarte will not initiate the Khartoum negotiations; instead, he will handle the service details here. That way he will monitor you and

"You will monitor him. Sam will monitor both of you. The stakes are tremendous, and I will see that our friends provide us with what we came for. Trust me, my boy!" He clapped Rick on the back heartily.

They signed the documents and paid the "fees" followed by handshakes all around. The genial bureaucrat had given them an approved building in an appropriate neighborhood. They all drove to the building to be sure it met their needs. It had a perfect facade in a neighborhood close to the foreign quarter where the other nation's bureaucrats resided. Rick thought it a perfect place for the kind of intrigue Ferrari had alluded to.

In the days following, the four men worked feverishly to decorate and equip the club. Ferrari had shipped in roulette wheels and other necessary gambling paraphernalia. They retired to a small trattoria; somehow Ferrari had found a man who could demonstrate the nuts and bolts of hiring appropriate types for the various tables, the bar, and waitresses. "This is more work than I thought," said Rick.

Ferrari was excellent at the organization of a staff. Ugarte extolled the logic of having a string of "girls" for the entertainment of the soldiers to allow a steady stream of useful intelligence. Rick thought ahead to the profits and the hardware it could buy for the anti-fascists. Sam was busy thinking of his back-up band and the hiring of a female singer.

On the advice of the Office of Internal Entertainment, they hired an "agent" (read government informer) who would assist them in finding the talent they needed. Italians were swarming to the Dark Continent, so fortune hunters were everywhere and disillusionment accompanied many of them. They had envisioned a new start, with money, servants, and power. True, opportunities existed, but the competition was keen. This was apparent in the faces of some of the potential employees. Women who thought that their street-walking days would be replaced with call-girl status, men who assumed that access to a fortune would be forthcoming. All seemed eager for an opportunity to work with gamblers for they equated gambling with money and upward mobility.

A week passed, the necessary people were hired, the machines and tables in place. Rick and Ferrari talked the staff at length about the need for discretion and diplomacy when dealing with the customers. "They all have the potential to make things uncomfortable for all of us if we don't treat them well. Any breach of this ethic will result in dismissal. Is that clear?'

Ferrari then read off he names and assignments. Some refused to work for Sam in the music and entertainment section and were released. A couple of the croupiers didn't like the bonus figures and suggested changing the house take. When Rick refused, they relented, but Rick remembered their names and made a note to check their tables frequently for any hank panky.

While this endeavor raced to fruition, war news ran rampant. Adowa had been liberated, atoning for 40 years of Italian humiliation. Stories were told of Abyssinian warrior commanders helmeted in lion skins racing troops into battle in the face of blistering rifle and machine gun fire. The Ethiopians didn't appear to have a chance. Rick knew it was important for them to provide those weapons for the blacks, and soon. On the ruse of obtaining further supplies, Ferrari and he traveled to Khartoum where large sums of money changed hands, and through Ferrari's limitless contacts, weapons were soon rushed to the encampments of the Ras Tayfu. He in turn would barter the weapons to his neighboring Ras' in exchange for cattle, food, and other contraband.

But what of the noble Ferrari? Was his contribution charitable? Not on your life. He exchanged the Duce's silver for Belgian and British hardware; his final payment was in gold. The piles soared, and his usual good humor with it. The gold became the temporary responsibility of the Bank of Rome and the accrued income returned to Asmara to pay for the additional paraphernalia they needed for the club.

The grand opening was set for the following Friday. Rick was happy, expectant. Despite the intended purpose the mind-numbing arrangements took his mind off everything else. News traveled fast in this insular war town, excitement was rare, and so the crowd exceeded any of their expectations. Additionally, the war news continued to be good, and the Italian mood was one of victory. Rick spent most of his nights in the gambling rooms, while Ferrari acted as the official greeter. Sam's musical revue was a great hit, with a Follies Bergere look. How he was able to achieve this level of professionalism in such a short time was a marvel to all.

Rick observed Ugarte speaking conspiratorially to shifty looking men like himself and wondered scam was being hatched. He often questioned Ugarte's sexual preference, so the contacts could be financial or prurient.

When he turned to the tables, The Greek stood directly in front of him. He smiled at Rick through a haze of cigar smoke and offered his hand. "Congratulations Mr. Blaine. Er, that is the name, isn't it? No matter. My friend Ferrari speaks well of you and that's enough. You know, of course, that I'm a silent partner here. Ferrari feels my, ah, special talent for beauty is too good to ignore. But I have said too much. If you need anything at all, please be advised that I am your friend." He winked, pressing his damp, puffy palm into Rick's. "Thanks for the offer. I might hold you to it." No sense in being arrogant or ungrateful, Rick believed. He might need this mysterious person at another time.

Several officers were talking animatedly while they watched the roulette wheel. "They can't hold up against what we have to give them. We have planes, armor, artillery, and automatic weapons against their antiquated rifles and spears." The speaker looked about slyly. "And, they don't have our little Chianti bottles. That's the one that really gets them. A few canisters bouncing about the battlefield scatters them like insects. Then all we have to do is to mow them down." They all laughed and turned their attention to the tables.

Rick sought out Ferrari and asked about the canisters. "Poison gas, that's what. They drop it from low-flying planes; it burns the skin and sears their lungs. They die, but only after horrible agony. Italy denies it officially, of course. The League is impotent because Italy just denies the charges."

Rick looked at Ferrari, slack-jawed. "I've heard about this stuff from the first war, but I thought it had been banned. This gotta be reported to the major newspapers!"

"Do you think that the censors will let that happen? Most of the international press is in Addis Ababa, without access to modern communication, hell they can't even speak the language. Besides, what will the world do about it? Do you think the world is ready to go to war again for a stone-age nation located God knows where? The economic depression is trouble enough, without spending a single cent for aid to some obscure band of rag-tag savages!" Ferrari's face had become red and contorted. "Rick, no one gives a damn, there is no love or concern in the world. It has become a relief for me to know this, because it allows me to ignore anything but my own welfare. While the world sinks in self-interest, I grow richer by acting in mine.

Weeks passed, and the club was jammed every night with people whose pockets burned with the money of the new empire. The profits from gambling alone were beyond Rick's predictions. Ferrari and Ugarte were happy, Rick was satisfied with the smoothness of the business and Sam was in love. His lady from Rome was in Asmara, and the two of them were inseparable. Rick felt envy, not only because he had enjoyed Sam's exclusive company, but also because he lacked someone to love. Women were more than available to him, but he had no interest in them and what they might give him, moreover, the women he sought were not available to him in Ethiopia.

One busy evening Rick was checking the numbers in his makeshift office. Ferrari walked in at sat down, huffing and puffing. "My boy, we have a project to see to."

"And what is the project, Ferrari?" Rick found Ferrari's approach to projects amusing and a little scary.

"I've made some contacts who want us to buy some guns from them for the people." Rick assumed he meant the Ethiopians. "One of us will accompany a contingent of British commandos to a rendezvous with an Somali Arab group for the purpose of . . . ah . . . commerce. You are the obvious choice for the project. You're young, smart, and quick, all of which are necessary attributes for this project."

Rick said, "Why do you take such pleasure in arranging my life? Do you ever do anything from start or is a middle man a Ferrari necessity?" They both laughed.

CHAPTER THIRTEEN

Commandos

Rick was chosen to travel with the Commando team and handle the moneys they were to exchange for guns for the Ethiopian forces. Ferrari told him, "There could be a problem with the payment and that the problem would be graft. No one in this part of the world will do anything for anyone without money exchanging hands whether the hands be on or underneath the table. The nature of gun-runners is such that there are no flags on either the money or the weapons." Rick listened to the wisdom of Ferrari's message but was having problems in digesting the truth of them. As if he read Rick's mind, Ferrari continued. "I want you to promise me you won't raise your American idealism or sense of fairness about this. Remember every one has their reasons and risks."

"I don't think I'm going to like these people," said Rick. "But I guess everybody's got to be somewhere."

The departure was scheduled for early morning, the rendezvous an elevated meadow beneath a jagged craggy mountain range, the peaks fringed in gold by the as yet unseen sun. Ferrari had arranged a meeting with a Somali Arab whose name was Muhammad and apparently was the boss of the gunrunning crew. Rick found himself in a mixed grill of Arabs, Ethiopians, and about 10 white skinned men who turned out to be British commandos. One youngish officer in a starched shirt and shorts came up to him and offered his hand. "Leftenant Baker." "You the Yank?" He eyed Rick's commando garb complete with sun helmet and the British pistol holstered on his hip with something like amusement. Rick was not amused but shook the extended hand "These damn Eyeties are a pain in the King's ass. I personally believe that we'll be at it with them before this is all over."

"From what I've seen I can't see how the locals can hope to do anything more than give the Italians a black eye," said Rick.

"That's a fact. And we know about the gas, too. Those poor bastards don't have a chance with their rifles that jam and shields made of lion skins. They're tough, we know that, but they still live in the 16th century, not the 20th."

The Somalis were an unnamed motley crew, all of whom looked like back alley assassins. Their traditional shoras with egals were filthy and ragged, as were their robes. Rick tried to make eye contact with them but they turned away as if to prevent him from identifying them later. Muhammad, the boss, was different; his clothing was clean and nearly new; he was friendly and ebullient, but then he pocketed the money.

Six rickety flat bed trucks pulled up to the group, their engines hacking, spewing and rattling like a pack of motorcycles and smoking like a grass fire. The vehicles stopped, then three more open roadsters arrived. They appeared to be Italian military cars with all the fenders missing. The Arabs clambered into the trucks while Baker waved Rick into one of the roadsters. The other commandos climbed into the other two touring cars and off they went in a cacophony of wrenching gears and shouted Arab gibberish.

The temperature rose considerably as the sun shot high above the mountains. Rick thanked the Gods for being in the lead car rather than behind the wheezing foul smoking trucks. Baker stood up, raised his arm and blew his whistle bringing the convoy to a halt. Two commandos filled large tin cups with water and brought them to the other commandos while the Arabs took their own wineskins and drank.

Baker sucked his cup dry then said to Rick, "It's about five more hours, uphill halfway and downhill the rest of the way." He smiled a gap-toothed smile then turned to his sergeant and said, "The Arabs can have their rifles when we start down the mountain." The sergeant saluted smartly and walked over to the trucks and told Muhammad about the rifles.

The hours passed like days as the convoy rocked and rolled up the mountain roads and cutbacks, stopping and starting while the trucks performed hair-raising maneuvers just to negotiate the hairpin turns. The heat was blast furnace in intensity, the sweat poured from Rick's head. One thing for damn sure, he didn't need a cigarette; inhaling the dust of

Ethiopia was enough for any lung. This was a shitty, smelly country filled with psychotic warriors and creepy Arabs. He wanted out. These thoughts somehow put him to sleep until a burst of gunfire awakened him. He was ready to dive into a ditch when Baker's rough laughter halted the move. "OK Yank, it's just the Somalis' was of greeting temporary friends. The effect is to keep others wary while maintaining their control.

Arabs came up out of the scraggy weeds and from behind rocks yelling in Arabic, and ululating. The fellows on the truck clambered down and joined them in the oral fracas. Rick felt frightened, dry mouthed and he wanted to move his bowels. Was it just the food or was did the sights and sounds of these desert savages disorient him? Baker said, "Blaine, you all right? Have you seen a ghost? Don't let these birds make you sweat; they're as spooked as you are. Macho is a highly valued behavior for them."

"Thanks," said Rick. He had happily regained his composure and his voice. He then noticed that most of the Arabs disappeared in the underbrush and Rick felt a resurgence of his anxiety, but was reassured when they returned lugging wooden gun cases. He watched as they began to load on the trucks. When one truck was loaded they placed some end posts, which they connected with side posts to prevent the cases from falling off. When all them were loaded, Rick walked over to his roadster and lifted up a sack of silver coins, then another. He turned to call Muhammad's name but he was standing right behind him,

"I'll handle those," he said thickly as he indicated that the bags were now his. Muhammad then turned and fired off a rapid string of orders in Arabic and the Arabs began to turn back into the brush and the boulders.

Rick saw something flash in the sun, then realized it was a knife, then many knives slashing the bodies of Muhammad's screaming Arabs. The British commandos fired their rifles into the melee and the screams of wounded men seemed to come from everywhere. Rick lunged to the ground and struggled out his pistol but was reticent to fire will nilly into the crowd until it occurred to him that he had to defend himself regardless of whom would die. A body plopped down beside him, Rick looked at Baker to see if he was hurt, but Baker gave him a grin and began firing his pistol into the underbrush. He panted, "Yank, we have here a reneging of this first order. Those damn Somalis want to kill us and take their rifles back. Fire at anything you see and we'll count the dead later."

The battle was short as the skill of the commandos out performed the Arabs. Baker shouted out, "Check 'em all if any one of them moves or breathes, kill them. The bloody wogs tried to do it to us." Rick began to stammer an objection but Baker cut him short. "Look around you, Yank and tell me what you see." Rick looked around at the carnage. He saw part of a bloody forearm and other clumps of unidentifiable flesh; mutilated bodies were strewn everywhere, Weapons, rifles, pistols, and long bloody knives littered the ground.

Rick turned towards Baker and shrugged his shoulders. His long arms drooped even longer and his face was twisted. He thought of the scab cops he had killed in New York. "You're right, Baker, it was them or us."

One commando staggered towards them, blood pouring from a neck wound. Baker whipped off his scarf, balled it up and pressed it to the wound. Then he checked the wound, saying, "It's a vein but not the jugular. Get out the kit and let's wrap it. Rick had seen more blood in the past 10 minutes then he had seen in his life. He sat down on a rock and put a cigarette in his mouth and let it dangle. "You ok Yank?"

Rick nodded weakly. "Yeah, I'm ok. I just don't think I want to see any more of this shit. How can you be so blasé, Baker?" Baker said nothing and continued to wrap the commando's neck. When he finished he said, "Good job soldier. Take it easy and I'll check that spot out again later." The man nodded in gratitude and walked over to one of the cars.

Only one of the Arabs who left Eritrea that morning had survived and even he suffered a knife wound to the head. The other Arabs now lay in shallow graves at the site of the attempted coup. Rick had done his best to wipe the sweat and dust from his body but nothing could dispel the stench of his day's work. The others were no less ripe, redolent with the odors of fear, blood and dirt. "Now we gotta get rid of the ordinance the Somalis brought us," said Baker, shaking his head.

"Baker, I'll bet when you open those crates they'll be filled with straw. These guys had no intention of gun running, just running us into the ground." Baker grunted and ordered a crate to be opened. Straw.

By now it was to late to negotiate the mountain roads Baker ordered them to spend the night. It was already getting cooler as the sun floated below the mountains but Rick wax not prepared for the cold. The winds, which had picked up, grew colder. Rick was thirsty but their water supply was low so he decided he would delay slaking his thirst. A stagnant stream stood nearby but the water was not safe to drink. The commandos gathered wood and started a huge fire but the blaze was no match for the piercing winds. The humidity was high despite the desert and by midnight their outer blankets were soaked through. Rick shivered throughout the night and blessed the rising sun.

Baker was already organizing the loading of the trucks. Rick noticed the crates hacked to bits in the brushy periphery of their campsite, the straw littered everywhere. Baker gestured at the wreckage and said, "Good morning, Blaine, we're traveling light today." They both laughed and climbed aboard the stuttering trucks.

The trip back over the mountains was worse than the trip out. They drove against the white-hot sun and the dust, the effect was blinding. There were frequent close calls and stops to clear the road of rock falls. By the time they returned to Asmara the entire team was exhausted. The commandos left Rick on the outskirts in an attempt to avoid detection and Rick took a rickety cab back to the hotel area hoping he wasn't seen by any agents or other members of the Italian army. He stripped and showered, then hit the hay for a much needed sleep. He realized that he hadn't had a cigarette in 12 hours.

CHAPTER FOURTEEN

Addis And Beyond

Ferrari's call came early; Rick was momentarily confused as he grappled with the phone. The voice crackled through the archaic system hurting his ears and exacerbating an already pounding headache. "Come to breakfast now, and bring a raincoat." The click was abrupt and commanding. Rick walked to the window. The streets were empty but for sweepers and a few military vehicles droning along. His pajamas were drenched with sweat so he took a quick shower, dressed, and then joined Ferrari in the breakfast room.

"Aha my boy, how wonderful it is to be alive when there is so much to be done." He sipped his coffee while waving grandly for Rick to sit.

"Why wasn't he asking about the Commando raid? Someone apparently had already briefed him?" thought Rick. Instead of asking he said, "For me early mornings are for sleep first and duty later."

"That's a point of view I've always had trouble with." Ferrari shrugged saying in in a low voice, "Eat rapidly. We've a plane to catch. I'll explain when I can, but we fly to Addis Ababa today!"

Rick was incredulous, and felt his stomach twist and flop. What is going on? He hadn't seen an airplane he would fly in since they arrived! Now he had to fly over hostile territory to get to another nowhere. But, his newfound sense of excitement made even a jeopardous flight palatable. Plus, he needed time with Ferrari to discuss increasing the niggardly flow of arms to Haile Selassie's beleaguered armies. Where in God's green earth would they be able to find enough money and supplies to withstand the ordinance that Il Duce was pouring into Eritrea and Somaliland? The answer was simple. They couldn't. Rick knew he would have to watch another powerful bully beat up upon a weak and ill-prepared victim.

The two men waited while the mechanics and the pilot went down the checklist. To Rick's relief, the pilot was going through his second check, even though the first one was flawless. The plane and the pilot were British; their destination was to be British Somaliland. Ferrari explained, "We are supposedly going to Somalia to pick up more gambling equipment. While in flight, we will digress slightly, turning south to Dessie, where we will refuel. Then on to Addis Ababa where The Emperor has granted us an audience." The fat man turned to Rick. "What do you think?"

Rick was alarmed. "Criti knows we are going, he probably has paid this pilot to report every move we make. I think the idea is suicide."

"Let me tell you about the pilot. Yes, he is in the pay of Criti. It just so happens that British MI also pays him, and always more than Criti. Finally, I pay him more than both. He hates the Duce and his fascists. MI supports our activities because they want this part of Africa for themselves. If Mussolini is successful here, Hitler will not refuse the competition. The Germans want their East African colonies back, and badly. Their claim to be a world power is dependent upon their ability to strike from long distances and win short wars. Il Duce is trying to beat them to the score."

Rick could not conceal his admiration for the man and his schemes. "What about this war? Why don't the British interfere? There's got to be enough support for some intervention there."

"My friend, even I cannot explain the complexities of international politics."

Safely in the air, they followed their flight plan, landing at Dessie to refuel and take stock. This being a holy city, Rick wanted to take some time to see how the Orthodoxy lived. But Ferrari?? When the plane rose gracefully from the narrow strip, Rick marveled at the majesty of the arid mountain peaks. Altitude achieved, the thunder of the engines relaxed to a drone. Ferrari began to speak in an uncharacteristic impassioned tone. "Rick, do know of the Englishman Evelyn Waugh? Rick nodded his assent. He's in country now and I don't understand him. The British establishment is rotten with fascists, but of all the English writers, but I would have thought Waugh above the contemptuous stand he has taken against this unfortunate country. Because he is such an iconoclast, perhaps he thinks it clever to hobnob with an ass like Mussolini.

Rick interrupted Ferrari, saying, "In the main I assume that most of the writers and journalist are left wingers, especially in this cause."

Ferrari continued, "The Duce created a cause the way a writer creates his fiction. They both use fact to metamorphasize it into some forme frustre that pleases them. Further, they want it to please their following. To me, it is the lowest form of ingratiation, a kind of pandering to the lowest impulses. Writers and journalists upset me because of their arrogance towards the rest of us. 'I have a pen, a typewriter, and I have forged my words that they may turn the hearts and minds of those who would be informed.' Their penchant for misinformation is beyond redemption, and the damage possible from their eructations is limitless. In war the first casualty is the truth, and we must realize that the truth is not what they seek. They would rather the truth be subjugated to their Pygmalion fictions. How heady to run about the world transforming events into personal opinions and attacks on institutions. Mark my word my boy, the day will come when the press will be as hounded as any other league of scoundrels."

Rick said, "I await the day. When I was a union organizer most papers were highly critical of our attempts to help the working man."

"I have been a student of your American yellow journals and predict that they shall suffer the indignities of those they have hounded. Addis is filled with men of this stripe, Americans and Europeans alike. They cheer the lion as it rips the gazelle, and then criticize both, the one for being ruthless, the other for being weak. Points of view? I think not. The more I observe men of character the more I think of Junius' aphorism,' 'An honest man, like the true religion, appeals to the understanding, or modestly confides in the internal evidence of his conscience. The impostor employs force instead of argument, imposes silence where he cannot convince, and propagates his character by the sword.'"

Rick replied, "Junius is not in my lexicon. I took a philosophy course at Chicago and dozed through it. Don't mind if I doze."

Ferrari continued, "Unleashed, despots like Mussolini and his cohorts release that repressed national or personal core that no other idea can match in horror or malfeasance. I'm sorry to go on thus, but the world is rapidly dying, and the smoldering mistakes we make today will burst into a fiery holocaust tomorrow. We suffer these autocrats too gladly; every slice we give them sees them demanding the rest of the pie. The British

Embassy told me that both England and France have weaseled out of their threat of sanctions. France tacitly now supports the Italian expansion.

"My God, we're back in 1914! Nothing has changed."

"We waste our efforts here, my boy. Our Maria Theresas against the Italian treasury. Selassie has to fight his own internal battles: the Rases, the Coptic Church, a country 2000 years behind Europe, and his own limitations. Swords and lances against iron and steel, a paltry few aircraft against the best that Europe has, and, regrettably, the yperite. This latter weapon drives men mad with a substance they cannot fight. Ethiopia is a candle in the wind." Ethiopia is a huge country and the borders are generally unguarded and porous. Even the few areas that have border controls, bribery was rampant and few smugglers were denied because they had the money and they had the guns that this country needs."

Rick asked Ferrari, "Which parts of the country are getting the most guns now?"

"That's easy, Rick. The entire eastern half is swarming with gunrunners, from Djibouti to Somaliland. The problem is that the various tribal leaders are stocking the guns for another day. Those guys believe Italy will win the war and they want to be first in line for the next step. It's a mess." Rick shrugged but didn't respond. What could he say? One thing for sure, he felt he was growing up. Idealism will get you nothing but dead.

Ferrari continued, "There's a place called Harar, well east of Addis, wonderful site, that is the center of all smuggling in Ethiopia. Ethiopia is Christian but Harar has many Muslims whose specialty is the transport of 'goods' from Muslim Dijbouti and Somaliland. Quantities of drugs are exchanged for guns and ammunition."

Rick found this fascinating but it made him question, "Why do we bother to run guns if they're already pouring across the border?"

Ferrari laughed his booming laugh. "Users, my boy. We make sure the guns go to our side."

An open roadster awaited the men as they exited the airport. Rick lit a cigarette as the car pulled away, but soon found himself choking both on the tobacco and the combination of thick, chewy dust and the 7500 foot altitude made him breathless. He never had seen a place quite like it. The capitol of this huge country was a rank smelling, grim hovel. Evidence of the Italian bombing was almost obscured by the general dishevelment of the place. The stink of open latrines, shallow ditches paralleling the roadway, made his eyes water and nose sting. The driver pointed out the wreckage of the American Hospital, which had been bombed by the Italians. He proudly told of the letters of indignation received from all over the world. Rick snorted, but held his tongue. Indignation. What the hell has world indignation ever done for anyone? Indignation! What a bunch of crap!

They were surprised to learn that only the main street of Addis was paved. The driver described its paving for the coronation of Ras Tafari, The Lion Of Judah, Haile Selassie. Some shabby shops along the way offered shoddy European imports in their windows. Rick inquired, "Why would anyone spend a penny to conquer this God-forsaken place?"

Ferrari turned to him patiently. "Simple, my boy. A victory in a strange, exotic country, especially one with biblical roots, is great news to people who have never seen it. Despots need victories to maintain their sway over a reluctant populace. Being number one becomes infectious, the industrialists loosen their purse strings, parents offer their youth for slaughter, and everyone sings the national anthem louder. Quite simple, indeed."

The auto entered the gates of the palace and halted as armed palace guards checked their papers.

Ferrari spoke in hushed tones. "This is called the 'little Gebbi', a small palace. The Emperor has . . . ." Ferrari was cut short as the car stopped in front of the entrance, and liveried men began opening doors.

"Welcome to Addis Ababa!" The speaker was a man who introduced himself as Ras Hailu. Tall, light-skinned, and very elegant in a bemedaled white uniform and a clipped British accent. After introductions and handshakes, the Ras invited them into a dark, cool drawing room, resplendent with coats of mail, heavy brocaded curtains, and portraits of distinguished looking black men. Some wore lion skins over their heads; others were in uniforms or tuxedos. An officer offered Rick and Ferrari comfortable chairs facing a small throne. There they sat until in silence until the door behind the throne opened and a small slim heavily medalled black man strode in. The Europeans all stood and bowed, while the Ethiopians lay prostrate before him.

"I wish to welcome you to Addis Ababa. I want you to know that my country is grateful to you for the aid you bring us. As you know, only the Belgians have seen fit to offer military aid against the Italians. I fear the League of Nations is a toothless old tiger and I know that it is only a matter of time until the invaders occupy my capitol. It is then that my people will realize that our internecine squabbles must be put aside in the national interest. We are not a sleeping giant, but we could become a wakened tiger. Their occupation will be one of great discomfort. We are an ancient country and so will rise again."

Rick looked closely at this man, his first emperor. The shiny black face, the Semitic nose so often caricaturized into the fierce beak of some flesh eating bird. He was dressed in a white uniform drenched with gold braid and medals. He could not have weighed more than 120 pounds. Rumor had it that he had tuberculosis. The stories about him in the Italian press portrayed him as a blood soaked tyrant who maintained control only through murder and torture of his enemies and a despotic grip on the citizenry. Rick was aware that this might be the way to deal with the other Rases since they practiced the same tactics with their subjects. Slavery was rampant in Ethiopia, and the system was not about to be changed by the Emperor's singular fiat to abolish it.

Servants appeared with trays of drinks for the guests. The Emperor sat on his throne with the others maintaining a respectful distance. Rick glanced around the room at the motley assemblage, Indians, Moors, a few unscrupulous looking Caucasians. It was obvious that the gold they earned was the only motivation for their smuggling guns. Rick lit a cigarette and watched as Ferrari moved easily among them. He seemed to know most of them and they him.

Ras Tafari stood, the room grew quiet, and he spoke again. "Thank you again for your efforts on behalf of my government. When this war is over I should like to talk to each of you about opportunities in my country." He then turned on his heel and left the room. Rick felt the weight of irony in his voice. Rick decided that it might not be a good idea to take him too seriously for too much gold had left the treasury for weapons that may or may not work, as well as some that never arrived. He would not want to be an enemy of this small but redoubtable man.

Ferrari said to Rick, "I have arranged a meeting with a member of the weapons procurement committee," as Rick followed him into a room where three rather confused looking black men, stood along the same motley crew of desperados whom the Emperor had thanked. Ras Hailu then strolled into the room with an air of dignity and assurance. His presence seemed to relax the other council members.

"Gentlemen, we need to talk seriously and to the point." His accent was British, his meaning international. "We are a in serious danger of losing our sovereignty to a nation of bandits. Your weapons sales to us will not make a difference unless some of you can persuade your governments to come to our aid now! Yesterday!" He stopped and mopped his brow. Rick felt tremendous compassion for this beleaguered man, a patriot soon to be without a country. "We must have aircraft that flies, tanks that will start with cannons that shoot, and artillery. Without these things you may as well cease your efforts for us. The Duce's canisters, which he denies knowledge of, can defeat us without any other ordinance. My men are brave when they face the enemy, but when they cannot see and breathe because of these noxious, deadly gases, they run like whipped animals until they die."

A man wearing a fez stood up and said, "Ras Hailu, what of the bandits? It is said that they steal more weapons than are delivered. Is that to be our fault? Can you not control your own people? In my country, we all would stand as one against the infidels."

Ras Hailu took a deep breath and looked at the speaker with hatred. "Ah yes, effendi. Might I tell you of a small rumor that had just arrived in our capitol? They say that you have had dealings with our criminal rabble, and that they steal the weapons and give them back to you that you might sell them back to us again, cash in advance. It was you of whom the Emperor spoke when he offered that some of you return here after our victory. Your departure will be delayed that our intelligence agents might talk to you of patriotism and treachery."

The Fez sank to a chair with a look of horror on his face and began a diatribe of denial in a foreign tongue. Several men in civilian dress pulled him from his chair and half dragged him from the room. Rick looked at Ferrari who smiled back. Imperial justice?

Ras Hailu asked again if anyone could foresee his own government interceding. The silence was enough; The Ras bowed stiffly and left the room.

A tall, disheveled looking man ambled up to Rick and held out his hand. "Hello Blaine. Remember me? Matthews from the New York Times?" He said "New York Times" like some might utter the name of their most sacred deity. The sarcasm in his voice was apparent, making Rick even happier to see him again.

"How long you been in Addis?"

Matthews grimaced. "Too long. The eyties are going to be here before you can say 'siccum.' Any foreigner will be considered an enemy of the

Duce, and will prosper accordingly. I'm getting out, going to Spain. Lots going on there, the eyties are there, too, involved up to their ears, and the Spanish Falangists love them. The Germans will be in soon, they tell me, and then goodbye freedom for those other folks. Should be good stories, a lot of writers and reporters are there, and my paper would like nothing better than to scoop them all. I've done what I can here; no one gives a damn about a few lion-skinned savages. Spain'll be different. People care about it, people on both sides. Besides, no one read the paper here. Maybe I'll see you there." He laughed, nodded his head and walked away.

The others were talking in soft and worried tones. Ferrari nodded at several who caught his eye, took Rick by the shoulder and half-pushed him from the room. "My boy, we must hurry or we'll miss our plane."

Rick and Ferrari returned to Asmara without speaking a single word. Sam and Ugarte met them at the airport and drove them to the club. Sam was animated, bubbling away about the money they took in. Ugarte was evasive even in his silence. Rick waited until Sam's animation dulled, then snarled at Ugarte, "What have you been up to while we were gone?" Ugarte threw a dirty look at Sam, but said nothing. Rick lunged forward, grabbing Ugarte by the throat, snarling, "What the hell have you been up to?"

Ugarte's contorted features turned reddish purple, but defiant. "I have done nothing, Rick! Nothing! I have done what you have asked; I stayed out of trouble, and watched the dealers for cheating. Why do you blame me for nothing?" The last utterance came as a bleat, for Rick's hands were increasing the pressure on his larynx.

"Because you're a creep, Ugarte! I trust you like I'd trust one of those jungle snakes in my bed! If I find out you're a liar, I'll . . . ."

Ferrari seized Rick's arm and said, "Leave him alone, my boy. If he's done wrong, we'll soon know it. If he hasn't, you punish him for feelings you cannot deal with."

Rick knew the fat man was right. Ugarte seemed the paradigm for all the evil he saw in the world. He saw him as one of the human hyenas of the world, picking at carrion.

He took his hands away from the terrorized Ugarte and nodded his head. Assent to what? Should he accept evil as it is, or should he fight it when he saw it? Or should he just become like the others, picking their way absently through the rubble, oblivious to the anguish of others.

Later, he and Sam sat at a table in the hotel bar. Sam looked at him with concern, asking, "What's the trouble Mr. Richard? We got it good here, business be fine, we got no trouble. Ugarte hasn't done nothing that I catched wind of. In fact, he spent most of his time talking to Major Criti."

Rick jumped to his feet, hissed at Sam, "We've got to get out of here, and fast. That piece of trash has sold us to Criti! I felt it, now I know it! He didn't get in on the guns and he's going to get his money by spilling the beans! I'll get the cash from the safe, you call Ferrari and fast!"

Sam raced off to alert Ferrari while Rick opened the office safe and slipped the large bills and the gems (a nice way to transport your loot!) into a leather portmanteau.

Sam and Ferrari were waiting at the bar. Ferrari looked flustered but not bewildered. "I have called the British Embassy. They'll fly us to Khartoum. I trusted Ugarte, but I now know you were correct in your recent assessment. They have a source in Italian M.I. who confirmed the treachery of our little friend. He didn't tell Criti everything, just that we had gone to Addis and that he 'wondered' if we were illegals. Humph! I believe he was going to play it out, get a little something from Criti, then a little something from us. He would then disappear and we would have to bluff it out with Criti. I believe we could win, but I'm not a gambling man. Not when the stakes include my person!"

A cab pulled up, the three got in and sped to the British compound. An hour later they were in the air, destination Khartoum. Rick looked from the window at hostile ocher landscape, wondering about his next exile.

Chapter Fifteen

Khartoum

Rick was jolted awake when the wheels touched the rutted sand runway at Khartoum. Sam was still sleeping, but Ferrari was sitting in the co-pilot's seat talking to the pilot. The man was a constant ideation, a totally improvisational being. What ever he was up to, it was certainly for self-improvement.

He glanced back at Rick and smiled broadly. "I feel a little safer now, my boy, I don't wonder but that Criti may have friends here in Khartoum. Shame to leave him so abruptly; I would ordinarily have said 'good-bye.' In spite of it all, he knew about kindness to his fellow man, and I respect that."

Sam awakened with a start, looking at the two other men, he asked, "Is this Khartoum? I sure hopes so, I'm damn sick of flying in this plane. Besides, what do we do now? I sure would like to see some friendly faces again."

They were driven to the British Embassy in a special car, apparently the Brits were interested in these alleged gunrunners and their assessment of the antagonists in Ethiopia. They would know of the recent meeting in Addis and wanted first-hand reportage.

Following the interrogation by the embassy MI staff they were housed on the embassy compound. "You fellows might be in some danger here," the MI officer mumbled into in his mustache. "I might suggest that you make your stay here as brief as possible. Your presence on our grounds makes our position a little tight should the Italians find out."

"Typical," Rick muttered to Sam. "They use us and then throw us away. They'd toss us back to the Eyeties in a minute if it served their fancies." Sam looked gloomy and said nothing.

They had dinner in their quarters, served by several British military strikers. "These men are our guards," said Ferrari. "They serve to keep us in as well as keep others out."

Rick looked at the men with disdain. "I'm getting out of here as fast as I can, I don't know where I'll go but it sure isn't here."

Ferrari leaned back, his chair creaking ominously. "My boy, my plan is to go to Casablanca. It's French, and the commercial opportunities there are boundless; the Algerians hate the French, the Moroccans hate both the Spanish and the French. Franco is sending his entire army to Spain for the war, and nature and I both abhor vacuums." He chortled at his little metaphor.

Rick was curious. He knew nothing of Franco, and the whole Spanish intrigue still remained an enigma to him. Too many governments in 10 years seemed to be the root cause. "Tell about this Franco. Does he have a chance of winning?"

"Oh, my boy! Not only does he have a chance, he will. He has the Italians and the Nazis on his side. The French and British have declared a blockade of Spain in an attempt to isolate the war and so as not to antagonize the fascists. This means that the Republican forces have no direct source of aid. Smuggling is not the way to equip a modern army. The Germans have committed their "Condor Legion," an elite air group, and a number of observers and technicians. Italy has sent 50,000-plus combat troops, as well as tanks and air support. Their navy patrols the southern coast of Spain. Majorca, and the Balearic Islands are theirs. If Spain is a walnut, Franco's role is that of nutcracker. Oh, his opposition is considerable, but theirs is a doomed struggle. Spain, whatever else it is, is a Catholic country. Franco has the support of the Church because much of the opposition is anti-Catholic. No, the sands of time are running, and they will run out for the Republicans." Ferrari stared out at the vision he had created, and then shrugged his shoulders. Sam looked sad and lost in a private reverie.

"Spain sounds like a place I might want to visit," Rick said. He inhaled a great wad of smoke and stared at nothing. "Who will you support in this conflict?"

Ferrari smiled wryly. "Do you want to be with the winners or the losers? Remember, the winning side is always the most cheerful one. Losers do not fare well in our world."

I'll stick my neck out only to save my neck." Rick was darkly intense. "Saps may stick theirs out, but there is nothing I believe or want to believe that I would stick mine out for."

"My but you're a real cynic, aren't you. Why don't you try believing in the power of money, or the power of power?".

"I've seen both and have nothing good to say about either, I don't like what the smell of both does to people. You know far more about this than I do, Ferrari, what's the fascination for you?"

"My boy, I love the game. I love the feeling even more than the game. Some day you'll learn how to feel something, and when you do I hope it is the feeling of power or the game that empowers you on the way."

Sam and Rick said their good-byes to Ferrari the following day. The two men then had lunch in the garden of the embassy. "What'll you do? Mr. Rick? They tole me I've got three days to decide. I'd like to go with you, if it don't mean fightin. I've had my fill of that and a lot of other stuff, I want to feel good and make others feel good. Nobody ever shoot the piano player, now did they?"

Rick chuckled at the thought of Sam under fire at his piano, then turned serious. "Sam, I think I'll go to Madrid. There's a war there, but maybe there's something to be learned, something that can be changed. Maybe a better chance to help in a cause I can sink my teeth into. Ferrari says a lot of journalists are up there looking around for a story, maybe I can find one for myself."

"What about your neck, Rick?"

I know it's sticking my neck out but the whole story sounds like a good cause."

"Mr. Rick, I just can't go there. Wars are not for me. I was scared the whole time since we left Rome. I heard some Negro jazzmen have gone to Paris and done OK, and a St. Louis girl name of Jo Baker is doin all right, too. Could be that's the spot for old Sam." His warm black eyes pleaded with Rick to go with him.

Rick turned, dropped his head, and lit another Camel. "Not yet Sam. But you go, and send word to the embassy in Madrid when you're settled. Maybe I'll see you there someday." The two men shook hands, then Sam moved to embrace Rick, but Rick was already walking away.

CHAPTER SIXTEEN

Mc Dowell's Khartoum

After the others had left Rick asked Captain McDowell for permission to see some of Khartoum. "I believe we can allow that, Blaine. And, if you don't object, I'll go along. Always interested in what the Wogs are up to."

"Fine with me," Rick replied. McDowell ordered a car to be brought around and it arrived immediately.

After climbing in, Rick asked, "Tell me, why do you Brits call all these natives 'Wogs'?"

"Well, I must say that it is something of a racial slur like your word 'nigger.' One of our Labour people described that 'Wogs began at Calais.' Guess it meant all foreigners were less than our own Brits. I feel it is just a way of speaking about the local people."

"Yes I've observed the European's superiority over the Africans," said Rick with sarcasm edging his comment.

"Hmm, yes I suppose you have," said McDowell, "But you're talking about the Italians, I'm sure, and they certainly wog-like."

"Oh boy," said Rick, "Let's just hear it."

"Sorry to offend you, old boy, but that's the way we think and nothing will change that." Rick just shrugged and looked out the window. Another example of British arrogance, he figured.

Khartoum City was brown, the people were black and the sky was a brilliant blue. And was it ever hot! McDowell laughed as Rick mopped his brow with his handkerchief saying, "Blaine, how can this be hotter than Ethiopia?"

"I don't know but it is. Maybe it was the mountains."

"At least you missed the mosquitoes. When General Gordon first came here they came in squadrons that darkened the skies. We took care of that and the malaria for the Wogs by eliminating standing water. Poor savages weren't even that grateful." He cleared his throat, tapped his pith helmet with his swagger stick and then elevated his chin.

Rick watched the people moving slowly, almost drunkenly, "Seems like all them are ready to drop."

"Like you, it's the heat. Poor buggers can't stand it either. Most of them live in lean-tos, roofs of corrugated metal. No respite. They are all just waiting for God knows what. Oh look, Blaine, there's the camel market."

Rick looked out at a huge cloud of dust but opened the window to be greeted by a cacophony of sounds, lots of camels lurching around, and the olfactory insult of camel stink. "Jeez, what a hell," he said making McDowell lose his dour affect long enough to laugh briefly.

The driver wound his way through the packed dusty streets past the souks and the Kasbah. The vehicular traffic was clotted with donkey carts, camels, and British military trucks and cars. Rick asked about the trucks and McDowell scowled. "You're not supposed to notice that and I'm not supposed to comment. I will only say that the Eyeties are big thunderous bullies and may need some cutting back." Rick laughed but said no more.

"Tell me, Blaine, what are your plans; surely you don't want to remain here in Khartoum."

"You're right, Captain, no plans to remain in Khartoum." They both laughed. "I was thinking about going to Spain. That new war fascinates me, seems like another Ethiopian dilemma. Good guys and bad guys again. I hate the damn fascists and their belief they deserve to own the whole bloody world and don't give a damn how they do it."

McDowell said, "Blaine, I've a brother at our embassy in Madrid. If you want to be in the fight, he surely can help you. Sub Rosa, of course. Our government has made it clear that we're hands off in this affair. Gregory, my brother, happens to disagree with that policy."

"That would be great, Captain. Rick surprised himself with his response. The decision had been made without much thought.

After an hour's driving they returned to the Embassy, a wide, framed structure that looked to be on stilts and surrounded by a high wire fence. McDowell invited Rick to dine with the officers, and then he reached into his briefcase and pulled out some papers. "This article was picked up from the cables. It's by your friend Herbert Matthews. Cheerio, old chap."

"Thank you and cheerio to you, too." Rick returned to his room and began to read the cable. Why were his hands shaking and dripping with sweat. Was it because he might have died there?

SPECIAL TO THE NEW YORK TIMES
(Via Cable from Addis Ababa)

On October 3ʳᵈ, 1935, fueled by the need for revenge and expansion by colonization, Mussolini's vaunted Roman Legions rolled down from Eritrea and west from Italian Somaliland into Abyssinia. These newly mechanized legions under the command of Field Marshal Rodolfo Graziano blundered and slaughtered their way with enthusiasm and vigor towards Addis Ababa, and within a month were 80 miles into Abyssinia. Poison gas and bombs, death's angels from above, plus modern rifles, tanks, and artillery weapons massacred the half-naked warriors in their anachronistic dress The lion skin shields and robes that they thought would insure the bearer invulnerability against death offered only guaranteed slaughter.

Still, resistance was heavy throughout the country, so Graziano began to rule with an iron grip. He destroyed the Intelligentsia, and killed many of the priests of the Coptic Church in reprisal for partisan attacks. Field Marshal Pietro Badoglio (1871-1956) took command later in 1935 and immediately resorted to mustard and other poisonous gases on a number of occasions to quell the unrest. General Badoglio is arguably the best leader in the theater and he marshaled his 400,000 men to occupy 25,000 square miles in three weeks. In one singular battle The Ethiopian Emperor's vaunted Imperial Guard, spoiling for a fight, conceived a plan to attack the Italians over a five-mile front through a double pass in the mountains. General Pirzio Biroli, Badoglio favorite, had personally studied the terrain and constructed a bold counter plan that would allow the Guards to move through the pass. By strategic positioning his forces could cut the attacking columns in two and destroy the attack at its inception. An Ethiopian deserter, an officer, gave the Italians the time of the attack guaranteeing them their massacre. The Ethiopians broke and scattered then reformed and finally broke again. Then came the final attack by the Imperial Guard. They charged with a grim fury but were immediately mowed down by heavy machine gun and rifle fire followed up by a pounding by the Italian and Eritrean mountain guns. But they still came in waves and hand grenades and bayonets killed them in droves, piling up bodies so high that the muzzles of the heavy guns had to be raised to avoid them. At one point the heroic charge actually breeched the Eritrean lines but a determined pincer movement dulled then halted the charge.

The Emperor and his entourage, despite the brilliance and heat of the sun, observed the twilight of their empire. He could not acknowledge this reality and ordered another attack by his Imperial Guard. It was total carnage despite the bravery and audacity of the charge. The Eritrean troops crushed them for the final time in a vicious pincers movement and a hand-to-hand confrontation. The Ethiopians retreated in an orderly fashion, a tribute to their courage and discipline, but they left thousands of their fellows on that carmine field of valor and slaughter.

By early 1936, the hard-hitting campaign crushed all organized resistance in the country. On May 5, 1936, the Italian army marched into the capital of Addis Ababa and Ethiopia surrendered. On June 30, 1936, Emperor Haile Selassie, who escaped the invading Italians, spoke before the League of Nations in Geneva, Switzerland, in protest of the attack. He was an emperor without a nation. "It is us today. It will be you tomorrow," he warned. The League of Nations decided not to respond militarily and imposed only minor economic sanctions against Italy. These sanctions did nothing to cripple the Italian economy and were lifted two weeks after Emperor Selassie spoke to the League.

BYLINE HERBERT MATTHEWS

Rick carefully laid the paper down and began to think about his future plans. "Us and them," he thought. "Selassie's right. Everywhere I've gone since New York it's been us and them. The big guys, the powers that be vs. the little guys. Goddamn, it's just not fair. No one of any force of personality stands up for the little guy." He felt a surge of anger, then his anger turned to resolution. "I've spent my life fighting for myself and it's gotten me little satisfaction. How 'bout we just forget about the 'us' and concentrate on the 'them'." He lay back on his bunk and closed his eyes for a few minutes, allowing his thoughts to flow. Then he got up and poured himself a scotch, raised the glass and drank a toast to the little guys.

CHAPTER SEVENTEEN

Spanish Civil War

Captain McDowell assured Rick that his brother Bruce would meet him at Barajas Airport in Madrid. As the plane bounced down the runway Rick could see broken segments of the runway caused by Nationalist bombs. Fortunately the skies were clear of both rain clouds and the Condor Legion. Rick deplaned and walked along the tarmac to the terminal entrance. A rugged looking young man in a British army uniform waved a large card with 'Blaine" printed on it. He was hatless, his red hair flapping in the prop wash. Rick noted that he looked like his brother's twin as he raised his hand and shouted over the engines' roar. "Blaine here!"

Rick shook his hand and the two men walked through the terminal out to the waiting embassy staff car. "Right on time, Blaine. Lucky that the Condors aren't flying today. They've been raising bloody hell here but most of the action now is over University City and the Campo. Franco's boys are raising hell there and Madrid could fall any day if the government can't hold 'em."

"I'm here to see that it doesn't happen." Said Rick.

"I've taken the liberty to inform the Spanish liaison to our embassy about you. They would prefer that you be a part of the American contribution to the International Brigades, the Lincoln Battalion. The American Embassy told me that there is a planned but unsanctioned American involvement that was anti-fascist but that you must avoid any political alignment."

"That sounds like a threat," said Rick.

"Your words, Blaine." McDowell smiled impishly. "I must say that if you have any problems call me as soon as you can. Lots of bloody shit going on these days."

The driver took Rick directly to the headquarters of the International Brigades. The young uniformed receptionist who gave him a sheaf of papers to fill out which he quickly completed. The clerk disappeared into the office behind him and returned a few minutes later, pointed to Rick and beckoned him into the office. Two uniformed officers eyed him warily as the studied his papers and then the political officers began interrogating him. Abruptly, one left the room returning quickly with a tall, bushy mustachioed fellow with a New Jersey accent and, apparently, no name. "So where in Jersey did you live?" The voice was ice.

"Near Princeton."

"How near?"

Near enough. Tell me, do you want men or are you looking for door to door salesmen?"

"Blaine, I know who you are and where you're from. Nice job you did with the scab police in New Jersey, and a nicer job in Abyssinia. Welcome to our war."

"That's it? What now?"

"We need leaders and we believe you' may be one. I'm putting you in charge of one of our Lincoln units. The men need a reliable stream of information about what's going on with the rest of the war and I think we can depend on you to be straight with them. We'll take care of getting the material to you, For now, we'll have you billeted at University City, then probably at the home of Sr. Navarro. He's a member of the Cortes, and a good friend of the movement." He shook Rick's hand and left the room.

The others in the room came up to him to shake his hand, smiling broadly; they suddenly all had names and shared them with him. They took him to the University City location and helped him settle in his quarters.

"Who was that fellow who questioned me?" Rick asked a helper named Fred.

"His name is Sokol, and he is our political officer," came the reply. "He screens all the new guys from the states that didn't enlist there."

"What is this, an election or a war?" muttered Rick.

"You'd better stop thinking that way, not aloud anyway. These political officers are rough, and no one questions them nohow. The higher ups don't like a lot of questions and backtalk, They're beginning to talk a lot about Russia and communism, and how good things are there now under the Reds. They kinda scare some of us who just came to help the Spanish against the fascists."

Rick looked at the man, understanding it all for the first time. Damn it all! What were they up to? They had a tiny role in Ethiopia, but Spain is the big leagues! They want Spain to be Red! Or do they? He was suddenly buoyed; was this something to sink his teeth into? He knew he had to be sure.

After spending the night at University City, a chauffeured car took him to the house of Senor Navarro. House? A walled compound with several buildings of formal Spanish design greeted him with an entrance that was protected by a large iron gate with two armed guards standing expectantly behind the walls. Documents exchanged hands, were scrutinized, then reluctant entre was allowed.

They drove to the main entrance of the house as servants appeared, ready to take his belongings. A short, slim, swarthy, elegantly dressed man came out of the door and welcomed Rick in flawless English. "I am Isaiah Navarro. Welcome to my home. We are proud to have you with us. Our cause has too few friends these days. We have heard of your work against these fascists in Ethiopia and are grateful for your concern on our behalf." Rick nodded in embarrassment and said nothing.

While the servants took Rick's bags to another part of the house, Navarro led Rick to an informal dining area where a well-stocked buffet table awaited. Rick had not had breakfast and was grateful for the opportunity to satisfy his hunger. Their coffee poured, the servants disappeared. "What would you like to know about this conflict, Senor Blaine?"

"Why don't you tell me what you think I should know?" Rick looked intently at the older man.

"Spain had never recovered from the loss of its colonies. They may well have been the worst thing that ever happened to us. Reliance on the new blood and treasure of our possessions led us down the road of complacency and self-indulgence and in the process never left the 17th Century. That era made us incapable of competition in the world industrial markets. We are a nation of Quixotes and mystics who feel we have secrets the others don't. Unfortunately, we elected these lotus-eaters to the Cortes where they attempted to create national policy from their spider webs.

"That's fascinating. I knew about the past but not the present. I like your analogies."

Navarro continued, "We created the Second Republic with a coalition of left leaning groups that espoused land reform, a lessening of the Church's power, and democratization of the Army. Intellectuals, poets, and a democratically elected government now faced an angry group of rightists: bakers, landlords, the clergy, and the army. Oh yes, the army is rightist, and the Generals are under the sway of the wealthy, the landed, and the Church."

"You're a wealthy man, Sr. Navarro. Why are you in the left-leaning camp? It seems odd to me that you would support those people who would take your livelihood away from you."

"My family deals in agriculture, that's true. We grow and process olives for use in Spain, with a large export market. My lands have been divided among the farmers, who function as a kind of cooperative, with my family as broker for their fruit. I do not want to have or to be perceived as having slaves. There exists another reason. My family is Jewish, and Jews have had a hard time in Spain under despotic and authoritarian regimes. Are you aware of what is happening in Germany? Hitler's dictatorship will bring back an era of pogroms against us."

"Senor Navarro, what of the Reds in this outfit of mine? I am not one and I don't particularly like the idea of working with them. I worked studied and worked with some and they behave like religious fanatics. I don't like that."

"You must be careful of your criticisms. They take umbrage at criticism, enough so that people who do disappear. I, too, am uncomfortable in their presence, but my reasons are as old as my religion."

Rick felt comfortable in the company of this gentle, intelligent man, but he felt that further exploration of the Red issue should be delayed.

They finished breakfast while Rick asked tourist type questions about Madrid. Then he saw her, dark, with beautiful black hair and eyes, like a gypsy. Her mouth was wide and strong, with full, voluptuous lips, and her smile reflected enthusiasm and accomplishment, but without hauteur. He had always believed there exists a beauty of strength and virility in dark eyes. Her body was that of her father's, except for a modest swell at the breast. She wore a beige blouse with some kind of hiking pants, and boots to mid calf. Ignoring Rick, she strode into the room, gave her father a peck on the cheek and sat down. Only then did she turn the heat of her eyes towards Rick who was already standing.

"Mr. Blaine, this is my daughter Imelda." Imelda smiled at Rick and then drank her juice in an unconcerned fashion, apparently she was used to guests in her home, and Rick was just one more.

"Are you in Spain for the war Mr. Blaine?" She smiled provocatively over her juice. "That's what seems to bring you Americans here. Yanks everywhere these days. Many of the Americans I have met seem to think theirs is the only contribution that means anything, little do they realize that they cannot provide what we really need since your goberment has seen fit to support the blockade. The blockade serves Franco as thoroughly as aid from the Nazis."

Rick smiled at the way she said "goberment" in the Spanish fashion. "I must apologize, Imelda, I haven't heard about the blockade, I've been in Ethiopia fighting the Fascisti there." Imelda's face flooded red.

"You must forgive my daughter's unmannerly remarks about the Yankees. She is correct about the need for heavy materiel from your country, but her attitude towards your brigade has been shadowed by the conduct of a few of its members whose politics are more militant than their contributions."

Rick turned to Imelda and said, "I'm not political, Imelda, I don't easily stick my neck out for this or that government or persuasion, I merely refuse to tolerate people running roughshod over other people. I'm afraid you'll have to teach me the proper political attitudes." He smiled pleasantly at Imelda, but she looked directly into his eyes, transmitting approval beyond his wildest expectations, he felt a wild yearning for her company and her person. How long had it been since he had a woman? She lowered her eyes and finished her meal in silence. Rick stared at her until he was suddenly aware of Sr. Navarro's eyes, and he turned his gaze to the older man. "Tell me about Franco," he asked.

Isaiah Navarro stiffened. "Franco is like Spain, inscrutable, inexplicable, monastic, mystic, an aesthetic man amongst men whose primary need is power. He is like our church; a need to nurture and provide succor for the people while demanding that they go about on their knees, and obey orders like sheep obey the sheepdog. Mother Church, Father Franco; obey me and I will bring you peace and salvation, disobey and I will excommunicate and disenfranchise you."

"Sounds like the Pope," said Rick.

"Those of us who make our own decisions and see the need for a democratic voice cannot support such an institution or such a man." He stared down at his cup with a look of sadness. Looking up, he said bitterly. "We couldn't do it, our coalition of dreamers and malcontents, we couldn't make a single decision that would satisfy the right, no compromise, no giving in to the enemy. So, the call for Franco came, and from Spanish Morocco came this aesthete king, like some old world Quetzalcoatl, to save the republic. To save it, he must first destroy it, that is the tragedy; some of the alleged atrocities committed by the Republicans include 60,000 people killed behind the lines, many being old scores. Nuns, thousands of priests, monks, and even 12 Bishops have been murdered. 800 persons were thrown down a mineshaft. But, some of the stories were exaggerated, blown out of proportion, gruesome massacres based on flimsy evidence disseminated by professional propagandists. The dispatches are lurid. Catholics see the murder of a priest as a wound in the body of Christ and the Catholic Press is quick to report and exaggerate the mutilations of the bodies of priests and nuns. The Anarchists are the church burners while the communists stand behind the scenes and applaud. I believe that the primary goal of the Reds is to eliminate the other parties that they might have Spain for themselves."

"Is that the only reason they would destroy the others?" Rick asked.

"It is also possible that they don't want a strong Spain. We are told that their own house is in disarray, and they fear any strength outside their borders."

"Are you a communist then?"

"I am first a Jew, second a Spaniard, and I have little use for third level rankings."

Rick smiled, "A clever answer will always beat a truthful one. I think you'd better tell me where I go now, there must be war somewhere around here."

"Senor Blaine, there is more war than your soul can take in. Come, I'll show you the grounds, your room will be ready soon."

The two men walked from the dining room, with Imelda between them, her arm linked with her father's. Rick longed to touch her but it was not to be this day. His heart bounced suddenly, and then resumed its regular cadence. Coffee or Imelda?

Later, after the grounds tour, he sat in his room thinking about what had just passed. Imelda had seemed to ignore him, talking animatedly in Spanish with her father. Rick knew Spanish reasonably well, but the conversation made no impression upon him. He was reading what wasn't there, what she seemed so bent on eluding. It was suddenly important to him what she thought and did. He felt something emerging that had not known light since he left the States. He thought about Imelda for a few more minutes, and then took out his orientation pamphlet. He was about five minutes into his reading when a knock came at the door. "Yes?" he said.

"It's Imelda, How about my showing you Madrid tomorrow? I can work my schedule around yours."

Rick opened the door to a smiling Imelda. "Sounds good. I'm free tomorrow."

"That's nice. I'll have the cook prepare a picnic."

CHAPTER EIGHTEEN

Imelda

Next morning Imelda and Rick got into the chauffeured car and began a tour of the beleaguered city.

"Madrid is an important city both to us and to the fascisti," said Imelda. "Franco wants it for his capitol city and he doesn't want to lose our beautiful buildings to the Condor Legion or the Rebel artillery. That's Chicote's Bar on our right. That's where the journalists have come; they get lots of stories from the young officers who visit there frequently. Up ahead is the Telefonica, the communications heart of Madrid. You can see it's been hit by some artillery shells but hasn't yet been bombed." The driver skillfully steered the big car through and around the debris.

Rick looked around at the devastation, buildings in ruin, smoke from old fires, charred wood and splintered concrete and said, "Doesn't seem like the best reason to save a city full of his enemies," said Rick.

"Well, there is another important fact; many of his supporters own the buildings. The Condors have been at it since August so we see how careful they've been. They want a fearful citizenry, not a city of ruins."

"Why doesn't that surprise me?" Rick replied.

The smell of cordite and dust pervaded the air. Sandbags were piled against many of the buildings to protect them from the fragmentation bombs. "Look Imelda, is that the cathedral?" Rick pointed at a dome that was half in ruin still oozing smoke and debris.

"Yes it is and one can see some of the art still hanging on the wall." Her face was twisted. Rick could see clearly through the trees the interior and the devastation against the bright blue cloudless sky.

Despite the ominous surroundings the cafes dotting the street were filled with patrons coming and going. The women in their bright colored dresses and the sharply dressed men zigzagging around the rubble made a sharp contrast to the debris and craters that littered the streets. "Interesting how the people ignore the risk of sitting in a cafe or bar," said Rick. "I'm impressed with how prosperous they look. I expected them to be shabbier."

Imelda said, "If they didn't dress up and go to these places there would be nothing else to do," as the big car zigzagged down the avenues avoiding the man made barriers.

Rick noticed a number of well-dressed young men sitting with the women and said, "What about those young men in street clothes just sitting around drinking and flirting?

Imelda looked at Rick grimly, saying, "Those Caballeros are rich and in a politically favorable position. Our peasants fight for them, too."

"What the hell am I doing here, fighting for these parasites?"

"Your choice, Rick." Imelda's tone was icy. "We'll all responsible for our destinies. They chose non-involvement." She sat forward, "Now see, there is our government building. You notice that there is little damage. The top Republican officials set sail for Valencia last November. We've become accustomed to deserters."

"What about the antigovernment people. What are they doing?" Rick said intently.

"Franco insists that there is a group of people he calls his "Fifth Column." They are the traitors who sabotage trains full of our soldiers; throw grenades from the rooftops onto fire engines, or signal the location of special targets to the bombers."

"Where are the police and the army?" asked Rick.

"They are too busy guarding the fascist officers we've captured. There are so many that we have to commit too many of our men to keep them in the jails."

"I've heard that the number is getting smaller, thanks to the new death squads." Rick waited for Imelda's response, and it came quickly.

"The only death squads here belong to the fascists." Her tone and face were grim.

The car made a left turn onto a wide, gracious avenue and Imelda pointed at a pillared neoclassical building. "There is our jewel, the Prado," Imelda said. "Most of the art is now hidden in caves around the city. After the war you must return and see what treasures we have there." Rick shook his head in silence. Return? When would that be? Would he be around when the war was over?

They drove west, down the Grand Via past the Plaza de Espana towards the western edge of the city. "Those buildings in the distance are part of University City. Look at the women, see the tents? Those are soup kitchens for the troops, some are for the wounded. My God, so many wounded." Imelda choked a sob. A number of men lay on stretchers in front of a larger tent that had a red cross on top. "Oh Rick, that's an operating tent. Those poor men."

They came to a stop as a soldier in a mono had raised his hand, then his rifle and pointed it at them. "No pasaran aqui," Broken concrete and rubble filled the streets while a pall of smoke and dust obscured the actual damage. Rick could see a line of trenches protected by sand bags through the damaged buildings that marked the periphery of what was the battle zone. He and Imelda climbed out and began walking, picking their war down the ravaged street. Shells began to fall into the trenches as cannons growled in the distance. The soldiers seemed oblivious to the small explosions. A few Loyalist artillery pieces were dug into the red earth, surrounded by men in dirty dark blue "monos," the ubiquitous Republican uniform. They raised tired eyes to the limousine, some smirked, others looked away. The government had requisitioned most of the autos in the city and everyone knew it. Plutocrats were not indulged in war torn Madrid.

A young lieutenant and two enlisted men, assault guards, came towards them. "Papers please," said one soldier. Rick and Imelda handed him their papers, which he in turn gave to the lieutenant. The young officer saluted them smartly, saying, "Senorita Navarro, welcome to the front." He then turned to Rick and said, "Senor Blaine? Are you here as a tourist?"

"Lo Siento, Teniente but I have come to fight with you for Spain."

The Lieutenant shrugged and stuck out his hand. "Teniente Pena. Welcome to Madrid." He waved at the mountains in the distance and a rumble of artillery answered his gesture.

I guess they know I'm here," Rick quipped as he stared down the long road sweeping down to the Manzanares River. Shell holes pocked the area as if the scrabbled ground had a bad case of small pox. Rifle cracks followed by a stuttering machine gun caused Rick to seek cover.

Lt. Pena called out, "Don't worry Senor Blaine, the action is still further down by the river. We only worry today about the artillery and the airplanes." He laughed a nervous laugh.

Rick looked to his right and saw through the trees a row of bombed out buildings, or what used to be buildings. The walls were rent and torn, floors sagged onto lower stories strewn with desks, chairs and tables. "What the hell is that place?" he asked.

"That's our University City, or was. The bloody fascists have destructed all our hospital, bacteriology center and cancer center. They've killed relentlessly and without discrimination; patients, doctors, nurses, lab technicians, workers. Nothing or none of them can ever be replaced."

"Is that all from artillery?"

"No, the dive bombers shared in the shame. And, we pushed back the bloody Moors who were trying to take over the area. They got far enough so their grenades and rifles inflicted more of the damage. So Sr. Blaine, do you feel ready for all this? Do you feel our Spanish soil is worth putting your life at risk?"

"I don't believe your Spanish soil is the only one at risk with these buggers," replied Rick. "From what I've seen the entire planet is up for grabs to these guys." He saluted the Lieutenant and took Imelda's arm and they half-ran back to the car. Imelda told the driver to take them home. "I tell you, Imelda, I thought I came to Spain to help make a difference, not to get sneered at. None of the military people seem to want any help. Why?"

"It's very complicated, Rick. You want a simple answer, I'll tell you, politics. If you want the whole answer, it's politics."

Rick laughed and then said, "Imelda, you are a true philosopher, and what's more, a real cynic."

Imelda spoke in rapid Spanish to the driver, and they walked back to the car and drove off, leaving the devastation behind.

"This is what we have to keep Franco out of the city?" Asked Rick. "I expected more substantial fortifications. These sandbagged nests will be useless against heavy artillery."

Imelda sniffed again, saying, "The corazon my Yankee, the heart. Do not forget the heart." Rick nodded his head in puzzled agreement.

They drove past some more substantial buildings, some appeared to be apartments, others were more like small palaces. Suddenly Manuel turned, speaking in staccato Spanish to them. Imelda called out, "The bombers!"

The limousine careened onto the grassy terrace. A Stuka dive-bomber roared low down the avenue but did not belch fire from its machine guns or drop a bomb Instead, hundreds of leaflets poured from the fuselage as the plane catapulted over the skyline and disappeared. Manuel opened the door and retrieved one of the leaflets and handed it to Imelda. "What does it say," Rick asked.

"It is a warning that future planes will carry weapons of death to the Madrilenos."

"Nice of them to warn us," said Rick.

Manuel steered the Hispano off the terrace and again they were in motion. "This is the Puerto del Sol, the heart and center of the old city. All roads in Spain begin here." Rick smiled out the window at the monuments and the City Hall with its clock tower. Imelda followed his eyes and offered, * "Older than anything in your country." Rick just nodded.

The streets were now quite narrow, then widened again. A large stadium-like structure filled the street view. "Las Ventas," said Imelda. "The cathedral of bull fighting."

"Why cathedral?" asked Rick.

"Because it is the only place of worship remaining in Madrid," said Imelda. She leaned forward and said something to Manuel who nodded. They returned to the Grand Via and turned right. "This is the Royal Palace. Just beyond is the Retiro, a park where we will have our picnic." Rick smiled in anticipation, aware for the first time of his hunger.

Two guards wearing clean blue monos stopped them at a checkpoint acting as an entrance to the park. Manuel showed them his papers, and then the men looked gimlet eyed at Rick and Imelda. Imelda showed them her special papers and they were waved on into the parking area. They passed numerous stone statues that, according to Imelda, were statues of long dead Spanish kings and queens.

When Rick and Imelda got out, Imelda said to Manuel, "Manuel, you stay with the car. Senor Blaine and I will walk to our picnic area. Keep your papers handy." Manuel nodded.

"You handle that driver like American planters handled their slaves," said Rick. He did not approve of arrogant behavior towards servants.

"It is easy for you to say that, but in these times it is important to keep a distance between servants and their masters. The peons are restless, the lines between us have blurred and they no longer want to wait for change. They want what we have and they will take it if we weaken."

Rick shook his head but said nothing; this was not why he had come to Spain. This is the North and the South all over again; their history has to play itself out in its own way.

Imelda looked up at Rick, her face flushed, her voice fervent. "Let me give you an example. created this park in the 15th century. It became a public park in the 19th. That's progress in the eyes of Spain's elite."

Imelda led Rick to a secluded beach along the man-made lake. She spread the blanket while he unloaded the picnic basket. After uncorking the wine and pouring out two glasses he sat down next to her. She turned to him, smiled and then kissed him full on the lips. Her tongue met his, but then she pulled away. "I'm sorry Rick, but I have been resisting and now I'm embarrassed."

"Then why did you pull away?" He put both hands on her cheeks and moved towards her but she stood up and a turned to towards the lake. God how he wanted her!

"I have my reasons and you are not among them. I am truly sorry." Tears erupted and flowed down her cheeks.

Rick did not hesitate. "Sit down here and let's have a picnic. The other stuff we'll deal with later. Please say more about your thoughts on servants and their masters." His heart was hollow, his mouth dry and thick. He had allowed desire to replace caution, now they would talk of fools and kings. He bit into a sandwich of fatty ham and cheese.

"Rick, that is something I can tell you about. We Spaniards have spent more centuries dealing with this than you Americans. It is such a part of our philosophy that it cannot be erased by a single act of denial. We have had to deal with both domination by other cultures as well as the Catholic Church. We are now in charge of our country but the church is its own entity and its politics Byzantine if not Machiavellian. Now they hold the robes of the fascists in this eruption and all our freedoms are again at risk. It's breaking my father's heart as well as most of the members of the Cortes." She opened another bottle of wine and refilled their glasses.

Rick sat for a few breaths, sipped his wine and then said, "But Imelda, it looks to me like the communists are running the show for Spain and not the Spanish government. That's my impression but I'd like yours." In his heart he didn't give a damn about much right now.

Imelda shot a glance at Rick that made him regret his comment. Then she grimaced and nodded. "You make a point I cannot deny. But I must tell you that I am close with General Walter and you must be careful what you say about the Russians in my presence. In fact, be careful always. They have many spies amongst us and they love their work."

"I've not heard of General Walter. Who is he?"

"Rick, I've already said too much. It's enough to say he heads all the International Brigades. Again, be careful what you say and who you say it to." She bravely raised her glass and said, "Enough of politics. Salud."

Rick raised his glass but he knew that his idea of a picnic was over. They sat and talked of the day, the bombing and a few chunks of life in general. After an hour or so it began to drizzle so they cleaned up their refuse and walked slowly back to the car. Despite the attraction he now knew there would be no intimacies between them. He shrugged off his emotions although his long arms felt as though they were dragging on the ground. Now he had a new track; he was determined to find out about General Walter.

CHAPTER NINETEEN

Greta

He was expected at University City sector at 1500 hours, but his driver arrived early, allowing a more leisurely trip through the city. The driver became very chatty after a few pointed questions by Rick. "It's been tough here alright, the air raids, and the bloody Fascists who still hide out in the city. They are constantly disrupting things with their damn bombs and assassinations. We nab a few everyday; we put them up against the nearest wall and shoot them. The bloody priests are worse because they hide those fellows in their churches and then cry sanctuary. You senors in the brigades are an odd lot; you come in and brawl with each other and us, you have no respect for our women and you are yet to fire a shot. I must say that you Yankees are a bit better than some of the others, but no bargain either. Your first commander here went out of his mind and had to be replaced by another, seems he got drunk and raised holy hell in the barracks. Gotta get things like that straightened out before you fight those Franco boys, they're mean and they're tough. Looks like the Jarama River is going to be first on your list, and good luck to you. Bad terrain, ground's too rocky to dig a trench or even a hole. And, I know we need a lot of help here, but those Russians are an arrogant lot. They sell us a few guns and they think we should be on our knees to them. Bloody French and Brits won't help us, we got to take charity from bloody Slavs."

Rick was fascinated with the man's diatribe, passionate yet articulate. "Go on, tell me more. If I'm going to be here I want to know as much as I possibly can about all of the factions. Which one do you support?"

The driver chuckled and said something under his breath in Spanish. "I'm an Anarchist, can't you tell?" "You foreigners treat us like laboratory rats, always pushing and probing. Oh yeah, do you know about the Alcazar in Toledo?" Rick shook his head, and the driver went on. "We have surrounded the Alcazar which is full of bloody fascists. We have their Colonel Moscardo's son as our prisoner, and we tell the Colonel that we will shoot the boy if they don't surrender. The Colonel asks to talk to the boy, and tells him to remember what his name is, and to be brave. He will not surrender, so we shoot the boy. That's what it means to be Spanish! It's all there it is our way." He turned to look at Rick, and his face told the story of his sincerity in what he had said. Words of iron, words of pride.

"Good God," thought Rick. "This war won't end until the last two men face each other in a bull ring."

He reported to the headquarters area on arrival, and was greeted by a tall American major dressed in khakis. "Bob Moreman here, welcome aboard. I'm told you've had combat experience and we need all the experience we can get. Let me brief you first, and then I'll take you around to your unit. Your men have been here for about a week and they're spoiling for a fight. You can't imagine how difficult it has become to come to Spain, what with the blockade. Our people have to leave the States on pretext, then make it through France down to Perpignan, then hoof it over the Pyrenees, we pick 'em up and truck and rail them down here. Guys from all over the world are joining the International Brigades, all hoping to get a lick at the phalange, but so far the only action for us has been here in Madrid. Franco thought he could walk into Madrid early, score a psychological death blow, and negotiate his terms on the government."

"Yeah, my driver was telling me about some of the action around the city."

"We're real proud of our contribution here, and now that the Russians have sent us new ordinance we think we can kick the tar out of the General. We have the world on our side; every journalist, every writer here is against Franco." Rick thought about Matthews and wondered who spoke for the fascists; maybe they didn't need advocacy other than the military backing of the Germans and the Italians.

"What difference does it make what the press writes when the blockade prevents any aid from the countries they write for?"

"We believe that we will change that when they learn what is really happening here. We must stop fascism here or Spain and all of Europe is lost to it."

They entered a room in what had been the old math building. The room reeked of strong, cheap tobacco, and visibility was poor because people were crowded around, smoking and talking. They jostled with each other while pointing their pointers at a large map of Madrid. The arrows pointing across the Manzanares River were Franco's legions, and they seemed to overwhelm the little cartoon fortresses that signified the Loyalist defensive.

Rick looked around the room, but saw no one he knew. A short man with several cameras draped around his neck and stuck out his hand. "New, eh? You guys all look alike when you first come. Name is Capa; I'm the court photographer and jester. You are?"

"Blaine, Rick Blaine." Rick shook the hand while he observed the remainder of the man. He wore a mono, the blue cover-alls affected by many of the Loyalist forces, no hat, peasant sandals, and a red bandanna. His eyes were large and dark with jutting forehead decorated by bushy eyebrows. Thick lips curled in a smile that spoke of warmth, friendship, and wit. His accented English was sensual yet manly.

"I've already heard about you and Ethiopia. A place I'd like to see. The word is that you're a hero there." Rick flushed at the praise as he popped another Camel from his pack. "Camels! My God man, give me one, these Spanish specials will rot a man's lungs out!"

Rick handed him a cigarette, lit his and then Capa's. "Been here long?"

Capa laughed and looked around. "Been here twice! Lot's of things going on here, and pictures are worth a lot of cash. Not enough cash brought me here, and enough cash will take me back to Paris, besides, I like the adventure."

Rick replied, "Are you political?"

"Hell no! If the picture is good, who cares who it supports, I am only interested in good pictures. Why do you ask?"

"Seems that everyone else here is. I feel a little uneasy about being so close to these commies."

Capa smiled conspiratorially. "That's one story I wish would photograph, or that I could write well enough to sell the story. This is not the place to talk about that, though."

Rick nodded assent, but said nothing, for a banty rooster of a man was coming towards them, accompanied by Moreman. "Blaine, this is Colonel Marty our Brigade's political officer. "Oh God," thought Rick, a living, breathing commie. Marty nodded his head curtly, but made no offer to shake hands, and Rick responded in kind. "Welcome to Madrid, Blaine. I see you already know Comrade Capa. Be sure he doesn't charge you for any picture he might take of you." He curled his mouth at Capa, turned on his heel like a drillmaster, and walked away.

Moreman flushed at the man's incivility and shrugged his shoulders. "Very involved in the campaign," he said.

Rick waved his hand as if to dismiss the issue, but Capa muttered quietly, "Another Red hatchet man. He's a frigging French commie who would cut off his mother's head if he could climb another rung up the Comintern's ladder. He's trying to make a name here so he can take over the entire arms distribution for Spain. That way he can arrange to get his enemies killed for lack of supplies, while he feeds his friends. I have never met a French Communist that wasn't a jackal at heart and this one sees spies everywhere, even among his closest comrades. He has been known to conduct paranoid interrogations lasting for hours."

"How do you know all this about him?" Rick responded intensely.

"My friend Tarocco is French, and she knows him from his reputation in Paris." He started to go on when Moreman began speaking.

"Franco's columns are closing in on the city. But, his numbers are not that great, and his air support isn't strong enough yet to do us too much harm. What we will do is counterattack him when he is just across the river in the Casa de Campo. The Lincoln Brigade has been assigned to General Walter, the commander of the 35th Division. We are fortunate to have him as our commander and he comes highly recommended. He speaks Polish and Spanish, a little French, but here's the twist, he doesn't speak English. We shall have to rely on Colonel Copic, who does, but he is not the greatest at dealing with Americans. He sees us as unreliable, headstrong, and spoiled, incapable of putting together any kind of offensive show of our own. Maybe he's right, we haven't fought anyone yet, but I am out to show him we are the best he has."

He stopped and looked into the eyes of his listeners. "If any of you have doubts about your ability to perform your duties, say so now, and you can go and not be judged by any man. God forbid that you be tried by fire and found lacking." The passion in his voice was real, thought Rick. This is a gent other men will follow. He felt a sudden surge of regret for having chosen to come here. A stranger in a strange place surrounded by zealots of all stripes, political, religious, military, and, those who pursued violence for its own sake. He sat with a handful of other men, also members of the Lincoln Brigade and listened to Moreman's lecture.

Moreman described the battle lines and marked the units, showing each one's place on the chessboard of war. When he finishes he said, "That's it, Rick, that's the briefing. But there's something else we have to talk about, and that's the journalists. You'll find them of all stripes here, and they're all aggressive. They'll pay for any crumb of information they can buy and they don't care whether it's true or not. They'd rather sit on their duffs in Chicote's than risk their necks out in the field. There's a number of Americans here, so let me tell you a little about each of them."

They then withdrew into small groups, talking of things other than the impending mayhem. Capa sidled up to Rick and whispered, "I gotta tell you, that Copic is one dangerous fellow. He doesn't know beans about combat, yet sees himself as the cock of the walk. I was with him at the Teruel retreat, and he was terrible; he wasted two battalions of his finest men because he couldn't admit he was beaten. I think he was afraid some high commissar would rap his knuckles. Say, what do you say we go to the Florida and have a drink and forget about tomorrow for a while.

Rick agreed, saying, "Let's go, and, by the way, may I call you Capa? Capa and Rick on the back.

After a good-bye to Moreman, the two men hailed a staff car heading downtown. They smoked in silence as the car rattled through and around garbage and rubble, the bastard children of the air raids.

The Florida's bar was smoky and dimly lit in deference to the recently enacted blackout orders. Capa greeted the faceless crowd as if he were king of the Cabaret, and the response acknowledged him in return. A young woman appeared out of the smoky miasma and threw her arms around the droll regent, kissing him on both cheeks. Capa held her at arm's length and roared, "Greta! When did you get back? There were some rumors that you hitched a ride with a Stuka. Is it true?" He steered her directly under Rick's nose, saying, "Rick Blaine, Greta Tarocco."

As Rick shook the girl's hand he studied her carefully. Reddish blonde hair styled short, a waif-like body, startling green eyes that probed to the soul. Her smile was one of openness yet shrewdness. She wore a blue mono, and she wore it tightly.

"Mr. Blaine? But surely you've acquired some kind of rank? Are you a spy, or one of those political people that seem to be moving this war along?" Rick could not decipher her accent. Viennese? German maybe, with French fluency. "But, give me five minutes with you and I'll tell you all about your business." She flashed a Hollywood smile.

"I'll bet you could," laughed Rick. "But what is your business here? There isn't much call for dames in the front lines."

"You've been in hiding Mr. Blaine. Women are everywhere today, except in whatever cave you've been sleeping in." Her eyes were clouded and her jaw was set, then suddenly she laughed and threw her arms around Capa. "How's my old lover today? Any good pictures?"

Capa said to Rick, "She is almost as good a photojournalist as I. Plus the men take care of her better than they do me. It's not fair, but that's war." It was obvious that Capa cared intensely for this stunning creature. It was also obvious from her body language that the affair was over.

"Photography it is, then. I'll bet some of your experience came from the other side of the camera, dames and pictures just naturally go together."

"You are a mind reader, Rick, she was a fine model in Paris before I convinced her that there were more exciting things in the world." Capa looked at Greta proudly.

The three sat down at a small table and ordered Rioja while nibbling on the tapas that the waiter delivered. "Where are you staying," Greta inquired of Rick.

"With Senor Isaiah Navarro."

"Have you met his daughter Imelda?" Greta's tone was guarded.

"Yes, she was with her father when I arrived. Why do you ask?"

"Because she is so damn smashing, and she has a major crush on Greta," laughed Capa. "No need for you to look any further at her, Rick. She's not for you or any other man. She belongs to the PSCU, a communist group that controls all of the arms shipments to Spain from Russia. They are the only faction that has all-women units in combat. Real Amazons they are, and man-haters to a man!" They all chuckled at the entendre. "Imelda has had the eye and the heart of every eligible man in Madrid, but she heeds them not. She wants a communist Spain, and she wants whatever else she wants." Capa winked slyly.

Rick felt a sense of disappointment over the gender preferences of Imelda Navarro, but the hurt was eased by the presence of Greta Tarocco.

They had another round, and talked more about the war. Both Greta and Capa had tasted combat, and both were excited about the opportunity to forge a reputation with the publication of their work. They had contacts in Paris that would print anything about the war they could get their hands on. Their romance had flourished in the cauldron of violence that was Spain, but it could not survive the boring tedium that was blinding all to the oncoming Fascist juggernaut. Capa opened by saying, "General Mola's four columns of Moorish Cavalry was rolling over the Republican defenders south of Madrid. He brags of a fifth column already within the gates of the city that will bring the city to its knees even before the other four arrived." Rick was amazed to learn that Mola had only 20,000 men in his assault unit. He had assumed at least 100,000 veteran troops were responsible for the decimation of the Republican forces.

Capa continued, "Don't forget the dagoes, Rick. They are tying up some of the best troops that the Government has. There are 80,000 Italians fighting in Spain, plus several squadrons of fighters and bombers, and excellent pilots. Their tanks are both fast and well armed, and the drivers are maniacs, but their infantry is another matter. They look so good in their combat gear, but they prefer not to stain their clothes in honest combat, the Italians have not been fighters since the Roman Empire, I think the barbarians knocked the starch out of them and they've never recovered."

Rick flashed back to the Ethiopian conflict, and wondered about Ferrari and Sam, wishing they were here with him to figure some way to pull a few more hairs out of IL Duce's nose. "Have they used their secret weapon yet, their canisters?"

Capa looked at him curiously. "What do you mean, canisters?"

"Gas. Poison gas. They used it in Ethiopia against any target that looked like it might win a battle."

"I don't believe it! The League bans gas! I've never seen it in print, never heard it talked about."

"Take my word for it. I'll never forget it, and I'll never forgive the megalomaniac who made it happen. That's why I'm here, sticking my neck out where I shouldn't be sticking it. And I wouldn't be surprised if he called for it here. The world let Ethiopia down, they're already letting Spain down."

Capa shook his head in disbelief. "Such animals! As a child, I believed that all people were good, now I know that all people are evil. What does it take to loathe and hate to such extremes? Gas!"

Both men looked expectantly at Greta, but she was staring at Rick.

"I'd like to interview you about Ethiopia and take some pictures for the Paris papers. They'd love the continuation of your struggle against the Fascists." Greta smiled at Rick primly, but the unspoken invitation had been extended.

Rick agreed to the interview, but there was no attempt by either of them to make an appointment, Rick in deference to Capa, Greta's reasons being less well defined. Capa mumbled something about having a photo session, and left the table. Greta watched him go without comment, then turned to Rick and smiled. Without a word they left the bar and took the creaking lift to her room.

CHAPTER TWENTY

The Brigades

Another siren awakened Rick and Greta from their exhausted sleep. They dressed and took the stairs to the lobby while plaster fled from the walls and ceilings with each bomb blast. They walked out into the street to observe the carnage and to get out of a building that could easily collapse if hit by a bomb. The Condors had already left but the smoke and dust filled the air. A few fires were being quenched by a fire platoon. No one seemed to be injured, there were no screams and little noise other than the fire brigade.

The air raid was just another page in the war history of Madrid. As he watched Greta taking photos, she came towards him, moving lightly through and around the rubble and the shocked crowds. Her face seemed to change, she became somehow transparent, a filmy, misty wraith, and a soufflé of evil portent rattled him. She stopped, smiling, waiting for him join her. Capa walked out of the crowd and they strolled to Chicote's. This hot spot was the most interesting place in Madrid these days, for it was the bar most frequented by the foreign journalists. It was important to know these men, for they were useful propaganda organs. Tell them anything bad, horrible, or degrading, and they would print it just the way you told it. Andre Marty, the commissar of the International Brigades, had told his political officers. Buy them drinks, find them comforts, and then convince them to subvert their reports to our persuasion. They ordered aperitifs and talked about the air raid. Their conversation was interrupted by a loud argument between two journalists who had apparently spent the day hunting a story in the bar. Greta recognized one, a thirtyish, burly

American writer with a bristling moustache and demeanor. She turned to Rick saying, "That's Ernie Hunter Ernie Hunter. I don't know the other guy"

The other guy seemed less in his cups and less interested in the combat. Greta said, "The journalists did not always have the appropriate first hand data for argument, and used their political hunches more than field research. Many make money reporting the news as their benefactors would have them. They say the Italians pay up to $1000 for such propaganda.

Hunter continued his side of the harangue by assuming a boxer's stance. Greta whispered, "Hunter is a legend in the bars of Madrid. He's said to have a prodigious appetite for the flesh, drink, and the intellect. A guy I know says he has so many sides that you couldn't make a sketch of him in a geometry book. His present paramour calls him a genius, that uneasy word, not so much in what he writes as in how he writes it. Her name was Mary Gilman, works for Colliers magazine."

Capa whispered to Rick, "Hunter brags about his connections with the Republican in-crowd, and is always willing to lend a hand to anyone who lends him a larger one. Plus he doesn't always deliver on his promises. Col. Jose Robles had been a friend and translator for a well-known American writer who was suddenly arrested on trumped-up charges. Hunter and the writer were friends, and Hunter had agreed to investigate the case, employing his vaunted 'network.' He sent word that Robles would get a fair trial and probably receive clemency, when in fact Robles had already been executed. When he had learned the facts, the writer was furious with Hunter, who coldly told him he was just another bleeding heart American liberal. It's obvious to all that Hunter plays all sides to get a story and to collect material for books he intends to write."

Rick felt an immediate disdain for the man' but stayed out of his way for Hunter appeared to be a formidable opponent. Hunter turned, looked at Rick with interest, and then strode up to him, holding out his hand. He was a strapping, bear-like six-footer with a bushy moustache and wide-set dark eyes that blazed fire beneath large bushy brows. Hunter's voice bellowed into his ear. "Hi, I'm Ernie Hunter and I understand you've come to fight the bloody falange.

Hunter turned, looked at Rick with interest, and then strode up to him, holding out his hand while yelling out, "Pedro! Here a drink!"

Rick looked at the man implacably and returned the handshake. "Hunter? Seems to me I've read something of yours. I'll have scotch and water. Name's Rick Blaine."

Hunter peered at him quizzically. "Read something? Not everything?" He turned to his audience and laughed. "I like this man, he pleases me." He turned back to Rick and roared again into his ear, "Blaine, let's get out of here and find some action! These pantywaists just sit here and wait for some lackey to come in and give them a story. I know a story that's about to start. Let's go!"

Rick took out a Camel and lit it, blowing out his match in Hunter's face. "Forget it, Hunter. I've heard about your story gathering. I heard about the time you went out to teach soldiering. You brought down all the mortar fire the Fascists could find, and then you left. Our troops had to take cover for hours. No thanks, pal. I don't like your style."

Hunter glowered at the smaller Rick. "Are you saying I turned tail? I won a medal on the Italian front in 1917 for bravery under fire. What in hell were you doing then?"

Rick chuckled and replied with a substantial exhale, "I happen to know you got your medal while you were peddling chocolate and cigarettes during a bombardment. And I was 15 years old and peddling papers."

"What the hell, Blaine, let's shake and have a drink. This stuff kills the worm that bites us."

"No thanks, Hunter, there aren't any worms chasing me."

The other journalists in the bar gave Rick appreciative glances. There were few among them that dared stand up to the bellicose Hunter, who had already turned his back to Rick.

Rick sat sipping his drink and making small talk with Greta about the bombings and the disrupted parade. After a bit, Greta excused herself and headed for the ladies room. Rick looked at his drink and floated back to the past. He thought about Gretchen and how his father had laughed his head off when he heard about it. "My son the Valentino. Shit, you'll never hold a woman, you're too much like them." Because of his father's taunting he wondered if he could ever hope to hold women such as Imelda or Greta.

CHAPTER TWENTY-ONE

Jarama

The next morning, Rick land Greta left the Hotel Florida and joined the American contingent, destination Albacete in the Jarama Valley. Albacete was the key destination for all would-be members of the Lincoln Brigade, and the jumping off point for their first campaign.

Moreman and he were in the lead truck, along with other members of the staff, as well as a "liaison officer" from division headquarters. Most of the "liaison officers" were political officers whose job was to spy for division. This one was ferret eyed and obsequious, clumsily feigning disinterest as the Americans talked intensely about the up-coming battle.

The trucks stuttered and stumbled along the rutted Spanish back roads, making map reading and coordinate spotting almost impossible. After a few hours, the convoy halted for water and personal relief. Rick spied Greta talking with Capa, and joined them. Rick's night with her had been beyond expectations and they swore lifelong devotion before dawn. Capa was no fool; he accepted what he knew to be reality. He liked Rick, still loved Greta, and accepted the emerging but changing bond between the three.

The break over, the trucks started again, the old engines sending up a huge blue cloud of foul oil and gasoline fumes. The passengers coughed and covered their faces. The requirement for night travel making driving an act of blind navigation on the lousiest, most breathtaking roads Rick had ever been on.

Albacete was a small provincial capitol with amply stocked stores and shops, full of good things to eat and drink. Moreman allowed his men to roam the streets, bars, and 'public houses' for a few hours before the general brigade assembly.

The city was in the La Mancha region, and the image of Don Quixote rose in his mind along with tilting at windmills.

The first assembly of the Lincolns gathered in the sun-drenched bullring, which as the temperature warmed grew more redolent with the odor of manure of bull and horse. Rick wondered if, maybe, in the heat of battle, a little human waste had been added to the farrago. Commissar Andre' Marty was the official greeter; the man the party had chosen to indoctrinate the Brigades in the correct political cant. He talked to the Americans in a rich, heavily accented baritone, his syntax dotted with indecipherable French idioms. Capa had told Rick about this martinet; a devout French Communist adding his bullshit to the existing piles.

Capa said, "The French Party convinced the Russians that the Spanish war would lead to military lessons about the Germans. It could assure Russian control of the political aspects of the Spanish conflict. The Russians do not want a major Communist government outside their borders."

Rick said, "My God, this is more intrigue than I ever imagined."

Capa continued, "Revolutionaries exiled from their own countries found refuge in Russia and Stalin found them politically undesirable so he decided to use them as a nucleus for the International Brigades and the world would not know of their Russian connection. The OGPU investigated every volunteer fro to insure their political purity, weeding out the undesirables, and sanitizing the potential spies."

"What did he do with them?" asked Rick.

"Some of them became soldiers or political officers, others were assigned to espionage. Marty had been a member of the French parliament until his radical leftist leanings became too much even for his own party members," Capa concluded.

Marty ordered the men to fall at ease and break formation. They were to return in 15 minutes.

Rick led the Lincolns into the bullring to receive their weapons and ordinance, and to hear last exhortations from their commissar and their commander. When Marty had finished, shouts of "No pasaran!" and "Oles!" rose from the bullring. As they marched smartly from the stadium, Rick thought their crazy-quilt blend of uniforms made them appear slightly ludicrous. Moreman announced to his men that they would be leaving for the front at sunset, traveling to the small town of Morata that would be their staging area.

Somehow, despite security and the blackout precautions, the Nationalists discovered the presence of the convoy, and began, at daybreak, an aerial and artillery bombardment. There were aerial dogfights, with the Republican pilots having the best of the Rebels that day. Despite the shellings and bombings, none of the trucks was hit and no lives were lost, although many of the men were visibly shaken by their first taste of war.

Early net morning after a sleepless night the trucks wheezed to a halt at the position that the Lincoln's inherited, which a wag immediately dubbed "Suicide Hill." The officers and the NCO's began a head count and discovered that one of the trucks was missing. Moreman radioed this information back to headquarters, which brusquely informed him that the fascists had captured the truck. Moreman asked, "Why wasn't I informed of this earlier?"

"We will provide you with the information we feel you need, Major, the details of war are our concern, not yours." The line went dead.

Moreman turned to Rick, "This is a strange way to run a railroad." Rick just nodded.

Rick, as second in command, ordered the men to dig in and construct their earthwork fortifications and trenches. This led to a generalized moaning and bitching about the lateness of the hour, their lack of suitable entrenching tools, and the impenetrable hard Spanish earth.

Six hundred twenty men of mixed backgrounds, mostly east coasters, made up the Lincoln Brigade. One company was predominantly urban Jewish communists, another company a group of reactionaries, who gambled and drank far more than the others, had more desertions, but who were prime fighters. Rick had little rapport with the Jewish group and even less with the reactionaries. He did not understand the total intellectual involvement of the former, and did not trust the sociopathy of the latter. They spoke primarily to each other, constantly laughing and roughing it up like a pack of rowdy dogs.

None of the men had been able to bathe or change their clothes since leaving Madrid; soon everyone had body lice, critters that produced hive-like lesions on the skin. One of the guys called out, "Hey fellows, look at this." He ran the seams of his shirt over a candle flame, popping the lice like some bizarre variety of popcorn. This produced roars of laughter and cheers time after time. This act alone was the best morale booster yet.

Rick became concerned over the increasing frequency of the delousing, remembering what he had read about the Balkan campaigns of the British. They experienced more casualties from typhus than from battle casualties, and, they had the benefit of the best of medical knowledge and techniques for that era. The medical services available were skeletal and fragile. Medicines were scarce, bandages and splints were fashioned from materials other than classic; they soon learned that blood was in short supply and often contaminated, doctors and nurses under-trained and far overworked. He went to the tent of the Battalion Medical Officer with his concerns.

Dr. Warwick was an aloof upper class New Englander who did not mix with the other officers and ignored the men. During the campaign Rick was never able to determine whether he had any apparent political persuasion. Nevertheless he was a good man to have around since many units had only stretcher-bearers, men who had not even the basics of first-aid training. When he heard Rick express his concern, he became animated, walked briskly around in a circle, waving his pipe while he exclaimed, "You're exactly right, Blaine! These men are in danger of a whole host of plagues. I'm glad someone in authority has spoken up, and with your help, I'll do everything in my power to help clean up this problem. The men must not be required to face any more danger of death than they do already from the muzzles of their enemies. I'll get my nurses and medics on this immediately!" He pumped Rick's hand vigorously, his face alive with enthusiasm and color.

Several days passed with nothing happening. The men grew restless because the waiting (in war one always waits) seemed interminable. Food supplies rapidly dwindled, although wine, and anise were in good supply. Despite warnings and penalties, some drunkenness did occur, especially amongst the reactionaries. Desertions became frequent; some meant for a few days of hell-raising in Madrid, others just wanted out of the whole damn affair. Moreman ordered that those captured would either be put in penal battalions, or just "disappear." Inquiries regarding the "disappeared" were not encouraged, and were not considered to be healthy. Rumors of secret trials and executions were rife. "The Ferret", who had become the battalion commissar, would not discuss these incidents. Rick did not feel disposed to question this sinister and suddenly important man, although some of the reactionaries demanded to know the reasoning behind all decisions, political or military.

Finally, in the second week the plan of battle was issued. The Lincolns at the left flank of the Brigades, with the Thaelmans, the British, the Dimitroff, and the Franco-Belge making up the center and the right flank. To the left of the Lincoln Brigade was a Spanish unit, a group of grim-faced veterans of several other campaigns. The Spaniards were hostile and resented the presence of foreigners, especially Yankees, on their soil. Rick felt certain it had to do with the Spanish ladies and their quick acceptance of the Yanks. Moreman, who was something of a history buff, believed that it had more to do with the Spanish-American war and the seizure of Spanish colonies by the Americans.

Rick quickly discovered to his dismay that many of the Lincolns were devoutly communistic, and, as Communists, tried to democratize their units, with elected officers, and with day-to-day combat decisions decided by council. This really bothered Rick but he felt he had to tolerate it.

The Fifteenth Brigade Communist Party officers conducted tours of all the units for propaganda purpose; inviting foreign writers and journalists to come to the front to see first hand the operations that the Communists wanted them to report to the world. Rick and Moreman watched them come and go, and the two comrades shook their heads in amazement as the parade continued. "This is more like a political convention back in the States than a war being waged. I guess the General Staff knows best, but I really question whether or not we'll see any benefit from this. I guess they're trying to sway their governments into changing their non-alignment policies," mused Bob.

"That may be the case," argued Rick, "but these Reds make me nervous. We're being exhibited like a bunch of laboratory rats, and I wonder if they'll drop us just as casually. I don't like the way they use propaganda to create illusions and half-truths. This army is not ready to fight, some of our rifles are still packed with grease, and some of the men had never fired a weapon of any kind. I think we should tell General Copic about it, and forget this carnival crap."

Moreman looked soberly at Rick. "We can't let on to the men that we have dissatisfactions with our leaders. They're skittish enough as it is, so let's be wary of letting on to them that we don't like these goings-on."

Rick nodded his assent. His over-lying concern had become the ordinance called up by Command to back up the men in the trenches, which concern found him walking from one end of the defensive positions to the other, checking the number of Maxim guns, heavy machine guns, and small artillery pieces. It was useless to hope for any heavy artillery pieces, they were too much needed in the offensive campaigns presently being waged. Then he saw the tanks, the beautiful, swift Russian tanks purchased by the gold from the Spanish treasury. They roared about with their turrets open, the gunners smiling cockily as they caught the admiring gazes of the infantrymen. The tanks were manned by Spanish and Russian drivers, the Spanish drivers having been trained in Russia. Rick's morale took a boost when he saw these armored juggernauts roaring along at 30 miles an hour. He became convinced that they would hold the positions for the cause. He walked briskly back to the Lincoln' fortifications. Thanks to Moreman's urgings, the Americans managed to dig the best trench system in the whole front. The no-man's land was 300 yards from trench to trench, from the fascist bayonet tips to the Republican's barbwire.

Moreman called for a briefing and, he outlined the battle plans. The Nationalist offensive involved 200 tanks and 25,000 men, threatening the control of the Madrid-Valencia road. If this strategic route was lost, Franco's armor could drive unopposed to the outskirts of Madrid, with the fall of Madrid, the Republican war effort would never recover. Jarama was where they must be stopped. Moreman said, "The Rebels have already occupied the high ground, our reconnaissance reports indicate they will soon begin their offensive." Moreman carefully described the Lincoln's responsibility. "We take high ground to reduce the fire on the rest of the division. Intelligence reports say the attack is imminent. First we'll get an artillery barrage from the German "88" batteries, then aerial sorties will drop incendiary bombs. A ground assault by the Moors will complete the main offensive. No pasaran!"

When the attack came, a cold dawn had already shrouded the valley with fog. Rick thought to himself that no briefing could describe the terror brought by noise, light, and the shuddering earth, the shrieking of projectiles, the groans and screams of men in agony. He saw men with their bodies splintered and torn, the obliteration of all light by the clouds of dirt and dust, smoke and fine debris. Even before the bombardment ended, several men had to be physically restrained, one even tied, because their nervous systems could take no more. Screaming and weeping, they writhed and rolled into fetal balls of deflated manhood. The others, whose thoughts and terrors remained their own and ignored these few; ducking and blinking they shaped their thousand yard stares. Men learn techniques of survival even in chaos.

Abruptly there came an eerie, calm; debris no longer leaped and rolled over the ground and through the air, in the eastern sky a forgotten sun burned crimson through the mists, menacing like the devil's beacon. "What next," Rick wondered. "Oh yes, the planes. Too foggy? Not with that sun coming through. They'll be here soon, and the hell will come again."

He stood up slowly, slouching so as to remain below the trench top. "All right, everybody, roll call for each unit, find your dead and wounded and watch your heads! They've got the advantage up there! After roll, get ready, 'cause those planes are gonna come, and when they do, I want everyone under cover." He knew that the air assault could not last long, and if they survived that, the rest was routine. Routine? To risk your life is routine? To crawl through mud, dirt, rubble, to bring back bodies and body parts is routine?

Now the planes, a chorus of bees, the fighters with their high-pitched hums, the bombers with their low rumbling, then the Stukas. The Germans had marvelous planes, but the Stuka was the prize. Capable of maneuvering like a fighter, they carried both wing and fuselage bombs which we at the end of a steep dive, the plane then wrenching its way upward, producing a sonic tooth rattling vibration just before the bombs hit. He counted 15 of these birds, watching with fascination as they began to peel off in perfect formation and head for their hill. "Here they come," Rick yelled, blowing his alert whistle. Everyone but Rick hit the dirt, crowding up against the sides of their trenches, some covering themselves with their packs. A new sound now split the air, the wailing screech of sirens. The Germans had put sirens on their dive-bombers. "Just a touch of terror," Rick mused to himself as he joined the others on the bare scorched earth. More roars, lights, flashes, and contractions of the earth, somehow it seemed less terror-filled then the artillery barrage. It was over quickly. Abruptly the sirens were gone, the engine noise receding in the battering noon sun.

An angry roaring came from the west, and when Rick turned he saw a cloud of aircraft roaring in pursuit of the Germans. The swift little Republican Chatas brought down several of the Junkers, great lumbering shapes twisting slowly downward, smoke pouring from the fuselages, then crashing in a fireball. The Stukas retreated with full throttle and were soon out of sight. The Americans cheered, buoyed by the appearance of the Chatas. The jubilation was short lived as machine gun fire from the heights raked the trenches. When it stopped, sniper fire began. Rick blew his whistle and hit the dirt. The snipers were deadly, bringing down their targets almost at will.

During a lull in the fighting, the cooks brought in some hot rations, which the men greeted with gusto. Finishing his coffee, one man stood up and, with a grandiose gesture, threw back his head and howled. A sniper bullet crashed into his brain, blowing cranial contents onto the other men as he crumbled to the earth. From then on, no one stood up to do anything, and sniper casualties dropped.

Moreman, zigzagging through the trenches, lurched up to Rick, his large frame nearly doubled over, and said, "The new orders are here. We and the Spanish unit are to go over the top and move on up the hill. We've got to take it soon or we'll never get it. The other units are going to give us covering fire so their machine guns will be neutralized."

Rick looked at him with disdain. "Bob, how in hell do you expect to neutralize a machine gun nest with covering fire? Their guns are dug in, they're firing through a wall of sandbags."

"I know," said Bob mournfully. "I told Division that and they told me to obey orders, not question them. I wonder where they got their tactical training. I had some at Berkeley when I was in the ROTC, and they would have court-martialed anyone issuing the orders I just received."

"What are you going to do?"

"What can I do, but obey orders."

"How 'bout we say 'fuck the orders?'" Rick was angry but he knew they had no choice.

The men moved forward from their trenches with Bob and Rick in the lead. No man's land was a garbage dump of shredded grape arbors, gutted rocks, and cracked, gnarled olive trees, some still smoking from the incendiaries. Rick found one of his men hiding in a large shell hole, covered over with a blanket, shaking with fear. "Why are you hiding here?" challenged Rick. "There's no place to hide here, run away to the rear and hide if you must. I don't want you cluttering the field getting in the way of the others. If you change your mind, go forward and join your comrades."

The man looked at Rick gratefully, then grabbing his rifle and his blanket, he bolted towards the front where both his friends and death were waiting.

In the course of battle, the wrong ammo was delivered for the machine guns, resulting in an impotent covering fire for the attacking troops. Rick watched the Spanish unit came up out of their trenches, a number of them fell, then he tensed as the rest leaped back into the trenches. They were incapable of facing the blistering fire. Rick knew they would not win the summit without them. He crouched in his shallow crater filled with frustration when Greta appeared, camera in hand, her beret pulled back on her head. "Bon jour, lover! Que pasa?" she smiled at her linguistic melange. "I've been looking all over for you. I can't wait to show you the pictures I got of the dogfights, and wonderful shots of the men." Her face reddened as she smiled up at him.

Rick only frowned. "Where the hell have you been hiding? And what are you doing here? I don't think a dame belongs up here. Why can't you and Capa collaborate, you get the guys back there, he gets 'em up here. You're going to get yourself killed, or worse."

"Worse? The worst is being left behind. Besides, I'm armed just like the rest of you." she pointed to her tiny pistol in its snug Spanish leather holster.

Greta began framing his face in her range-finder. "You photograph so much better than you look," she teased. "Why do you always frown when you talk to me? Come on, my big macho man, give me a battle grin."

Rick couldn't help but smile, and as he did so, he took her wrist and pulled him to her. "What you need is a kick in the pants, and some lead from my piece."

Greta roared at him, "Which piece I get the lead from, hombre?"

Rick shook his head as he smiled a wan grin of defeat. Their interlude was interrupted by the Doppler-like screech of an incoming projectile. He slammed her to the ground and hopped atop her as the shell exploded behind them, showering them with rocks and dirt, the shock wave driving them even closer together. She turned her face to him and whispered, how about some of that lead, senor?" He covered her mouth with his hand and forced her down again as another, then another, and yet another shell blasted the ground, turning their light-hearted period of banter into a hellish earthquake. The acrid smell of cordite burned their nostrils and lungs, by this time they were half-buried in dirt and small rocks. Dirty tears ran down Greta's cheeks as she faced him when the barrage stopped. "It's not fair, we can't die now! I've waited so long to be happy, now I'm happy, and now one of us may die. Promise me you won't die, Rick."

Rick's face softened as he murmured, "kid, neither one of us is going to die, especially if you get that pretty little frame back to the rear. Now go!"

Greta shook the debris-covered camera and pointed it at him, suddenly laughing. "Go to hell, Rick Blaine, you can just go to hell!" She snapped several shots of him, then turned and ran laughing towards the other end of the trench, where she snapped more photos of the action. The men laughed and lifted her aloft that she might get some photos over the sandbags.

"Put that woman down, you damn idiots before some Sanchez blasts her head open!" They immediately lowered her to the ground with Greta tossing Rick an obscene gesture, and then gave him an angelic smile.

Despite the carnage, the initial Rebel maneuver had failed; the untested Lincolns had seen and tasted death and maiming, and, above all, fear, yet stood fast. The first test. It was a proud moment for them all, but no one celebrated. Too many bodies were strewn about the scene. Rick put his boot under a corpse and turned it over. A Moorish face smiled up, looking beyond the sky and seeing nothing. Corpsmen were running stretchers back to the aid station, some of the men bandaged their own wounds and refused to leave the battle area.

The second attack saw the Spanish unit again disobeying the order to counter-attack, leaving the Lincolns to go over the top alone. Moreman phoned HQ, talking to Copic and his staff, telling them that they would face impossible fire. Moreman was overruled. "We must attack at noon," he told Rick.

"I suppose those Spaniards had an election and the attack lost," said Rick bitterly. Moreman laughed and touched his finger to his head.

A torrential rain began to fall, turning the trenches and the no-man's land into a thick pate of mud. At noon Moreman ordered his troops to attack. A wall of machine guns were aimed where the men's heads would appear, and when the men went over, they were struck by a spate of fire, some thrown back into the trenches, dislodging the ranks behind them. Others were lying on the ground like turtles, their packs like canvas carapaces. The aid men were unable to provide for all the calls for help. The Americans were caught in crossfire. They had no air support, and no artillery, plus no support from the ancient machine guns. The promised tanks never materialized. The first shells tearing off their metal exoskeletons flattened a feeble sortie by two armored cars. Yet, firing their new weapons the Americans zigzagged through the olive groves towards the summit, yelling and hurling their grenades. Somehow, they found shelter in the arid, rocky soil, continuing their assault upwards. In the forward trench, Moreman raised his pistol and prepared to lead the next assault wave with Rick set to follow him. Bob vaulted over the sand bags, then spun around and fell backward onto Rick and both men fell to the ground. "Are you hit?" Rick yelled.

"Yes, I think so."

Rick ordered two men to drag Moreman to safety and attend to his wounds. He then crawled over the bags re-entering the death scape of no-man's land but the battle was over.

Every war has a hill to take. The hill was not to be taken by the Lincolns this day but despite the carnage the entire Nationalist attack was blunted, the road remained open.

Rick wearily returned to Brigade HQ where Moreman sat propped up against a shattered olive tree. "Just a shoulder shot, Blaine. Should be back at it in a week. Unless we hear otherwise, you're the boos till then."

"Ok," said Rick. "What's the tally now?"

"Looks like 50 killed and a bunch wounded. Ask the doc, he's got the sheets." Moreman grimaced as he stood up and walked into the medical tent.

Rick felt the wind blow cold in his face and he turned away from it. This Spanish earth now belonged to him and the Lincoln Brigade.

CHAPTER TWENTY-TWO

Madrid Fights Back

The Lincolns, relieved by another brigade, prepared to return to Madrid to relax and prepare for another assignment. It was obvious that relaxation would not come soon. The city was suffering daily bombings and shellings; the enemy was only a few kilometers away.

After seeing to Moreman in the ambulance, Rick rode in an old Fiat limousine with Greta by his side. Her beret was filthy and torn, her long hair matted and darkened with dirt and debris. She slumped next to him, head on his shoulder, and began to cry. He said nothing, wishing that he had some way to relieve the emotions exploding inside himself. He kissed her cheek and suddenly wanted this beautiful woman, fantasizing that they were on holiday. He felt a surge of tears but held them at bay.

Innumerable checkpoints riddled the rout, each of these roadblocks manned by dour-faced boys in ill-fitting blue "monos." They held the ID's upside down, diagonally, then side-ways, scratch their noses, and hand them back. "They can't read," thought Rick, "Illiterate," he whispered out loud. Greta turned her face to look at him, her expression was blank. "These kids don't know what the hell this thing is all about.

Greta pulled away from him, crying, "What do you mean? These boys fight for the same cause as we do. They know the difference between the fascists and freedom!"

Rick took her arm and said, softly, "You're right, Greta, they know. I guess I'm just tired, too," while in his heart believing his initial outburst.

They reached the outskirts of Madrid at sunrise; a black haze hung over the city, its bulk tinted pink at its edges. In some areas, fires flickered in the haze. Posters on every building spoke of the ultimate victory of the left. Mola's Moors had built the half-completed barricades at almost every intersection hastily for the coming assault.

They drove up to a barricade and stopped. Four men in blue uniforms flanked the vehicle, each carrying an automatic weapon. The driver presented his documents. One of the soldiers waved to Rick and Greta to get out. They dug for their papers as an officer came out from behind the barricade and shouted, "Esta bien, esta bien! Bienvenido camaradan!" Rick smiled at him and asked if he had a cigarette. The officer produced a wrinkled butt from his tunic, which Rick lit and smoked it by half in one motion. Greta took a drag, inhaled deeply, and coughed violently. "I'll never get used to these damn things," she wheezed.

Rick asked the officer for directions to the main command post in University City, and the car was allowed to proceed. They were stopped four more times before they reached the headquarters area. Loudspeakers mounted on small trucks blared 'The International,' while blue clad troops lounged about waiting for something to eat or something to screw. When the song ended, 'Bandera Rosa' blared forth, Rick resisted the temptation to throw a grenade at the sound truck, he had heard the tunes all too often. Further, he was not a comrade of the Comintern. How the hell had they taken over the war? The only evidence of Russian help he had seen were the tanks, and they always seemed to be somewhere else when they were needed.

Greta looked at Rick and grimaced, she too had tired of the martial dissonance. "Some day we must dance, you and me, and put these rancorous melodies to bed."

"I would much prefer to put them to the grave," Rick laughed and hugged her.

A plainclothes thug type interrupted his uncharacteristic public display. "Senor Blaine? Come with me to Coronel Beck." Rick and Greta fell in step behind the thug, whose small body was made larger by an ill-fitting suit and Charlie Chaplin shoes. They walked up to a sandbagged building that announced that it was once the Economics Building of the University.

"No senora," he asserted, as he turned as if to block Greta's entry.

Greta looked at Rick but he shook his head, whispering, "Wait for me here."

Colonel Beck was a big, hairy man, with a perfectly fitting gray uniform, unmarked except for a red star on the epaulets. His pointed Leninesque beard was streaked with gray and tobacco, a panatella smoked quietly at his desk. Behind the desk, a large map showed the city of Madrid, with red and black markers indicating the fascist positions. His desk was clean except for a folder marked in Cyrillic.

"Comrade Blaine?" The greeting was friendly but the voice was cold. "Might I inquire after the health of Major Moreman? Do you think his wounds are critical?" Despite the words of concern, the voice dripped cold.

"I think he'll be back in a short time," Rick replied. "He's a tough guy, and he's young, that is, if the doctors don't kill him with the blood they're giving him." He waited for Beck's reply.

Beck took a metal cigarette box from his coat, opened it and offered Rick one, Rick took it, lit a match, lighting first Beck's, and then his own. "Thanks."

"In the absence of Moreman, I must ask you to take over the brigade, the Moors will soon be here, and we must all be ready." At that moment, Rick heard a whoosh and dove to the floor. Beck remained motionless as an artillery shell rattled the windows of the room. Rick looked up, admiring the coolness of the man, while not feeling the least embarrassed by his own actions.

He sat up, put his elbows on his knees and said, "Colonel, next time you should join me, those German gunners are really good."

Beck smile retorted, "And how do you know they are German, Captain Blaine?"

"We learned at Jarama that the Huns won't trust their bloody guns to anyone, just as they don't let the Spaniards fly their planes. Very superior, if we were smart, we'd import a few of them."

Beck laughed harshly. "We have the Thaelmanns, and they brought no planes and no artillery, only Russia has been generous enough to send major ordinance."

"I understand that they have been paid well for their ordinance, and if they continue to keep it out of battle it ought to last forever."

"I know of your sarcastic tongue, Herr Blaine, and I would advise you that the leadership has concern about it. Please be advised that you are under watch." He smiled through small, dirty nicotine-browned teeth as he hissed out the last four words.

Rick looked at him and shrugged his shoulders. "OK, comrade, if that's what it takes to get along, I can get along."

Beck walked to the map, pointing with a baton at a specific location. "You Lincolns will be located here. You must defend it with the same loyalty as you defended at Jarama. Now go to the Florida, get drunk, and fuck your French tart."

Rick stepped one step towards the insult, then turned and left the room without saluting.

Greta was waiting, and when she saw Rick's face, she blurted, "My God what happened in there!"

Rick took her hand without a word, walked to the car, and told the driver to take him to the Florida, on the way, he told the driver what to transmit to the troops. He then turned to Greta and told her about the interview with Beck. Greta reddened, but said only, "Please be careful with your words of cynic."

Their room was ready at the Florida; they went straight there. As the lift door opened, Rick heard Capa's laugh ringing from the bar. The door closed and they ascended to their room. Once there, they fell into each other's arms, and drained their bodies dry.

Three hours later, they took their cold showers and went down to the bar for a drink. Capa met them there, embracing Greta, kissing both cheeks. He then shook Rick's hand, embracing him, too. "Have a drink, here, sit here, tell me about your fight with Colonel Beck!"

Rick looked at Capa with astonishment. "How do you know what Beck and I talked about?"

"It's all over the Florida," Capa said with admiration. "You really faced him down, didn't you?"

Rick lit one of Capa's cigarettes but said nothing. Capa turned to Greta and asked, "What happened?"

Greta smiled and said, "I know nothing, Capa." Then her face clouded and she whispered something in French to him. Capa stepped backwards, looked at Rick with great concern. "That's all I'll ask, Rick."

Ernie Hunter roared up to their table, pumping Rick's hand, and then lifted Greta up and hugged her hard. "Swell to see you both safe! I have some questions I'd like to ask about Jarama. I'd of gone there myself, but the bombardment here seemed to be as big a story. And, you wouldn't believe the sniping! The bastards! I'd like to form a posse and just go from house to house rooting them out like rats. But now, let's hear the stories. Blaine, tell me about your row with Beck. Is he as hard a rock as they say? By the way, Blaine, the Passionaria's bride is looking for you, since meeting you, she is having gender difficulties!"

Rick glared at Hunter, but Hunter just pounded him on the back, implying some great masculine bond between them. Rick smiled sullenly and looked at Greta. She shot him a jealous sneer and turned back to talk to Capa.

Hunter added, "That Imelda. Now that's some woman. I wish I had your luck with the ladies, Blaine."

Rick frowned at Hunter and snarled," Hunter, why don't you learn to shut your big mouth!" He whirled and left the bar, walked to the concierge's desk and asked about messages. "Yes Capitan Blaine. There is a message from Senor Navarro. He has invited you and a guest to his home for coktels. He said he would send a car for you.

Rick thanked the man and walked back into the bar looking for Greta. Spying her, he asked if she would like to attend the Navarro function with him. She nodded and the two went up to their room to change. Greta was quiet and Rick put his arms around her. "Anything wrong?"

"I don't like your being attracted to that woman." She kissed him lightly.

Navarro's car arrived 30 minutes later and they roared out into the night. The situation was blackout, and the lightless car blundered through the darkness. They arrived without an accident, with Rick wondering how. Heavily armed guards greeted them at the gates of the house. They were waved in after their papers were checked. He kissed Greta on the cheek as they waited for the bell to be answered.

The party was already in progress when they entered. Imelda rushed up, kissing Greta on both cheeks, then backing off and smiling up at Rick. Rick blushed, but was saved by Senor Navarro. "Rick, we are so happy to have you in our house again. Would you be so kind as to come to my library for a short chat?"

Rick nodded to Greta, who nodded back. Imelda threw a dazzling smile at him and waved daintily. A butch? Rick wasn't convinced.

Navarro and Rick walked into the somberly appointed library, Navarro proffered a humidor and they sat in silence for a few minutes, puffing on their Davidoff cigars.

"Rick, I have heard of your dissident attitude and I wish to warn you that your behavior has attracted great attention. With that in mind, please hear me out. Rick accepted his criticism but said nothing.

Navarro continued, "The war goes badly for the Republicans. The materiel gap between them and the Fascists is terribly wide, and will continue to widen. Unfortunately the Communists are subverting the war to their own ends. They are imprisoning, torturing, and even killing people who displease them. Others are being deported on threat of death. The Fascists are not my friends, but neither are the Reds, specially the Comintern Reds. Stalin is betraying the movement for a number of unknown reasons. Those of us who will live in a post-war Spain must prepare for detente between the antagonists, so that a new government must emerge from this chaos. A small group of us is preparing for these realities." He paused, looking at Rick with a penetrating glance.

"Go on, Senor Navarro. I get the drift of what you're saying, and I'll decide how far out to stick my neck when you're done."

Navarro continued, "Re-education through torture is not my idea of Spain's future. We have had our inquisition, and we Jews did our penance. It seems an irony that each time we have fought for everyone's freedom we end up losing our own. We were vital in the Russian revolution of 1917, now they are at us again. Many of us do not want to believe that will happen, but doubt is growing. If Madrid falls, we will begin a suit for negotiations with Franco."

"Why are you telling me all of this?" asked Rick.

"I understand that you are a man whose ideals do not interfere with his intellect."

"What happens if Franco takes over? That means the Nazis, and the Nazis hate the Jews." Rick felt his response was feeble.

"Friends who know Franco say he does not trust the Nazis, he will not give them bases in Spain. He is a unique form of aesthetic Spanish patriot as well as a Catholic mystic. Now to your first question. I am telling you because I believe our Russian secret police are on to us. We need non-Spanish people to know these things that we might get greater support from the powerful governments." When Navarro finished, he looked helplessly at Rick. Rick did not have the heart to tell the man he could not even return to America, let alone influence anyone there. His father had major influential friends, but had obviously disowned him long ago.

"I'll do whatever I can to help you," replied Rick. "I want you to take care of yourself, too, for you're treading on dangerous ground."

"One more thing, my friend. Be careful of Colonel Marty. You must understand the ruthlessness of these men and the power they wield. Now I must return to my guests. Go and beware, my son."

The two men walked back into the salon, unnoticed by the other guests. Imelda came up to Rick and looked at him quizzically. "You were with papa? Of what did you speak? Did you ask for my hand?" She gave him a smile and whirled away.

Rick shook his head and felt a sense of confusion. What's going on here? For a man-hater she can sure was a flirt. He then sought out Greta, finding her talking to a large, bearded man dressed in a nondescript uniform. His head was shaved and covered with scars. His head combined with his eagle-like beak gave him the look of a large predatory bird, the stars on the epaulets signified that he was a general officer. Greta immediately took Rick's hand and introduced him. "General Walter, this is Captain Blaine of the Lincolns."

The smile froze on his face. "So, you are Blaine." He then proffered his hand and smiled. "Your Lincolns did well in their baptism at Jarama. How is Major Moreman? I trust his wounds will not keep him from assuming leadership."

Rick met the General's eyes. "He will be back in no time, and yes, he will assume his position as head of the Lincolns. Say, General, at the risk of talking business, what are you going to do with Colonel Copic? He doesn't seem to have a grasp of military tactics. Furthermore, did you know he tried to hold a kangaroo court . . . ?"

"Enough," hissed Walter, "You are in trouble enough, and I'll not hear of junior officers criticizing my staff!" The man walked away. Rick was stiff with anger, yet totally aware that he had made a serious error.

Greta's face was transfixed by terror. "Rick, how could you possibly have said that to one of them? They have the power to eliminate any and all of us."

"Don't worry, sweetheart. These toadies can't tolerate a challenge and maybe things will change for the better." He barely believed what he was saying and Greta knew it.

Both then heard Walter laughing lustily, and turned towards the sound. Imelda was holding his hand and smiling brightly at the General. "Oh, General Walter, you are a true Spaniard!" Walter held himself proudly while Imelda winked quickly at Greta.

The abrupt drone of airplanes interrupted the party; the blackout curtains were drawn, and the lights extinguished. Then came the thunder of distant bombing, followed by the cacophony of retaliatory anti-aircraft fire. The action was over in a few minutes, and the lights came on.

Rick scanned the room, noting that Walter and Imelda had disappeared, while Senor Navarro seemed tense and distracted. Greta whispered, "Let's get out of here." Rick agreed and, after paying their respects, awaited the arrival of their car. They did not speak during the trip to the hotel, avoided the bar at the Florida, going directly to their room, and made desperate love. Later, Rick sat at the desk, smoking, as he thought out the events of the evening. Greta asked, "A sou for your thoughts?"

"I stuck out my tongue further than I stuck out my neck," said Rick wryly. "But I can't stand that pompous Walter and his Slavic stupidity. Who dropped the ball so that these communist radicals have taken over the war? Aren't there any Spanish generals left?"

"What you really want to know is what Imelda and General Walter have going, mais ouis?"

"What do you mean?"

"My naive Yankee, you mean you don't know that Imelda is sleeping with General Walter? If you don't know that, then you also don't know why, that she sleeps with Walter to keep you and her father alive! Do you think you can insult important commissars and officers and get away with it just because you're the marvelous Yankee? Imelda is a Red too, but she loves her father and she loves anyone he loves. I also think she favors you in the other fashion, the man and woman thing. Know these things, Yankee, and watch yourself in the future. Your string is running out!"

Rick looked at Greta, he knew what she said was true; he had blown off his mouth without wondering how he continued to get away with it.

Next morning, Rick and Capa had breakfast in the Florida dining room. Capa spoke first. "President Azana left Madrid last night for points unknown. 'Touring the front,' they say. Front hell. An amigo of mine told me he's heading for Barcelona and for good. He thinks he'll end up at Montserrat or some other monastery. Then if the Nationalists win, he will have the protection of the monks, if the Republicans win, he can say he was protecting the government. Nice guy for a president in wartime."

Rick nodded absently, noting the arrival of a grim-faced Andre Marty. Realizing his tenuous status, he stood as the commissar walked up to his table. "Good morning, Colonel."

"Captain Blaine, Mr. Capa. May I join you? I would like to discuss the Lincoln's positions in our defense plan." The waiter arrived and Marty ordered. He then turned to the two men and told them the plans for the defense of Madrid. His monologue included the descent into madness of one of the Spanish Republican generals. Spying another commissar in the cafe, Marty excused himself and walked over to the other table. ·

Capa turned to Rick and chuckled, "Poor Marty. He tries so hard to be the perfect revolutionary. It becomes ever more important to him as his wife attempts her personal offensive with the Republicans."

Rick looked at him with curiosity, saying, "I'm not sure I know what you mean?"

Capa chuckled again. "She is cuckolding him daily if she gets a chance. Only thing is, he knows it and denies it at the same time. I 'spose that's why he struts around the men like he does, trying to prove his manhood. Hah! His manhood is kept in Pauline's purse!"

Rick pondered these insights into Marty, the quintessential incompetent. Marty returned to the table and sat down to his breakfast. The man looking like his breakfast. Cafe latte, brown bread with whitish globs of hard butter, and a murky glass of some concoction.

He gazed out at the street, suddenly aware of last night's bombardment, and saw the Madrilenos emerging from their potential tombs, ready for what the day might bring. One woman was furiously washing the blood from the sidewalk in front of her shop, pushing a foamy tide of water, blood, and pieces of flesh into the gutter. A couple of dogs scurried by, carrying objects in their mouths that Rick preferred not to identify. There was a smoking hole in the middle of the street with a small geyser of water bubbling from it.

"What does it take to keep from going bats?" he muttered to no one in particular.

Capa responded, "Madrid is like a castle under siege, the moat is full and the drawbridge is up. The besieged are at the mercy of anything the attackers can hurl, and we fight back with the same. We'll eat the tinned goods, then the horses, mules and the goats, and finally, the dogs, cats, and rats. The siege will end, no one will have won, and the city will go on. The people will forget the suffering because they will have eaten and drunk fresh water again. The nightmare will be over. Newborns will replace the dead and grow up to do it all over again, if not here, somewhere. It's all so amusing."

Marty took exception to Capa's philosophy and responded, "These people are prepared, determined to fight to the last man." He followed with some specious political sloganing. Both Capa and Rick pretended to concur with the diatribe, but neither was convinced.

"Time to do what must be done," said Andre Marty as he stood to leave. Both men stood with him, but Marty walked rapidly to the table of the other commissar, then turned and said to Rick, "I will see you at 0900 hours." He turned began and talking to the commissar. Rick and Capa sat down again, Rick feeling slightly off-center after the dismissal by Marty.

"Mr. Capa!" an accented voice rang out. "When did you come to Madrid?" An aproned waiter of vast proportions waddled up to them.

"Sasha? When did you leave Barcelona? I never thought you'd give up your taxi."

"I don't give it up, Herr Capa, they take it! The anarchists need it for their own ends, so instead dem cut off my hands I give it to them. Truly, dey is a dangerous lot of louts. I shall never vote for one again!"

Capa and Rick both roared. "Why would an anarchists even run for office? They shoot all their political opponents anyway."

"Dot's true, Herr Capa, but I tink dey don't know no other way to be. I tink it like the Coosacks dat love to beat the chews, dey chust can't help demselves." Capa introduced Rick to Sasha Szakall, the Ukrainian Jewish lawyer turned cab driver, then waiter.

"Nice to meet someone else on the lam," said Rick. "Why in God's name would you come here after Barcelona? Why not go to Paris or England?"

"Simple Herr Rick. Papers. I got no papers showing I come to Spain; I can get no papers say I leave. No passport, no money, no friends in high places. Only ding I got plenty of is me!" He chuckled loudly as he seized his large aproned belly and shook it.

"Sasha, Rick and I have to go to war now, but we'll be back here soon, and then we'll talk a lot.

Sasha frowned, then smiled. "Oky doky, Herr Capa, you be ever so careful. You, too, Herr Rick. I lose too many friends too soon." He pulled Rick to him and said, "If you need friends in Barcelona I can help." He gave him a kiss on both cheeks.

Rick and Capa hailed an ancient Fiat cab and drove to the Casa del Campo to begin the defense of Madrid.

CHAPTER TWENTY-THREE

Siege Of Madrid

The shelling began as the little Fiat careened through the rubble-strewn streets. The two mattresses atop the car were welcome safety additions, although the driver's recklessness made Rick wish he were on the front of the car as well. Capa whistled as a shell burst in the air behind them.

"Whatsa matter, Capa? Don't you guys celebrate the Fourth of July?"

"Independence is not what I look for today, Rick. I have always feared the first day of battle, so ignominious to die without knowing the outcome, and without a single picture to show for the tragedy. In fact, look what I did in my darkroom." He produced a 5X7 photo from his camera bag and handed it to Rick. It was an image of a soldier, taken from below upward, the man's arms thrown up, the rifle dropping, and the head thrust backwards, a man shot as he went over the top.

"That's quite a picture, Capa. Where did you take it?"

"Shall I say it's Jarama? Or, shall I say it was specially posed by professional models?" Capa winked at Rick.

"You don't really mean it's posed, do you?"

"I mean it to show a man dying for something, or for nothing, a man's life snuffed in its prime. Such a man can only be remembered thus; only the powerful do not let their dead die quietly and without some meaning. This photo celebrates 'everyman.' I believe the truth is always the best picture."

"So it is! Why don't you ever take my picture, Capa?"

"Because I am a superstitious Hungarian. My people believe that the camera robs a man of his soul and I don't want you to lose yours." Rick laughed and wondered to himself if he had any soul left. He suddenly felt homesick for the first time but he didn't know why.

They arrived at the Casa del Campo, where they found hundreds of soldiers and civilians, men and women, digging trenches and building barricades with any and all materials available, including mattresses, doors, and shattered auto metal. It began to rain, the dark November skies reflecting the darkness of the hour for the Madrilenos.

Colonel Beck called his officers together ordered all units into position. "Madrid today must become the tomb of fascism. We must hold! We will hold! Each of you will hold your men together by force of will. There is no retreat. That is all, Arriba Espana!"

Rick returned to his battalion and told the men of the predicament, knowing full well each of them knew the seriousness of the situation, but they responded with a loud "Arriba!" The Jewish contingent began to sing "The International," while the reactionaries laughed at what they saw as a bogus show of patriotism. All waited for the tanks.

They were not long in waiting. The first armored column appeared before the fortifications. Rick ordered the defenders to fire their antitank weapons and throw their gasoline bombs. This action thwarted the first wave. The second wave came too quickly because antitank ammo was in short supply. Rick saw this, realizing that the gasoline bombs would be their ultimate weapon. This required brave volunteers to roll out of their trenches and roll the bombs beneath the tanks. Rick's group then directed their fire on the Moorish infantry that followed the tanks. Doggedly the defenders repelled the second wave, but not without a major loss of men and exhaustion of their ordinance.

The field telephone crackled and the signalman handed it to Rick. "Copic here! Blaine, move your battalion back to the science building. Moors had occupied it and are sniping at the rear of the defenders."

"Yessir!" Rick handed the phone back and gave the order. The Lincolns responded with Indian war whoops as they entered the doors of the building with fixed bayonets. They quickly purged the first floor, then they prepared timed explosive charges and placed them in the elevators. They then sent them to the floors above. When the doors opened, the charges blew apart any troops foolish enough to check the cages. Rick was amazed at the ingenuity of this.

Moving in from four doors, they systematically cleared each floor, ascending to the next floor and moving inward. Rick, a Thompson sub-machine gun cradled in his arms, kicked open doors and sprayed the rooms with bullets, killing the hapless Moors within. They found a small group of Moors gagging in a laboratory room, clutching their throats and their stomachs. It seems they had eaten some experimental animals inoculated with various diseases and chemicals. They were quickly put out of their misery. Rick, along with his men, felt exhilarated. They had not lost a man.

Rick contacted Copic. "Well done, Blaine, now move across the Manzanares River and dig in there. With luck, we've beaten them back for a while, and then our air power will complete the victory. After an entire day of bombing by Fascist dive bombers, Rick was curious about the whereabouts and the reliability of the Republican air power, but said nothing and issued his orders. Capa came up to him, his face flushed. "I've got fabulous pictures, fabulous, especially of you kicking in doors and firing that thing of yours!"

Rick asked Capa, "Have you seen Greta?

"She's been with me and she's happy as a clam."

Both men were sobered at the sight of the wounded troops slumped in the courtyard of the science building. Their heads, hands, arms, legs swathed in bandages, their uniforms dirty and ripped. But their sooty faces were wrapped in an aura of victory. Ah, victory! He thought of high school football, when the most important thing in his life was making that "all important" third down, or the decisive touchdown. Life had become series of "all-importants," too much time and energy devoted to short-term and meaningless goals. He thought of death and reminded himself that the ultimate death rate for the entire world is one per person.

A ring from the radiophone interrupted his reverie. General Beck's heavily accented voice shouted over the phone, "Well done, Blaine! We want to start our river crossing now, and we would have your troops ("twoops.") lead the assault . . ."

Rick interrupted, yelling back into the phone, "We haven't even seen to our casualties, let alone counted our dead. I can't tell you if we have enough men to make a crossing."

Beck's voice roared over the 'phone, "Get your twoops to their location now, Herr Blaine! I will deal with your insubordination later!" The click sounded like a gunshot.

After relating the message to Capa, he looked at Rick with concern. "Let's get the men together Rick, I'll help you with the triage of the wounded." Rick called the senior sergeants, and ordered, "Muster your units."

Rick walked up to Dr. Warwick and asked the casualty report. "29 dead, 77 wounded and unable to serve, 55 slightly wounded and ready for duty. However, the men are tired and won't be at peak performance." He jutted his chin at Rick and awaited his reply.

"Doctor, I agree whole-heartedly, but General Beck has some kind of special hostility towards the Lincolns, maybe because of me. Nevertheless, we gotta be among the first to cross the Manzanares and there will be no acceptable excuses. Anyone that cannot perform, exclude them now."

The Doctor looked at him obliquely, and then nodded his head in agreement.

Rick led the brigade Indian fashion through the hills, trees, and gullies of the Casa de Campo, warily eyeing the dead and wounded Moors. Despite the shelling from Mt. Garibaltis, they reached the river without casualties.

Beyond the river, the terrain sloped steeply upward, dotted with clumps of shrubs and small trees. Each clump, each tree, posed special danger for the men.

Rick and Capa stood in the entrance of a concrete bunker and watched an Asturian unit busily preparing small catapults to hurl grenades towards the enemy positions. The Asturians were primarily miners whose expertise in explosives made them valuable in any assault. Capa and Rick watched with fascination as they prepared their ancient weapons. Capa said, "Did you know that these hombres tunneled under the Alcazar in Toledo and blew the whole thing to bits? Only trouble was, the Fascists knew they were down there, and moved their entire defense back beyond the mined area. They're still under siege, but they haven't surrendered. General Mola' son was a prisoner of the Anarchists, but the General told him to die bravely and to remember that he loved him. The son died for the Alcazar. Now they will never surrender."

"Yeah, I've heard that story. On the other hand, Capa, a man is lucky to be a martyr. How many men have died for great causes without recognition?

The drone of aircraft interrupted their conversation, and they looked up to see squadrons of Republican Chatas diving down on the enemy emplacements, across the river, strafing and dropping their 100-pound fragmentation bombs. The attack lasted a good 30 minutes, and when the planes thundered away, they saw the fascist troops heading for the high ground overlooking the river. The positions there were apparently safer than the pebbled shores of the river.

With this action, the men from the diverse brigades began to sing "The Internationale" in their own tongues. It was a strange but stirring sound to Rick, who was not used to seeing men united together in a cause. There was a naiveté about it that made him sorry he could not feel as they did, this international patriotism towards a common movement of the people. His cynicism was his own personal burden, it prevented him from extending his own inner needs to the empathy of others, thus, he bled alone. He lit a cigarette and allowed the emotions of the others to wash around him.

One of the runners came floundering up to Rick and panted, "Captain, the entire front had been secured and all the Moors have scrambled back to their spot on the hill." He then half-staggered as he set out for the next unit position.

The radiophone crackled again, Beck's voice roared out, "We are sending in your replacements, on their arrival you will remove your men to the University headquarters where they may be dismissed for three days." Beck added, "You must know their whereabouts for emergencies, and you must be available on an immediate basis. A job well done, Herr Blaine. Your irreverence takes on a different light in combat. The cause owes a great deal to you and your Lincolns." "Huzza!" rang out, and the men clapped and hugged each other.

Greta appeared from out of nowhere, hugged Rick and wiped the tears from her face. "I'm so happy, and so proud of you, so proud of all the good things that this war stands for. Let's get out of here and celebrate!"

Rick was too tired to protest as Greta half-dragged him to a waiting car. The ancient limousine belonged to General Walter! "How do we rate, riding in the General's car? I'm not exactly on close terms with him."

"Imelda," Greta said.

Rick ordered the liveried driver to take them to Chicote's, where Greta had said a celebration was in progress. "Imelda is in pretty deep with this guy if she can push his car around like this. What's the story?"

"Senor Navarro has provided the General with a more progressive vehicle, complete with radio-telephone. He is beside himself with pride! He has been sitting in it, calling everywhere just to talk."

"Navarro did that? But I thought . . ."

"Rick, he has Imelda to thank for this thing, not Senor Navarro. I don't think he would otherwise approve of it. Imelda seems to be totally smitten by this man."

Rick frowned, lit a cigarette, and looked out the window. What was going on? Navarro would not just give Walter a car to make Imelda happy.

"Please Rick, I know you've a lot on your mind, but put it aside for awhile and let's be happy." Greta's voice and eyes pleaded with him.

"OK kid, that's just what we'll do."

She snuggled against him, took a drag from his cigarette, and they both were silent for the remainder of the drive.

Chicote's was a bedlam, officers and reporters everywhere, spilling out of the front door, all of them in their cups.

"Do we really want to do this, Rick?" She smiled a wan but alluring smile at him.

"Hotel Florida, driver." Rick's said. The driver was unable to move through the crowd of reporters that suddenly surrounded the car. Hunter pounded on the window and yelled, "Open up comrade, looks like you've won them over!"

Rick opened the door and stepped menacingly towards Hunter, who backed up, raising his fists as he did so. "Whoa, Rick! Save it for the front! The last I knew, you were on your way to the disappearing center, and now you're cruising in the General's private limo. Not bad, pal." He held out his hand in a conciliatory gesture.

Rick said, "Hunter, you have a way of talking that will get you in deep trouble." He just didn't like Hunter and wasn't sure why. Too macho?

"Trouble? What's so bad about trouble, if it has literary merit?" He guffawed at his own joke.

Rick tossed his butt to the ground. "So, Hunter, how goes the war of words?"

"If those fascists keep on blasting at the Telefonica, we will lose it. The only reason we hang out here and at the Florida is the access to the wires."

"Is the only reason you guys are here is to sell stories? I believe you don't give a damn who wins if you get your name on the magazine covers. You don't even get the story yourself, you sit around drinking and whoring, waiting for your gophers to return with something factual or fictional. If it sounds good, it sells good. You all make me sick!" Rick turned and got into the auto and slammed the door. "Let's get the hell out of here!"

Greta hugged him as they moved through the rubble-strewn streets of Madrid. She watched the children, pale and skinny, playing their new game of searching the rubble for toys, food, and even the bodies of friends. By the time they arrived at The Florida, she was half sick with sadness for the Madrilenos of all ages. She and Rick stumbled into their room and made desperate, passionate love.

CHAPTER TWENTY-FOUR

Dinner With Cuddles

Their intimacies over, they changed for a dinner that Cuddles was preparing for a few friends, old and new. He was proud of his new café that he called "Le Gros Homme." Cuddles' dinner, given the limited larder, it wasn't all that bad. Tinned beef warmed with potatoes and a thick gravy made from potato starch, beef stock, and wine. The red table wine was tannic and furry, but existed in unusual quantities, hoarded for such a celebration. Capa joined them later, bringing a bottle of fiery Spanish brandy liberated from one of the Moors. They sipped the brandy with a watery coffee, the brandy burning new holes in their guts. The tables were mostly empty; the brawling, hungry crowd had long since dispersed. The immense bulk of Mr. Szakall appeared at the table, and Rick offered him a chair.

Rick said, "I want to know about the scene in Barcelona. Have a drink and let's hear about it." Cuddles was much younger looking than Rick had realized, his face unlined despite the white hair. His most aging (and most prominent) feature was the immense bulk of his abdomen, which rose high and proud like the abdomen of a first pregnancy.

"When I arrived in Barcelona, it was a great time to be a Jew, the Catholic Church was in shambles, the fascists had been purged, and the people seemed to be in command. Then it occurred to me that the burning of the churches, the slaughter of priests and nuns was just another kind of pogrom. I, as a Chew, did not have to be afraid, but I found my old fear emerged anyvay. They threw from the churches the caskets of long dead nuns, spreading their bone parts and ashes over the steps of the churches, they dragged the priests, still alive, through the ashes, beating them with clubs and rifle butts as the women cheered. Many of the priests clutched their rosaries and prayed aloud to their saints, some even begged for forgiveness for der jeering torturers. As dey tore the dignity from the priests, dey lost their own, and became inhuman jackals. Dey den entered the churches again and destroyed the marble and wood statues, broke the beautiful glass windows. I see one group drag a statue of Christ on the cross into the square, form a firing squad, and execute. I knew, as a Chew, that the best way to preserve an idea is to attempt to destroy it. I leave for Madrid the next morning. I never go back to dat Barcelona!"

Rick smiled, more in sympathy than in humor, for the fat little man had struck an empathetic chord. To be from someplace where you were something to a place where everyone seems to be crazy had become a recurring theme for him. "What do you think is going on there now?"

Cuddles rolled his eyes upward and said, "Insanity. Every group distrusts every other group. I hear the word "Trotskyite" is being used against intellectuals and idiots, babies and the very old. Mishuguna, all of dem de Reds will get all the groups to fight each other, den dey take control. Dey do it once again over and over!"

Rick accepted Cuddle's scenario without comment, but he believed the Reds intended the same actions over all Spain. What was their ultimate plan? Did they think they could dominate a Spain victorious without including the other factions? Not likely. What the hell did they think they were doing? Scratch a Spaniard and you find an anarchist, scratch him again and guilt ridden Catholic appears, yet both will turn on anyone who might criticize anything Spanish. Sometimes it seems that the Reds want the Fascists to win. Did this have anything to do with what Sr. Navarro had told him? What of the detente to which he alluded the night of his party? Rick hadn't had time to think further about their conversation since that night. He was determined to discuss this in detail with Sr. Navarro at their next meeting.

As the group sipped their watery coffee, a ruckus began at the entrance from the street. Hunter and Matthews were trying to get in, while a small group was attempting to bar their entry.

Cuddles left the table and waddled swiftly to the door. Rick and Capa jumped up and followed him. "What the hell's going on here," Rick yelled. One of the waiters said, "We have orders not to allow Sr. Hunter to enter, orders from the highest authority of the PSUC!" Rick recognized the acronym for the Communist organization, and asked, "Why?"

"Lo siento Senor, no sabe!"

Capa yelled in Spanish, "Let them enter and we will find out the reason!"

The waiters looked at each other, suddenly confused. "I take responsibility!" Cuddles' voice boomed out. The other waiters shrugged and went back to their stations.

"Hunter, I have no doubt you are the instigator here, so shut up while I ask someone else for the details," growled Rick. He turned to Matthews, who nodded at him.

"You're right. Hunter was addressing Sokol, the political officer for the brigades, and asked him how they ever let you get by with that business with him. He got angry and threatened to pull Hunter's press pass and kick him out of the country, so Hunter pulled out his pistol and threatened him. When he came to his senses, he put the gun away and tried to apologize, without success. Sokol told him that all hotels, bars, and cafes would be closed to him until his exit visa was ready. Hunter says let's find Marty. Well, he saw Marty in the lobby and tried to persuade him to talk to Sokol but Marty just stared at him for a minute and then told him he had no room in his life for someone who would cuckold him. He had already received information about Sokol's decree. You know the rest."

"Well, Hunter, it looks like your big mouth have finally done you in. Now we'll have to find some way to take care of you. If I were you, I would not wait for the exit visa, it could be a death warrant." Rick turned to Cuddles and half whispered, "Can you get this man to Barcelona?"

Cuddles wrinkled his brow and looked around hesitantly. He turned back to them and said, "It is done." He disappeared from the dining room, and the small group sat down, Hunter remaining by the door.

The other diners resumed their own conversations. Cuddles soon returned with a bottle and 6 small glasses. He set the bottle in front of Rick, as he did so, he slipped him a note. Rick fumbled in his pocket for a cigarette, then fumbled for a match. He deftly slid the note on top of the pack and glanced at it. It was an address with the name "Nasci" scrawled on it.

Hunter approached the table and took a drink, then another. He caged a cigarette from Rick, and lit it with a tremulous hand. "The man is really frightened," thought Rick. Hunter then went back to his position at the door. "Let's all go to `Chicote's`," said Rick in a loud voice and they left with Hunter in tow. Rick whispered the name and address to Hunter and then urged him to leave quickly.

"To think I produced a film for that bastard," snarled Hunter. "This is one story that will really be told!"

"Just leave town, Hunter," muttered Capa. He laughed, and Hunter laughed, but it was not a laugh of camaraderie. He left them at the next block.

Chicote's was booming, the press and writers corps was in full swing. Matthews pointed towards an empty table. A man in a Boiler suit walked jauntily up to their table and said, "Hello Matthews, where in hell have you been?"

Matthews introduced the man as Sefton Delmer of the London Daily Express. He sat down on the table, inserted a cigarette in his holder, and raised his head loftily. "And Hunter, where in hell is he? He owes me cigarettes, a drink, and an introduction to one of his muscular friends." He coughed. "My God, these cigarettes are dreadful. You Yanks have one thing over the rest of the world, and that's your tobacco, I still get upset over that damnable George the Third and his stupidity. Other than that, civilization has escaped you chaps." He winked at Rick. "You know, Rick, Hunter just thinks the wooorrld of you!" He began to laugh but then the cough took over, shaking his frail frame with great violence. Still gasping and laughing, he repeated Hunter's version of Rick's altercation with Colonel Beck.

Rick said, "Things ain't quite as funny as you would think, Selmer. Your pal Hunter has disappeared after a run-in with Sokol, and I don't think he'll be back to Madrid."

"Disappeared? My God, man, do you know what that means? They've got him, that's what it means. We've got to use influence to save him! Come, let's call Marty and . . . and . . ."

"Relax," Rick replied, "I think he's safe. We think he knows enough people who will help him get out of here." He was reticent to share his involvement in Hunter's escape with this man; there was something sinister in his cackle and faggoty concern for him. Apparently the others felt the same, for no one volunteered any information to him.

Selmer's face sobered, "Orwell's been arrested," he volunteered. "Seems the POUM didn't like him either. His press dispatches were verrry unkind to the Republicans. It's just as well, he is such a bore, he's just like all those other colonials who resent those of us who went to good English schools."

"Wonder what this attack on the writers is all about? mused Capa. "Maybe we photographers are next."

Matthews looked at Rick, "Maybe it's time for all of us to go home. Reporting this war has become impossible because of the retaliation. St. Xupery told me this is a period of summary judgments, and I cannot disagree. The heart of an ideal has become a charade for the power mongers of all stripes. We see the generals and the schemers, the politicians and the commissars, the millionaires, hiding. The ordinary man fights and the psychopaths scheme." He paused and then continued, "I'm a more a pacifist now then when I came here. When friends of mine in the press corps said they were going to Ethiopia, I told them the buzzards would pick out their eyes and livers. For some reason, they didn't believe me. I don't know, but as much as I like Africa, I wanted nothing to do with the Lion of Judah and the Eyeties. A bad lot, both of them. It's a fact that the Italians used gas on the poor buggers." Rick nodded assent.

Matthews said, "I remember one reporter who dashed about in a red motorcycle, "An Indian, as I remember."

"Good bike," said Rick.

"It had a sidecar, which no one ever rode in."

Rick took a big drag and ground the butt out in the ashtray. "A wild place, and no resolution yet. You press people did a real job there, just like the one you're doing here. You got your info from some wog, and you printed it as gospel. One of those wogs must have sold the same information to all of you."

Matthews grinned, "I have nothing to say."

Rick snorted triumphantly. "Mr. Luce, of Time magazine, loved and still loves Mussolini. He was tickled pink when you guys got the shaft from the wogs and couldn't tell a lie from the facts. He loves such things as palaces that flew the Red Cross flag, and the Abyssinian officers using the Red Cross shelter when the Italians bombed Addis. Capa does such a good job with his pictures. I don't know how he gets some of the shots. In Ethiopia most of the photos were faked. The photographers did not want to die when they could mock up comparable action behind the lines. Someone once said that the first casualty in a war is the truth. I think that says it all."

"Let's forget the past for now," said Greta brightly. "I think the whole game of politics has been invented so that you men can find something to fight about."

"That's right, Greta, let's have some fun!" Capa's gaiety seemed forced.

They drank, they sang the few Spanish folk songs they knew, but the conversation gradually came back to Hunter and his movie. Capa said, "The piece was sent all over the western world to persuade governments to intervene on behalf of the Republicans."

Selmer said, "Actually, the movie is second rate, as you might expect. Looks like something an aspiring adolescent would present to his film class. I'm sorry, I don't mean to be unkind but his work is puerile." Selmer hissed out the last sentence.

Greta stood up and leaned over the table, "You have no right to talk that way! What have you done or contributed to this cause? At least Hunter tries to present the real story to the world! You think that, because you are an upper class British snob, that you need only resent yourself to the world and it will sing paeans to your greatness! We all know the reasons why you here, and they aren't altruism! Nice young masculine men without sexual outlets, and Joseph Stalin. Your preferences are obvious, and your politics preceded you! You are a secret agent of the Kremlin and don't think your prissy ways can disguise it!"

Selmer's smiled sweetly, saying, "And what of you and your ex-lover, Capa? From my point of view, your juvenile picture taking is neither art nor journalism. It is, at best, a feeble attempt at both and a monumental waste of effort. And we all know of at least one attempt to create reality through posed action!"

Jutting his head forward, Capa said, "No one can say I have created false images of this war. Everything I've shot is genuine, real to the action we've all seen."

Rick noted that no one had picked up on Greta's revelation about Selmer's ties to the Kremlin. He filed it away, it would be useful, he was sure.

Selmer stood up and left the table.

Greta said, "Now let's do something fun!" She grabbed Rick's ear and pretended to lift him from the table. They all laughed and spontaneously broke into "Banda Rosa" as they swarmed out the door. Rick felt that he had found family for the first time in his life. "On to The Gran Via!"

They laughed and sang through the rubble-strewn Paseo, the broad boulevards pocked with shell holes, the holes filled with water. The singing and the laughter continued. Capa said, "Madrid was once gayer than Paris, let's bring it all back!"

The jovial band arrived at The Grand Via, an old hotel with a basement restaurant favored by some because it was perceived as a bomb shelter.

A large group of foreign journalists were whooping with laughter over some salacious joke, and the narrator was none other than Hunter. They all turned and waved at the newcomers. "Come on over," he roared, "Everyone's here but Shakespeare!" Rick frowned at Hunter, but did not say anything, for his "Belle du jour" was hanging all over him. Instead, Capa approached him, "Hunter, get the hell out of Spain before they live up to their reputations! This is foolish behavior."

"Oh what the hell, they wouldn't take me with all my friends watching!" Hunter was obviously drunk.

"Don't kid yourself, Hunter, you're a marked man!" Rick warned.

"Don't be such a spoil sport, Rick. This war is fun, and the Russkies are great comedians! Whaddysay we play some poker? How bout it, Greta, strip poker maybe, eh?" He smirked with satisfaction over his little joke.

CHAPTER TWENTY-FIVE

Ebro Planning

General Walter called to a surprise meeting at Brigade Headquarters. The sun blistered the sky and the arid plateaus around Madrid. On arrival at the assembly they found the room crowded with sweaty stinking officers from all of the brigades in the 15th Corps. "That's General Rojo up there," Moreman whispered. "He's the head guy of all the forces in our army."

"Interesting last name," muttered Rick. "This looks more like a CP shindig to me." Moreman ignored the jibe and began shaking hands with the other officers. Rick knew many of them by this time but preferred to just listen and watch. Several of the Brits came up and shook his hand. "Great to see you, Blaine," said one. "Nice job you did at Casa de Campo. Did yourself proud." Rick felt heat in his face at the compliment.

"Thanks,' he replied. "You Brits know how to fight and that made it easier."

"Yeah, the bloody Spaniards are so tied up in hating each other that there's little left for the fascists." Three cracks from a gavel brought the hall to silence. General Rojo stood up and began to speak, his voice almost a falsetto. "Wounded in the throat from a duel," offered the British officer.

"Comrades, I am announcing a new campaign that I'm sure will break the back of Franco's drive to the sea, especially to Valencia." He grimly continued after allowing the opening comment to sink in. "The result will be twofold: the first will crack Franco's attempt to take Valencia, the second will be to reunite our forces presently divided by the fascists. We are committing the majority of our forces to take Gandesa and its rail hub, and then in a swift offensive we meet with our comrades to the north.

We will suck the fascist divisions dry and discourage then to the point of retreat and eventual surrender." He stopped and looked around as if to drink in the adulation of the assemblage. The entire group stood and applauded, enthralled by this Spanish Spartan.

"Sounds like the Supreme Soviet to me," he thought. He felt he could no longer trust Moreman who continued to clap his hands and smile his broad smile. "The rumors are true, Bob is one of them." Another friendship corrupted by the party.

Colonel Marty stood up and asked all but the unit commanders to leave the room. Rick patted Moreman on the back and quickly left. He saw Capa snapping pictures as a few random artillery shells fell several hundred yards away. They probably knew of the meeting but their guns didn't have the range to hit the buildings. When he saw Rick he trotted over to him. "What's the news," he yelled.

"News is that we're gong to bust up the Fascists with a one-two punch and the war will be over in three months.'

"New weapon? Between you and me Rick, the plan, whatever it might be, will not work without the milagro, the miracle." Rick nodded mutely, his thoughts affirmed."

"OK then, Chicote's it is, and the devil take what he can." He linked arms with Capa and they headed for the Metro.

The Madrid Metro filled the role that the Paris taxis played in WWI; it took combatants all around the city and in all directions. Safely aboard the underground car the two men relaxed for a moment. "Capa, I wonder what the temperature of the Ebro is this time of year."

"25-28 degrees Centigrade," said Capa. "Why?"

"Just thinking about having to swim in it,"

Rick and Capa walked from the metro station on the Grand Via to Chicote's. Several men in ragged uniforms stood outside, lurching about as they argued in loud, drunken voices. Rick saw a flash, a glint of blade as one man plunged a dagger into the other. The man fell to the sidewalk and the other ran away, lurching and staggering but continuing his rant. By the time the duo got to the scene he had disappeared down a side street. Other of the wounded man's comrades were already helping him to his feet, yelling and laughing as they carted him off.

The bar was jammed with men in uniform, reporters, and whores. Capa pointed to a door at the back of the bar and made a sexual gesture implying that behind the door one could find women and beds. Rick watched a young buck dressed in a tight striped suit sidle up behind two young assault guard officers. He took out a gun from his pocket and aimed it at the back of one of the officer's head and pulled the trigger. The officer flinched and turned towards his assailant, his face dripping with water. The fey civilian laughed raucously and squirted the other officer, who turned quickly, pulled out his pistol and shot the joker in the face. Blood and tissue erupted as he fell to the floor. Men and women were screaming as the two officers picked up the fool and threw him out the door. That was the end of that. The Spanish Nada. The people returned to their previous activities.

CHAPTER TWENTY-SIX

River Of Death

The convoy of decrepit trucks crawled through the darkness and the blinding rain, stopping as one, then another became mired in the greedy muck. Greta, Moreman, Rick, and Capa were in the same transport along with a radioman and three soldiers. They all wearing the traditional French helmets, orders from Moreman, for the Fascists maintained total control of the air. A guttering oil lamp suspended from the roof swayed back and forth, emitting smoke and the stink of partially burned kerosene.

Moreman said, "They're battering our guys with at least 200 batteries of artillery, and the commitment of lots of aircraft. The Italians are mad as hell about their loss at Guadalajara and are really out to hurt us and hard."

"Ah, the Italians fight with more bluster and fewer balls than any in the world," Capa said.

"This is different," countered Moreman. "They've claimed the Sierra de Capalls, and they're the most commanding position along the front. We have tanks there for counterattack, but the mud is burying them, the gunners fire their cannons and machine guns 'til they're empty, then they have to abandon the machine. Soon we'll see those things heading towards us, and we'll have none for retaliation."

"Where are we going to be located?" asked Rick. "Is there anything to occupy on the other side of the river?"

"Oh yes, we'll help defend Mount Picosa. Copic told me it's invulnerable to enemy attack, but you know Copic. He might better make it into a folk opera, with our tenors and basses trying to drown out theirs. I have no confidence in any conclusion he might reach. However, the positions are well constructed and supplied, according to Marty. The Command is relying on this position to bolster the others and hold the line, we certainly don't want to swim the Ebro."

Rick took a contemplative drag on his cigarette and said, "Sounds to me like the whole jig is up. If they need our 400 to seal this hole, we'll be washed away like the rest of the top soil." He looked at Moreman, but no response.

"At least we'll have a good view for our photo sessions," said Greta, a little too cheerfully. She then snuggled against Rick and he smiled.

The convoy jerked to a halt. Moreman and Rick jumped from the truck and peered into the rainy darkness. They were at the Ebro Bridge, and the demolition people were inspecting it for booby traps. The old iron structure did not appear to be a sturdy edifice, its spidery spans too delicate for mechanized units. "We'll move across in groups of three," he shouted to the drivers. "This thing is not long for this world, but it's all we've got."

The driver of their truck pulled out and waited until the last trucks had crossed, then they proceeded to cross alone. They drove without incident to the foothills of Mount Picosa where they were met by a small cluster of Military Police. One man said, "You can't drive any further, the mud is too deep. You gotta walk." Everyone involved in the discussion was wet and shivering, the rain had changed to sleet and snow.

They moved by foot to their positions on Picosa. The landscape was a scene from Dante or Goya: fires, shell holes, smashed and smoldering ordinance, and small hospital tents with gaping holes. Men wandered about with bandages on their heads, arms, and chests, and thousand yard stares in their eyes. Rick saw that this would be an untenable position when the rain stopped, too small not to be a wasteland after the gunners zeroed them in, say nothing of the Condor Legion's Stukas. He envisioned a nice warm swim in the Ebro.

Greta was waiting. Her face was pale and dirty, her usually jaunty beret dangled loosely from the side of her head, secured only by a large hairpin. "I'm so frightened, Rick, I can't understand why we had to come to this place. We're sitting ducks for those Italian guns. Why?"

Rick hugged her. "Because they said we must. This war is about over for the Republicans. They surrendered to the Comintern Reds, now they gotta surrender to the fascists; all we can do is hope we get to better ground before the rain stops. If we can charge down the slopes before the big guns open up, we may be able to secure a bigger perimeter. Stick by me and get your best shots of the war. I think it's best we go to our tent and get some sleep, morning will come soon enough."

Rick slept fitfully, but he was careful not to awake Greta until both were suddenly awake, thrown into the air by an awesome blast, then falling like large dolls into the soft, deep mud. Rick got up on his knees and called for Greta, his ears were clamoring bells, his vision blurred by the mud in his eyes. He spied her crawling towards him, her body misshapen by the clinging mud. He crawled to her and rolled with her in his arms into a trench. Another explosion filled the trench with bushels of mud. He was aware of two things, the rain had stopped and the sky reddening with the rising of the sun. "Oh God, this is it!" he thought.

The silence as devastating as the noise preceding it and Rick was aware that the shelling had stopped. He peered over the top of his muddy ditch and looked down the hill. Giant lizards? Then clanking of tank treads told him of the armored advance.

"There must be 75 coming at us," he yelled to Greta telling her to stay put as he scrambled and zigzagged towards the command tent that, miraculously, still stood. Moreman crouched in the entrance, shouting, "Gunners, fire at will! I want any volunteers to slide down that hill and throw grenades at the attackers. If you have gas bombs, throw 'em!"

Many of the tanks were hopelessly mired in the mud making them sitting ducks for the experienced gunners while the volunteers were able to damage enough of them to break the assault.

Rick kneeled behind a stone fence. He felt elation mixed with puzzlement. "Where were the Stukas?" His question was quickly answered as the screeching whine of dive-bombers added to the cacophony on the ground. The bombers using their sirens made three passes, each brief but terrifying in sound and destruction. Lurching up from his muddy universe, Rick saw a number of tanks burning and smoking, looking like nothing but blackened scrap metal. Again, silence followed by the crying, moaning yelling, cursing of the wounded.

Greta rose up from a shell hole, totally covered with muck, but unhurt, wiping off her camera with an unexpectedly white cloth. She moved about, snapping pictures, sobbing all the while. Rick urged his men into another assault group when Moreman appeared, shaken but not wounded, and ready to take command.

Rick described his plan to expand the perimeter as quickly as possible, and Moreman agreed. Once formulated, the Lincolns moved quickly down the hill. A radioman made contact with Copic and Moreman described their plan. Copic, hesitant, agreed and advised him that air support was on the way. Moreman raised his eyes to heaven and rang off. Rick was furious. "Lies, deceit, bullshit. We have no air cover. Let's get on with this before theirs come back and finish the job."

Fifteen Loyalist tanks supported the battalion as the men scampered behind the clanking, roaring machines while heavy machine guns opened. They had reached the enemy's perimeter. The fascists, however, were obviously prepared for this gambit. A tank wiped out a Rebel machine gun, and the fire ceased, they could see the Moors retreating rapidly to their fixed positions. The Loyalist tanks began to fire, almost in unison, and several large explosions in the enemy areas indicated telling hits. The tanks assumed positions that provided some cover for their profiles, stopped, and continued to blast away. Rick heard the whoosh of mortar rounds and buried himself in the muck. The first barrage was an insignificant one, the shells landing harmlessly well behind the new lines. He peered through the mist with his binoculars at the enemy's location, but could see no evidence of counterattack.

A new and more intense enemy mortar barrage began, with the explosions coming closer and closer to the Lincoln lines. A crippled tank blazed and hissed in the rain, followed by a giant explosion when the petrol ignited. Moreman zigzagged up to Rick and yelled, "Time to move forward, tell your group to be ready in exactly five minutes." The two men checked their watches. Moreman had a bloody bandage on his neck but did not appear weakened by his wound. His round Trotsky glasses were cracked and mud specked. "Copic has assured me that the air cover is coming, and should be here in about two more minutes. They'll bomb and strafe the lines for three minutes, then stop. That's when we go." He looked at Rick, slapped him on the helmet, and duck walked away. Rick looked after him and then turned to brief his unit on the new plan.

Two minutes later, three Chatas appeared, coming in low over Mt. Picosa. Rick watched as the Chatas released their wing bombs over the enemy lines, then turned away in steep climbs, rolling over Picosa and then roaring back, although only a few of the explosives appeared to hit anything material. The Chatas then strafed the lines; one was hit and dropped in a thunder ball of flame, crashing out of sight of the Lincolns.

Rick checked his watch, then blew his whistle. "This is air cover?" he thought. "My God, this is leading lambs to slaughter!" He raised his arm and stepped forward to lead the assault. The tanks lurched forward, the men yelled and whooped as they slogged through the barren mudscape. The counter-fire was blistering, heavy machine guns, mortars, and tank fire. Rick fell forward as a mortar round blew in front of him. When the hail of mud cleared, he saw none of the tanks moving forward, they were mired in the mud and in a split second all were smoking and burning. The attack had failed as if it had been planned to fail, the air assault had been worthless, and the succeeding attack suicide.

Whistles blew, and Moreman ordered all units to pull back 100 meters. All firing had ceased, silence prevailed. A temporary command post was set up, and the radio was cranked up to call General Copic. The squad leaders gave a casualty report that was grim; Of the 400 men who had been trucked across the Ebro bridge, 147 were killed, 74 seriously wounded seriously, the remainder had some kind of minor wound, psychologically, all were devastated. Their poor training, poor equipment, and poor high command had destroyed their morale. One final statistic, missing in action, 33. Had any or all of them deserted?

Copic's voice crackled from the set, "We have achieved our goal, we have put the enemy on notice that we will not be moved! Remember, comrades, no pasaran! Other units from the militia and the XlI and XlV International Brigades are moving in around you. When they are in place, we will attack again. A runner will bring the battle plan to each battalion. Our cause cannot fail. We have the means, the men, and we have the right!"

"Attack again? Moreman's voice was incredulous. "We haven't enough men to negotiate a retreat!" He turned to Rick for his reaction, but Rick's face was stolid. He knew that the order would not be rescinded, the Lincoln Battalion had just received a death sentence, and all contrarian opinions could not commute it. He lit a cigarette and stared his first thousand yarder as he awaited the inevitable.

Greta, where was Greta? He saw chaos everywhere; bodies lay in heaps, lumps of dirty cloth, ripped and distorted, looking like the discarded puppets of a mad puppeteer. Faces looking blankly at the sky, gray with death in an earth toned world. The Lincolns had been decimated by the ferocity of the battle.

Stunned wounded men reeled from dead man to dead man, peering in their faces for identification, then sitting down next to them and covering their own faces with their hands. Men were sprawled over the turrets of their tanks, some with body parts missing.

Rick began to run, sprinting this way and that, ignoring the cries of the wounded, looking only for Greta. He ran further forward, looking in all directions, afraid of what he might see. "The Fascists have withdrawn," he thought, "And she's chasing them, catching everything in her camera." It s occurred to him that the enemy would be back to anytime now to capitalize on the destruction wrought by their superior ordinance. Then he heard the roar of an auto engine and saw the big Hispano Suiza careening through the muddy ruts. There was Greta standing on the running board, holding her camera to her eye with one hand while she clung on the doorpost with the other. A Loyalist tank suddenly lurched into movement, and a guttural scream came from the primal depths of his soul. "Grrreeetttaaa!" He watched, as the big car swerved in front of the tank, and bowed his head as the tank struck the side of the car. Greta's body disappeared into the crunching metal.

He raced towards the horror, flying over the mud and debris of battle. The tank crew was already checking her body when he slid onto the earth next to her. Her face was somehow elongated and he saw her eye hanging from a stalk of tissue staring blindly at the ground. Her mandible angled abruptly to the right, rendering her chinless. Three great bubbling coughs came from her mangled mouth; she looked up at him without recognition. Her head slumped to the right and it was over. Bob Moreman came panting up, looked with horror at Greta, then put his arms around Rick and drew him away. "You can't do anything now, Rick. I'll see to it that she is taken to the rear, and we'll give her a fitting burial when all this settles."

"Settles? Settles? Bob, how can you say 'settles'?" Rick groaned. "There's nothing left, Bob. The Fascists own this war." He stopped, an immense feeling of anguish overwhelmed him, he fell to the ground and buried his face in his hands. No sobs, no shaking of the shoulders, just a vacuum of emptiness and loss. He saw her as he had seen her the first time, the jaunty beret, the tumbling hair, the fresh cheery face, the slight little body, girdled by the belt that held her tiny revolver. Greta. Greta the beautiful waif with the reddish blonde hair, Greta his wanton lover. An abject Rick wiped his dirty face down her arm, wept and looked soundlessly at the sky. Moreman, slipped away from his grieving comrade. He and two other comrades loaded the blanket wrapped body into a truck, never to be seen again.

The fascist counter attack began a few minutes later, and the Lincolns, along with the Xll and the XlVth battalions, fled the line. Rick and Moreman, along with Dr. Warwick, slipped and slid down and around the hills behind Mt. Picosa, their position no longer defendable. The doctor fell heavily onto a rock outcropping, striking his head and shoulder. He fell with a moan. Rick turned back to help him, Moreman continued on, disappearing into the rocky trail. As he attended to Warwick, Rick heard hostile voices calling out, "Alto! Alto!" Dr. Warwick said that he wasn't hurt badly, so Rick ran down the trail, his pistol at the ready. He saw nothing, neither Moreman nor anyone else.

It was as if Bob had never existed. Rick returned to the doctor, and told him what had happened.

Warwick **was very disturbed, "We'll have to swim** or we'll die like the rest." They reached the cold, muddy Ebro, kicked off their shoes, and discarded their blanket rolls. Both swam the river to safety, the water already spattering with rifle fire from the enemy. Both men were strong swimmers and readily managed the distance. Once ashore, they were helped to the lorries that waited in an area of defilade. The convoy slunk back to the staging area in Abril. The cost? Beyond any redemption, beyond any treasure.

Arrival in Abril brought them the news that the Catalonian front had collapsed which would further hasten the doom of the Loyalist forces. La Causa was dead. He felt his own loss far more keenly than the national disaster. Greta, Bob, lover and friend, comrades in arms, they were the war.

He recalled the posters, the brave and aggressive battle songs, 'Bandera Rosa' and others, the proud faces of boys and men marching to the cheers of the flag waving crowds For Rick the war was over. He would return to Madrid and leave the ancient Spanish dust.

CHAPTER TWENTY-SEVEN

Navarros

Rick's return to Madrid was less than a homecoming. Capa shared his gloom at the loss of Greta, the loss of the battle of the Ebro and the waning anticipation of a Republican victory. Madrid was still pulsating with the pride of survival but the fascists controlled the surrounding countryside and it seemed to Rick a mere matter of time before they would be marching into the city.

He sought out the Navarros but when he went to the house it was guarded by uniformed soldiers who denied him entry. They told him that the Navarros no longer lived there and that the home was now government property. "We don't know where the people are, Capitan, we know only that they are not here." Rick was desolate as he returned to The Florida to seek information about their fate. The first person he saw was Herbert Matthews. "Blaine! So good to see you alive and well. How did you survive the Ebro?" Rick told him of the battle, the death of Greta and the disappearance of Moreman. After telling him about the watery escape he asked Matthews about Sr. Navarro, Matthews' face tightened as he began to speak. "Navarro is under house arrest, no visitors allowed, and the rumors run wild. The most recent one alleges that he is a member of the Fifth Column, one of General Mola's saboteurs. The government suspects that this particular cell was trying to recruit Madrilenos to join in a peace accord with Franco. It seems that the rich guys here are afraid that if the war continues, their fortunes and properties will be lost forever."

"But Navarro is a key guy in the Loyalist government," protested Rick. His heart felt ever heavier, adding Navarro to his list of the lost. Once the accusation was made, no one escaped the ruthlessness of the GPU.

Matthews affirmed Rick's thoughts. "Once the finger is pointed, the assassination follows."

"Do you know who was responsible for turning him in?" Rick asked.

"Yes, that person is known."

"Chrissakes man, who did it? Smells like Marty."

"Rick, it was no GPU thug, no political zealot. It was his daughter, Imelda."

Rick was incredulous. "Imelda? You're nuts! She worships that man, she adores him! How do you explain that?"

"Simple. She loves the movement more. She sees her father as a person lost at sea, unable to find the favorable wind that takes him to the proper shore. She is totally dedicated to the concept that re-education will bring back his reason, even if that process means his death. That's it, Rick and it's a tangled one, one so byzantine that you might not believe it if this weren't Spain. It seems that Sr. Navarro was involved with a group of crypto-fascists that were trying to make a deal with Franco in order to save the economy of the country. Most are from very rich old families. They're predominately Catholic and Monarchists, purportedly an international Cabal of wealthy, conservative power brokers, a sort of super-government and don't care about anything except the preservation of their wealth and power."

"But Navarro is Jewish!" Rick countered. "What do these people want with a Jew?"

"Rick, think about it! What more convenient scapegoat than a Jew? They included Navarro so when and if the Loyalists found out about their plot, blame the Jew! It fits in perfectly with what Stalin has already started in Russia. Get rid of the undesirables as well as the opposition through arrest and spectacular public show trials. Maximize public paranoia and sweep your enemies out simultaneously while reminding the faithful that the Jew is ultimately not to be trusted.

Rick shook his head slowly. "Do you know where he's being kept?" Yet, he needed to see Navarro, to assure him of his loyalty, concern, and support. He began to have wild thoughts of rescue, knowing full well that they were impossible if only because he could not do it alone, and would not ask anyone to help him.

"No one knows, and if I were you I wouldn't try to find him. Your unpopularity with the General Staff could be fatal to you if they thought you had anything to do with this plot. The military set-backs are making them testier than ever, so whomever they suspect they eliminate, suspicion being confirmation of guilt."

Rick thought about Imelda. Why would she do this to her father? Was she really that fanatical? He doubted that, although her relationship with General Walter made him wonder. Then he realized what could have happened. Imelda was protecting something or someone more important than her own father. But whom? He would make it his business to find out. Then Matthews spoke in a whisper, "Rick, get out of Madrid. Now! Out of Madrid and out of Spain before they get you." Rick saw that Matthews was two men, one the nonpartisan dispassionate observer, the other a cynical but committed warrior, the first writing dispatches, the second seeing the war from a very emotion-laden participation. He thanked Matthews for his candor and left the bar, walked to the Florida and got slowly and quietly drunk.

Next morning Rick made a quick trip to the Brigades' headquarters asked the whereabouts of Isaiah Navarro. The sergeant-at-arms looked at Rick with suspicion as he traced his finger down the list of the jailed. "This man's an officer?"

"No, a civilian."

The sergeant looked at him with increasing distrust. "Civilian prisoners aren't listed here. You'll have to go to Party Headquarters for that information." He looked around carefully, then murmured to Rick, "Do you really want to know about this man? You must know that you'll come under suspicion when you inquire about any prisoner?"

Rick left the building and walked briskly towards the Hotel Victoria. Most of the Russian advisors and journalists lived there, and he knew a couple of people that might feel they owed him something. He showed his papers to the guard at the main entrance and was waved on. Rick noted that the guard was not Spanish but a large Asian-appearing man. Rick sensed that their obsession for secrecy knew no bounds, and the idea of anyone outside the GPU or NKVD had to be considered an enemy bent on the destruction of the Soviet system.

The lobby was surprisingly empty. A few ill-dressed men sat about looking bored, pretending not to notice Rick. For all he knew, they were photographing him. He walked into the bar, an imposing room with dark woods and leather chairs, low lighting, and tables located for privacy and discrete liaisons. The slur of Russian language conversations rose up from all sides, Vodka bottles decorated the tables, and a few "ladies" were plying their trade at the bar. The bartender was a thick-jowled Slav with a black bow tie slightly tilted. He looked at Rick with curiosity. Rick moved to the bar and ordered a scotch and soda.

"Vodka."

"No, scotch and soda."

"Vodka. No tenemos scotch and soda. Vodka."

"Fine, quero vodka con hielo."

"Lo siento, solo vodka."

Rick laughed, lit a cigarette and shrugged. "Vodka." The man nodded and brought him a bottle and a glass, even smiling a little at their word play. "Englese?"

"No, American."

"Americano? Why do you come to the Victoria? All of you go to the Florida. You not like Florida, you in trouble, or you work for GPU. Yes?"

"No. I'm looking for Comrade Kozlof. Do you know him?"

The bartender looked at Rick through slitted eyes. "He compadre of you?"

"I want to ask Comrade Kozlof a question about a comrade of mine who is missing. I need to know so I can tell his men the latest information."

"Name?"

Rick snuffed out his cigarette. "Have you seen Comrade Kozlof?"

He pointed to a table at the periphery of the gloom. "Ayi." Rick headed for Kozlof's table. His hopes were buoyed when Kozlof, alone, spotted him and waved him over. The two shook hands. "What brings you to the Comintern west?" He chortled at his little joke "I don't recall seeing you here before, Blaine. Is this your version of surrender or has the Florida run out of caviar?" Both men roared at this.

"I need some information about a friend of mine, Isaiah Navarro. Do you know of him?"

Kozlof looked at him impassively. "Yes, I know of him. Who doesn't? He's about to become the biggest story of the war if he will make a full confession. Are you aware of the charges?"

"Why don't you tell me?"

"Well, before I start, I need to know what he is to you, that is, what ties have you with him?"

"He was my sponsor when I first came to Madrid, and he opened his home to me."

"Good. I am glad there is nothing more. Or is there?"

"Are all of you guys GPU?"

"Your need to ask the question makes you appear naive, Rick. You are not naive, so I must assume you know the answer. But, let's go on. Navarro is simply a traitor. While he masqueraded as a loyal supporter of the Popular Front he was making deals with the fascists to sabotage the defense of Madrid. He is the chieftain of General Mola's famous 'fifth column.' Like all Jews, he just couldn't part with his treasure."

Rick could not help but be surprised at the naked anti-Semitism he heard in Kozlof's voice. Half the Lincolns were Jewish, and many of the other foreigners were anti-fascist Jews, including many of the Russians.

"Do you know where he is being held?" Rick's voice was cold.

"He is in the Carmelite Kremlin," Kozlof sneered. "Surely you won't try to see him! I'm told that he will not see visitors until after his trial."

"Take my advice, forget him. He is beyond redemption, and anyone seen as his friend is a marked man. Are you still sweet on his Imelda?"

Rick wanted to strike the man, but thought better of it. "I would like to know if she's under suspicion."

"Well, she was the informant, but even that is a suspect action. We in the press believe she is shielding someone, and if we believe it, the GPU has probably confirmed it. Imelda's feelings about her father are well known, but her action is such a paradox that she will not be detained until further complicity is determined. Have I answered your question?"

Rick asked, "How safe would it be for me to talk to her?"

"Blaine, your aggressive acts are such that nothing you might do would surprise anyone, especially the GPU. No, I don't think your talking to her would turn any heads, just confirm what has gone before."

Rick shook hands with Kozlof and left the hotel. He strolled aimlessly for a quarter of an hour, mourning for his friend, for Imelda, but most of all, for Greta. Love lost, love now wearing a blanket of the Spanish earth. Did his father win after all? He had lost Greta, and Imelda was never his. He shook off his reverie as he became aware of a man he presumed was shadowing him. He thought of his vow not to stick out his neck for anyone, yet, he had to know about Navarro, and why Imelda had destroyed him. Ignoring the shadow, he headed back to his room at the Florida. He was about to pick up the phone to call Imelda but realized the foolishness of calling. "They" would be listening. No such thing as an open phone at the Florida.

He left his room, heading for a quiet place where he might make a call, then realized they would be listening at Imelda's as well. He hailed a passing cab and gave the Navarro address. The cabbie grunted then Rick was aware of the driver's eyes on him in the rear-view mirror. "Oh fine," he thought. "I didn't even tumble to it! I'm losing my touch; this guy is GPU or nothing. I'll just have to see what happens, but one thing's for sure, I gotta call Capa and get out of Madrid. In fact, if Navarro is really in solitary, I'm already rung up. General Walter won't forget my private conversation with Isaiah; in fact, he's got a couple things up on me. Imelda, and my shaky standing with the Commissars." He pretended unawareness while he planned his escape from Madrid.

The old cab wheezed up to the gates of Navarro's estate, the driver opened the door, announcing, in heavily accented Spanish, the fare. This confirmed Rick's suspicions, and sealed his decision. He paid the driver and walked to the gates. He didn't recognize these two militiamen. "State your business Capitan."

"I have business with the Senorita Navarro."

"Senorita is not available and shall have business with no-one."

"I am under orders from General Walter to see Senorita Navarro, now let me pass!"

At the name of General Walter, the men looked at each other. The older of the two shrugged his shoulders, opening the gate, mumbling, "Pasaran." He walked briskly up the drive to the house, aware of their eyes watching him. He rang the bell and Navarro's old butler beckoned him enter. "Is Senorita Imelda home?"

"Si, Capitan Blaine, I will tell her you are here." He peered at Rick through his little round glasses, fear filled his rheumy eyes.

He returned in a few moments and said, "Senorita Imelda says she cannot and will not talk to you." He turned his palms up helplessly.

"Tell her what I have to say will be brief, and that I have only concern for her and her father."

The old servant looked at Rick, nodding his head in mute approval, and left the room. Ten minutes passed, then an almost unrecognizable Imelda walked into the room. Her black hair was tousled and matted, her face swollen from crying, her mouth a slitted scar. She stopped and hung her head, tears flowing down her hollow cheeks. Rick walked to her and took her hands. "Imelda, I am so sorry. I am so sorry. It must be tough, kid, I came as soon as I could find out anything. How is he?"

Imelda plunged into his arms. "Oh, Rick, I did it, I did it! I gave my own father to the death squad! Oh God, I want to die, I want to confess equal guilt, I want to lie, I want to save him! Why did I let him do this to us?"

Rick held her closely, stroked her hair, "Now kid, just tell me the story, get it out of your system. I can bet you one thing, you're not to be blamed in this affair."

She looked up at him, her terror still in command. "Do you mean it? Do you know?"

"I don't know, but I know him and I know you, and that's all I need."

"He thinks so highly of you Rick, I don't know anyone he trusts more. He came to me several days ago, very upset, I have never seen him so. `I must tell you something now, and you must hear me out before you say a word. They know about the Franco accord, they know only this fact; they do not know any names, at least not yet. We must provide time for the others and their families to escape the terror we know is to follow. Here is what we must do. ` He then told me what little I didn't already know about his group. Finally he asked me if I loved him."

She began to sob and the desperation on her face brought tears to his eyes. "I told him I loved him, then he asked if I would die for him. I said I would if I could save him. He shook his head and said, `you would die for me, then you would die for what I believe in.` I don't know why I said yes, but he then raced on, saying that I must turn him in to the GPU at once, and by the time they got what they wanted from him, the others would have escaped, men, women and children. We are only two, Imelda, and they are scores. They will find me out anyway, and then we all die. You will be able to submerge for awhile, then resurface and carry on our work.' I wept, pleaded, but he would have it no other way.

He then told me the real motive for his surrender. He knew that if the Franco scheme succeeded, the war would be shortened; the Nazis attention would no longer be directed to Spain. Then they would be free to pursue their European war. We Jews are well aware of terrible deeds perpetrated by the Nazis towards all Jews in Germany, and this, combined with Hitler's known determination for war was enough to convince me of the wisdom of his decision.

I rang up the GPU, they were here in five minutes and I haven't heard from him since. I have ruined my life and his, and I'm not sure why. I slept with that pervert Walter for `our work`, I have played the lesbian, I have played the tart, and now the only person who has loved me without qualification will die at my hands. Rick, tell me to wake up from this most horrible of dreams."

His mind sweeping through any and all alternatives without success. "It will do us little good to find him. They will be torturing him and won't allow us to see the results of their workmanship. We must make our escape plans, and soon. It's a matter of time before they take you in, and you will tell them how close they are to eliminating the resistance."

I must stay in Spain for the honor of my father, our family, and my country. I am a citizen conscript, a Spaniard; I have to show friends and enemies alike that the Navarro family were patriots to the end. Better I should share my father's fate than to creep away to survive." She looked up at Rick, put both hands on his face and caressed him, then kissed him. "Ah, Senor Blaine, my hands went cold and blood hot when I first saw you. Another time, another place?" She took her hands away and walked rapidly away.

The old butler came into the library and said, "Our driver will take you back to your hotel." The old man turned to leave, then turned again to look at Rick. "Thank you for your consideration, Capitan. You did more than most would do these days. I will watch over the little one . . ."

CHAPTER TWENTY-EIGHT

The Prisoner

Rick was fast asleep in his room at the Florida when he was awakened by the jarring sound of his door bursting open, blurred figures storming his bed. Someone jumped atop him, grappling for his hands and wresting away the pistol he kept beneath his pillow. He gasped with pain as his hands were bent back onto his forearms, then he felt a sudden burst of pain, then darkness.

An olfactory melange assaulted him; dampness, the stench of human waste, icy air filled his nostrils. He opened his eyes, darkness at first, then and a patch of pale light. Then pain, pain in his head and under his right eye, a searing pain in his chest wall. Attempting to stand, his right knee buckled, and he fell onto the damp stone wall. He cursed and sat up. The top of his head was sticky, he felt for, then found the laceration. "Musta beat the hell out of me," he thought. "But why the middle of the night? Bet they tailed me for at least two days."

His clothes felt damp, he had soiled himself; he smiled grimly. He patted his shirt pocket, found a mangled cigarette and a lucifer. He lit the thing and puffed greedily, then shivered in the cold. Was he alone? He crawled about the cell gingerly, found a bench and a small table, no chair, so he crawled onto the bench. He hugged himself and shivered against the frigid dampness, smoking his bedraggled cigarette down to a butt.

"What now, Blaine? I feel like I've been tortured already, and don't remember a thing about it." He wondered if he had put up a fight, then gave himself over to the pain.

He must have dozed off, for he was startled by the clanging of cell doors and loud shouting. "Arriba you red pigs! Time for your baths!" His cell door rattled open and someone threw a bucket of water into the cell. The door jangled shut as Rick turned his back on the icy waves. Then he sat up on his bench and rubbed his knee, already swollen to twice normal size. He began to limp about his cell, now dimly lit by the ceiling vent. At first he thought it looked like a cell in a dungeon, then he made out a symbol on the wall. A crucifix! Could this be an old monastery?

He continued his tour of his dungeon when he heard the rattle of iron gates, the sound of keys in locks. A voice rang out, "Breakfast, comrades, get out your hammers and sickles!" Laughter in the corridor. Rick's door jangled open, and two uniformed Falangists leered at him, standing behind a large steaming tub of what appeared to be coffee. Another tub was filled with small loaves of bread. "Your cup, Rojo?"

Rick replied, "I have no cup, no hammer, no sickle, no plate. I'm new here."

"Well comrade, here's your coffee." The man threw a ladleful of coffee onto the cell floor, the other tossed a loaf atop it, then a third, unseen man slammed his cell door shut, the keys clamoring on the iron door. Rick picked up the bread and ripped off a chunk, it was stale and half-done, but it felt good on his tongue, even better in his gut. He sat again, chewing and listening to the chatter in the hall. More light from the ceiling outlined his cell; Water on the floor, a bit of straw, one corner littered with small bones, none human. A large rat appeared a few feet away, eying him warily; the smell of the bread had invited his visitor. Ordinarily, he hated and feared rats, but this one seemed more like a companion, so he threw him a chunk of his loaf. Sniffing carefully, the rat located the morsel and crept toward it. He picked it up in his paws and nibbled daintily, never taking his eyes from Rick. Rick munched his loaf, then tossed another piece toward the rat. His guest squealed again, dropped his food, and raced toward his escape hole.

Rick laughed and pondered their parallel fates; the rat could hide, apparently had access to the building, yet he too, was a prisoner of sorts, relying on the prisoners for his daily bread. Smaller fleas have smaller fleas, thought Rick. Still, here he was, as much a trapped rat as his guest, relying upon the kindness of strangers for sustenance.

Noise in the hall, then a key in his lock. "Come with us, Rojo!" His two waiters from breakfast stood in the corridor, smiling with brown teeth. "The Capitan wants to see you. Hurry up now, Rojo, he is in a foul mood today."

Rick limped out into the corridor, stopping to look around. Grim cell doors with small barred windows stared back at him.

One of the men kicked him in the rump and pushed him forward, pain slashed through his injured knee, almost causing him to fall. "Watch out you jack-ass!" The two men took him by the arms and dragged him down the hallway and out into a courtyard. Despite the grayness of the day, his good eye slammed shut against the brightness. The courtyard was like a parade ground, with many soldiers leaning on their rifles, looking bored. Several looked up as he was dragged by, but no interest showed in their faces.

They stopped before a wooden door, which one of the men opened with a large ancient key, then they dragged him into a small office. Two wooden desks, two chairs, and two wooden benches. A young officer sat behind one of the desks, a large photo of Franco on the wall behind him. The guards shoved him up to the desk, then stood at attention still supporting their sagging prisoner.

The young officer smiled icily at Rick and offered him a cigarette. Rick took it and put it in his mouth. The officer lit his, then handed Rick the still flaming match. Rick lit up and inhaled deeply. The guards let go of his arms and retreated from the office. "Blaine? Is that English? But you are an American, no?" Rick nodded. "What do you think of Spain, Sr. Blaine? Is this your first visit? Have you enjoyed what you've seen? To be polite let me introduce myself. I am Capitan Diaz Ball."

Rick said nothing, sizing up the man. Young, slim, clean-shaven, short cropped blonde hair, clean uniform, he looked like a West Pointer. "Would you like to see yourself, Sr. Blaine?" He shoved a hand mirror into Rick's hands, and Rick assessed himself. His left eye was swollen shut, he tried to open it without success, his cheekbone was sunken, and his nose deviated in a C-shaped concavity. Stubble, dirt, and blood covered the rest of his face. "You are not pretty Blaine, and you smell like a goat. Sit down for a moment and listen to me. I will see that your wounds are cared for, I will obtain a clean cell for you, give you a bath, food, and cigarettes, and, I shall guarantee that you will be allowed to escape to France." The man paused, carefully observing his prisoner's response.

Rick felt his confidence returning. "Sounds like you want me to make a deal with you, but you haven't told me what that deal is."

The officer growled, "Think not to make any deals, Rojo gringo! Remember, you are the prisoner, your life is in the balance, and you have no power here. Don't forget that, even for a minute."

The man turned on his heel, his shoulders twitching. Minutes passed, silence filled the room. Rick's knee ached, and he longed to sit down. The Spaniard pivoted around and glared at him. "Sit, gringo." Rick sat down, feeling a great sense of relief and gratitude. "Now, gringo, here it is, we know that you are an amigo of a prisoner here, a Sr. Navarro. We want to know everything that you know about him. You know, of course, that there are other methods of obtaining this information from you, so why don't you just begin to tell us. It will make for less work for both of us."

Rick replied, "I have been a guest in his home. I know he is a patriot in the Spanish battle for liberation, I know little more than this. We are men from different worlds, different cultures, and we have a language barrier." The young officer wrote rapidly as Rick spoke, without a visible change in affect.

"Go on, Capitan Blaine. Just continue to lie, just let me get this all down, so that when we break you, you can wipe up your own slop with this paper!" The officer strode to the door, called the two guards into the room and ordered them to take Rick away. The two guards dragged him from the room and down the hall. He looked up at his escorts who looked like twins. Short-cropped hair, powerful lower jaws, with brownish equine teeth protruding from their lips. He wondered if everyone who looked like this was born to be a sadist.

One looked at him and sneered, "Rojo, we have a surprise for you. Your favorite traitor has requested an audience with you!" With this, they opened a cell door marked with two signs, one merely "Ojo, the other, "Incommunicado." They half-threw him into the cell, he slipped on the damp floor, sliding on his chest and face.

The stench was overwhelming and he retched uncontrollably. He sat up, rubbing his throbbing knee, and wiped his mouth with his hand. Looking around the cell he made out a cot in the corner, and what looked like a pile of blankets, then realized it was a human figure. Navarro sat up slowly, his face battered almost beyond recognition. He softly said, "Welcome stranger, and make yourself at home." The welcome was rich with irony, and then came recognition. "Rick! My God, can it be you?" Rick limped over to the man, sat on the cot next to him and embraced him stiffly. The older man winced, then groaned. "I'm sorry, Rick, but they have not treated me warmly."

"What have they done, how long has it been going on?"

"I have been here a week and it has been nonstop. They want more information than I actually possess, but I'm trying not to tell them anything because, if I do, I will open up and tell all." His voice cracked slightly, and the brutalized body flinched.

"Isaiah, you can't do this, they'll kill you if you let them continue."

"They will kill me regardless of what I do. I know you know that, do not pretend it could be otherwise. Other than Imelda, I have nothing further to live for except my honor, and they cannot take that from me, I will not allow it." His voice became full and resonant as he finished his sentence, his head jerked up, his face gaunt but defiant.

A key clanged in the lock, the door opened, two men with an oil lamp came into the cell. Two others stood outside in the hall, submachine guns at the ready. "Senor Blaine, you have seen what you wanted to see. Now come with us." They seized his arms and dragged him from the cell.

"Goodbye Senor Blaine, despite your words, you cannot make me tell what I will not tell, try your traitorous tactics in another cell!" Rick knew that Navarro was attempting to protect him by denying Rick's friendship and loyalty toward him.

Rick said to himself, (I will not see such a man again in my lifetime."

Walking down the long corridor, he could see eyes peering out from the door grates, voices muttering, "Keep your spirits, don't give the pigs anything," plus other garbled phrases he didn't understand.

Loud popping sounds, like Chinese firecrackers, came from down the hall. "Firing squads," he thought.

His life's statement seemed insignificant now. He had always assumed that he would die when he was ready, when the work was done. The idea of a death by firing squad, away from the eyes of his friends, seemed so ignominious. Strange that this American was about to die in the assembly grounds of an unnamed monastery.

"Rojo, you don't know how lucky you are," said one of the guards. "We have bullets today! When we run low, we lay all of you down and run trucks over your bodies." Both men laughed raucously.

More popping sounds, followed by a creaking, groaning sound of metal on stone, then the bray of a donkey. The door to the parade grounds opened, and the small entourage walked out into the blazing

Spanish sunlight. Uniformed men were picking up corpses and throwing them into a wagon. The jackass looked around at Rick, as if to say, "Don't worry, pal, I'll wait around for you." Rick grinned at the mangy creature, who then extended his head and brayed again, sticking out his tongue through his yellowed piano keys.

His guards took him to the wall, still running with blood from the last volley, tied his hands behind his back, blindfolded him, then thrust a cigarette to his lips and lit it. Rick took a long drag, and dropped the butt. Cursing, one of them picked it up and put it back in his mouth. The squad sergeant instructed his men where to aim, as if they had never done this before. A ray of hope? Maybe they would revolt against this injustice, shooting their commander, then cutting his bonds and freeing him. Sweat gushed from his head and brow, dripping beneath the blindfold, stinging his eyes. He spat the cigarette from his mouth. No sign yet of the anticipated mutiny, then came the sound of rifle bolts being activated.

He thought of something he had once read about a man wrongly accused of a crime, being convicted, and dragged before a firing squad. The man had felt terror, then calmed by the realization that, for the time it took to pull the trigger, the hammer to strike the bullet and activate the powder, start the bullet into motion, the bullet to pass through space, then strike his vital organs, he still possessed immortality.

"Alto!" Captain Diaz-Ball strode into the courtyard. "Release the prisoner." The firing squad looked at Rick, then at their officer. "Blaine, you live a charmed life. Your compadre Sr. Navarro has agreed to tell us what we have asked of him in exchange for your freedom. When we have heard him correctly you will be free to go."

Rick was totally speechless at this gesture. He slumped in the blood of the courtyard bowing his head. A few hours later he walked out of the Spanish jail, a free man who knew he had just become a condemned man. He had to contact Capa now.

CHAPTER TWENTY-NINE

Escape

A military vehicle took Rick back to the Florida. He ripped off his filthy rags and took a long cold shower, the water embracing his aching body. He changed into a mono and lit a cigarette and poured himself a scotch. He sat for a few minutes and then picked up the phone and made a quick call to the desk and asked for Capa's room. There was a short silence, and then the line clicked, followed by the line ringing. Click? Is it possible they've tied in another line, a device for snooping? Capa's voice appeared, "Qien?"

"Mr. Capa, this is Paul Fischer. I'm the reporter from the Hearst organization?"

"Yes, what is your business?"

"I wish to talk to you about swimming the Ebro." This was a prearranged code between Capa and Rick in case of such a crisis.

"Oh yes, what do you want to know? I am dry now, so the story is slowly fading from my memory."

"Well, in that case shall we meet in the usual place?"

"Certainly, give me 45 minutes and I'll be there. Ciao."

They would meet in the shattered laboratory in University City to finalize their underground journey to Barcelona, then on to France. There was little time to spare, for the GPU would be hot on their trail, ready to expose them to a skittish populace who saw fifth column traitors in every face, friend or stranger. Wouldn't the Comintern gang love it, a respected member of the Internationals, an American and a French photographer as traitors? No one but our brave Russian comrades can be trusted would be the party line, everyone else is weak and perfidious, the American and the Judas Jew selling out to the fascists.

He packed a few items in an old knapsack: a couple of tins of beef, his hunting knife, a bottle of red wine, passport, a French dictionary, and extra ammo for his pistol. Not enough provisions, but enough to see them through the first days of their escape.

The sun was setting over Mt. Garibaltis as he tight roped through the bustling streets, people hurrying to their diverse destinations: work, drink, mistresses, with the war on the edge of every mind.

The stench of death and garbage was everywhere. Rick saw the dead dogs and cats littering the streets; even an occasional horse's corpse. "Funny," he thought, "You'd think they'd be eating the dead horses."

Every other block he changed sides of the street, looking around furtively for any sign of being tailed. Everyone looked suspicious yet commonplace. There was no shelling tonight, no bombers threatened overhead, yet the city was already preparing for another blacked-out evening. He missed all the glass storefronts; they were now boards and corrugated tin, their glass long since history.

A large rat interrupted his musings, scurrying across the littered street. "Do I know this rat? Could it be the rat I met in prison? My doppelganger? What's his mission today?" He identified with the hated rodent realizing they were of the same genus today, both hated, pursued, and vilified. He wondered if the rat, the king of survival, felt justified, triumphant.

The wreckage of University City materialized, erasing his reverie. He found the lab building, no one in sight. On entering the building he waited in an anteroom that gave him a full view of the entrance without being seen himself.

He took his pistol from his holster. The minutes passed like hours still Capa did not come. Then, footsteps, more than one person. What now? A hatted, leather over coated figure loomed in the doorway. Not Capa. A curse in a heavy accent. Russian? Then another voice, same accent. Definitely Russian.

Rick aimed his pistol at the first person, waiting for the other to enter. How had he missed these two? No time to worry about that now, he had to take action. Two shots for the GPU, three more for any others, one for himself. He placed both hands on the weapon to steady it. The first overcoat was joined by the second; both had weapons in their hands. Rick aimed at the second man and slowly squeezed the trigger. The gun popped and the man dropped silently forward, pushing his companion down, forcing his gun down. Rick fired two quick shots at him as he fell, this one, too, crumpled silently to the ground. Rick bent down to look at them, heard a sound and swung his weapon towards the door.

"Rick, it's Capa!"

Rick lowered his weapon, saying, "Quick, give me a hand! He quickly searched both bodies: weapons, change, pen knives, nothing else. The absence of papers on both bodies was evidence enough of their pedigree. They dragged the bodies into the anteroom and covered them with rubble. They then left the building, heading in the direction of the river where two motorcycles were waiting. The password "Ste. Pilar" satisfied the man guarding the bikes, and he handed them each a packet that held their papers of passage. They kick-started the captured cycles and roared off into the darkness, headlights off.

They drove through the night, finally stopping just as dawn kissed the frosty mountains on the Madrid-Barcelona highway. Rick was amazed that they had encountered no roadblocks or vehicular traffic of any kind. Either the GPU had not yet found the bodies of its operatives, or they assumed that the fugitives were hiding somewhere in Madrid. They pulled their bikes off the road, covered them with brush, and then leaned against some rocks waiting for sunrise. They planned to hide out most of the day, and then resume their journey at sunset.

From his hiding place they saw trucks loaded with munitions, military gear, and men rumbling by in both directions, some bore red crosses, but contained boxes of munitions rather than wounded. Bored, Rick allowed his mind to wander, soon he was asleep. He dreamed that he and Greta were picnicking by the Mediterranean, swimming and playing in the waves, but as he reached for her to embrace her, he was awakened. Capa was snoring softly, his head lolling on his shoulder. Two P.M. No traffic now, only the distant drone of an airplane, and a few howitzer blasts, so far away they sounded like champagne corks.

He realized he was thirsty, and, reached for his briefcase, took out the bottle of Rioja, opened it and drank deeply. He opened the tinned beef and carved out a chunk with his knife. Capa blinked awake at the smell of the beef and wine and joined Rick. When they were finished, Capa asked for coffee and cognac. Rick chuckled and threw him the wine cork. "Go and make us some, I'm in the mood myself. Capa threw the cork back at him, and they both laughed.

Their revelry was suddenly ended by the muffler blast of several motorcycles. Rick and Capa dropped to their bellies and watched as the group passed. "Think they're looking for us?"

"I don't know," replied Rick, "but it wouldn't surprise me." They watched as the cycles roared by, the goggled men in their long, dark brown leather overcoats seemed to intimidate the roadway before them. In a flash they were gone, but in the thin air, the low drone of their engines lasted several minutes. The two fugitives sat up and looked up and down the highway.

It was now late afternoon, the shadows played across the highway as the light receded into dusk. The stark, brown hills were an alien scape of rocks and scrub smelling of sage and pine tar.

Rick said, "This Spain is a land where God is either revered and reviled. If we really knew God was not with us or the other guy, maybe it would be easier to resolve conflict without carrying God's righteousness into armed disasters." Capa was already dozing.

Later in the night Capa awakened with a snort, and said, "Is it time we started?"

Rick shook his head and pointed towards the north. "There's a bunch of trucks up there, I've been watching the headlights. I think they're out looking for us ready to do us in on the spot. We've got to wait until we decide what they're doing. If they're setting up a small base camp, we can ride our bikes north for a few miles, and push them at the point where they might have sentries out, start 'em up and blast north before they know what hit them.

Capa replied, "On the other hand, if I were in charge, I would have two outposts, then when we got by the first, the second would be alerted and we would be dead ducks, trapped between the two, with the mountains on our left and the valley on our right. I think we should abandon the bikes and start climbing the mountains 'til we get past the ambush. We should be able to find some way to get transportation from there, even if we have to swipe something."

Neither man relished the idea of walking, but Rick recognized the wisdom in Capa's plan. They pushed their bikes to a rocky outcrop, lay them down behind it and covered them with branches and weeds. "Well, Rick, what's the route. I hate walking, and I'm afraid of heights, so you lead and catch me if I fall."

Rick was amused but said nothing. He wanted a cigarette, but knew even the flare of a match could be seen for a long way in the darkness. Instead, he picked his way up the rock-cluttered mountainside with Capa close behind. They traveled in silence for more than an hour until they saw the lights of several campfires. "That's them," hissed Rick. "Be careful, one rock down the hill and it's curtains for both of us." Capa nodded his assent.

They moved carefully along the rocky trail. Soon they could hear the voices of the men below talking rapidly in Spanish, but couldn't decipher it, some of it sounding like the usual grumbling of the discomfited soldier. Patiently, soundlessly, they made their way past the encampment until they heard no more voices.

They picked up the pace; the moon was now high and bright in the sky. Capa started to speak, but Rick held up his hand, then half-pushed Capa down on the ground. Rick had heard the clanking of metal on metal, then the low tones of male voices. A patrol? He strained his eyes at the path ahead, then heard the curse of a man uncomfortable in his work. He looked down-slope and watched as four figures emerged from the darkness. They were lurching in single file and were apparently looking for the trail. They moved on until he could no longer hear them, then Rick tugged Capa's arm and pointed forward. They walked about five more minutes when they saw the campfires of another patrol, but well below their position.

Moving quickly, they soon felt themselves out of danger. As the first light of dawn came, they were on the outskirts of a small villa. A dog barked, then another, followed by the ridiculous crowing of a hardy rooster, Rick said, "Capa, look for a vehicle we can steal."

They didn't have long to wait. A Fiat sedan beckoned to them from the drive of a small, well-kept cottage, its black paint still shiny despite its vintage years. Capa stood guard while Rick crept up to the vehicle and looked inside. No keys, but cross wiring would be a snap. He checked the mechanical fuel gage, more than half-full.

He looked about the cottage grounds and spied a larger house. Telephone wires. They'd have to cut them. He looked for a central pole that would be the target for any of the electricals to the house, finally spotting it further down a long driveway. He crouched down and zigzagged back to Capa. "I want you to climb that pole down there and cut those wires while I get this thing started," said Rick.

Capa raced furtively down the long drive to the pole and began to clamber up it, a knife between his teeth, looking for all like a modern buccaneer scaling the mast of a Spanish galleon. Rick carefully opened the door of the Fiat and ducked below the dashboard. He grabbed the two ignition wires, and, used his knife to strip off the insulation. He heard a ferocious growl and saw a large mastiff racing straight for him, not barking, just a whining growl. Rick shoved his knife straight ahead as he covered his face with the opposite forearm.

The dog hurled himself straight into the blade, knocking Rick back against the steering wheel. The animal yelped, then convulsed, his gore gushing over Rick's arms and chest. Rick gagged and pushed the dead beast away.

Capa ran up with gun drawn and climbed into the passenger side. "Quite a mess here, Rick!" He watched as Rick crossed the wires, the Fiat roared alive, and they drove down the long road to the highway.

"I cut every wire I could find on that pole," said Capa. "Do you think they heard us leave?"

"If they didn't, they must be deaf! I just hope they don't have any other way to contact the militia 'cause if they do, we are in deep, deep trouble." Rick drove with his knees as he lit a cigarette.

"How come you never cough from those things?"

"Capa, there's nothing left to cough out," said Rick. "Someday, somebody's going to find out these things kill people, then what will I do? Probably nothing, besides, if we make it out of here it will be proof enough of my immortality." Both men laughed.

They drove for hours in silence until Rick saw a stone kilometer marker ahead. He slowed down to check it. "30 kilometers to Barcelona. I think we'll dump this thing now and wait 'til night, then walk into the city. In a few K's we're going to find roadblocks we can't handle."

Capa agreed, so Rick drove the Fiat into a old rutted road into some trees, put it into neutral and pushed it down into a deep ditch.

Capa in front, they climbed a small cliff that gave them protection yet a commanding view of the countryside. Rick looked back at the area they had just covered but saw no movement, no planes, no cloud of dust. "I just can't believe it's this easy," he said to himself, "what's going on?" There was apparently no available answer; at least none came forth.

At dusk they resumed their pace towards Barcelona, avoiding any villages that they might see at a distance. Once a small airplane buzzed high and to their left, but they were well hidden before the pilot could possibly see them. They walked well into the night, oblivious to any thought of capture or danger, for they believed themselves too close to freedom to be vulnerable.

They discarded their packs, hid their pistols and some ammo in their bulky jackets, and prepared to walk into the city. Their fabricated ID's identified them as members of the German Thaelmann Brigade, since both men were fluent in German.

Sunrise came as they walked into the factory district of the city, half-destroyed by fascist bombing. Sasha had given them names of people who would provide safe houses for them, Jews who had fled the rising terror in Germany and the countries of Easter Europe. Wasn't it an irony that their lives would be in greater danger here in beautiful Barcelona? Rick thought of Sasha, said a silent prayer for the safety of this gentle man, a man who had already suffered far too much.

They walked down the Ramblas, the great boulevard that bisects the city, and serves as the main mercantiling and banking district of Barcelona. Hopefully there would be safety in the anonymity of numbers. The two men sat at an outdoor café and feigned interest in the daily newspaper, while their eyes danced from the page to the crowd, hoping to see nothing, but looking for the thuggish faces of the GPU.

Posters were everywhere, the walls of buildings dripped with the scrawled graffiti of political cant. "La Tiera Es Vuestra!" "Fosig, de Cara A La Guerra." "Un Barracho Es Un Parasito. Eliminemisle!" A large poster appealed to Rick's artistic sense, a cartoon man with a huge biceps, captioned, "Aidez L'Espagne."

A group of about 20 men paraded down the center of the street, blocking traffic, carried a banner proclaiming "No mas POUM! No mas POUM!" Capa said, "Looks like the POUM is in real trouble here. I think the Comintern is out to discredit all the Trotskyites then take control. Tell you Rick, there's real trouble here. I want out and soon! These people are turning on themselves like cannibals, and I don't think you'd have to guess who'll end up with the fattest gut!"

"Think you're right, Capa, but we can't afford to travel out of here without help. We'll go the Sasha's friends tonight and put ourselves in their hands. Hopefully we'll get on a boat and bypass the border. We don't stand a chance on land."

Capa nodded and went back to his paper. At two P.M., they walked briskly down the Ramblas to a new building designed by one of Spain's most famous architects, Gaudi. The building was chosen because its unique design could not be mistaken for any other. Across the street, smoke poured from a building while men were tearing down a large sign, which read, "Solidaridad Obrera Diario de la Revolucion." Capa pointed, saying, "That's the headquarters of the Anarchist newspaper and it looks like they're burning them out. My God, the irony! People like me belong in monasteries, where the mysteries of life can be explored free of the realities."

He turned towards the building that they sought, and saw a curvilinear facade with fanciful wrought-iron balconies following the undulations, looking more like a large habitat for The Seven Dwarfs or elves than living space for ordinary people. Rick grabbed reluctant Capa's arm, while sensing his need to photograph yet another episode in the death of an ideal. Capa turned towards the whimsical address and gaped at the eccentric landmark. "Funny looking place, but another great picture. Damn it Rick, I'm missing shots of things that need to be seen by the world. The Condor Legion could easily turn this place to powder tomorrow with one 500 pounder."

"Yeah, pal, and the GPU could turn you into jelly in three hours if they catch you. Let's get inside and find our contact."

They entered the building. Sasha had told them to look for apartment 47. They found the name and rang the bell underneath that box, then walked to a small waiting area. Capa took out his handkerchief and wiped his brow, while Rick picked up a newspaper. A well-dressed, middle-aged man walked into the lobby, glanced at them, then walked to the stairwell and disappeared. Capa put his handkerchief into his jacket pocket, but allowed half of it to dangle out while and slouched low in the chair, covering his face with the paper.

Another man emerged from the stairwell and walked rapidly towards them, stopped a few feet from Capa, whispered in a language Rick didn't understand, Hebrew? He then walked from the building. Capa turned and said, "Follow me, and don't say anything." He half-trotted to the stairwell, held the door for Rick, and then bolted up the stairs. They ran up four flights, two steps at a time, arriving breathless at the stairwell door. Capa then cautiously opened the door and looked both ways, then moved into the hallway stopping at number 47. The door opened abruptly and a man with a machine pistol indicating they should enter by silently waving the barrel.

There were four other men in the room, each brandishing a machine pistol. Rick tightened, what the hell is going on? They indicated that the two men sit, and they quickly obliged. One of them walked up to Capa and extended his hand, speaking in a Slavic language. Was it Hungarian? Capa nodded and took something from his wallet. The man studied it, embraced Capa, then extended his hand to Rick, saying, "Andrei Voznesky."

Rick took the man's hand and replied, "Blaine, Rick Blaine. You guys have an interesting way of saying hello. You guys on the lam or what?"

Voznesky explained, "There's anarchy in the streets, brother against brother, ideologue against ideologue. We trust no one, because without identities, you're just another enemy. The people are cold, half-starved, exhausted, and they'd kill their mothers for bread and a bed. Half the city has been destroyed by the bombs the other half is threatened by gangs of Stalin's thugs. I apologize for the seeming lack of hospitality."

"Which side are you fellows on?" Rick asked.

"We supported Trotsky in Russia and had to leave when Stalin's purges started. Here also we are Trotskyites, and so they try to purge us here. The POUM is our party, a Spanish Leninist group supporting Trotsky; we've fought long and hard for the Popular Front. The Communists want complete control of the revolution. This means we, the Anarchists, the Socialists, anyone not a Communist go."

He drew back his shoulders and walked to the window. "See it burn. I've watched the Czar's Cossacks torch my village, now the flames have followed me here. I can and will go no further. I will fight them here, and when we win, I will go to Palestine and fight the British. I want a home and a homeland, and I'll fight to my death to get it!" He blinked back tears, then looked around the room. "My comrades feel the same way. There is no other way for us."

Rick nodded, then retorted, "We're running, but not for the same reasons. Can you help us get to France without getting caught?"

Vasilov answered. "We'll get you out of here tonight, but first let's all have something to eat."

The others laughed, for the pickings were apparently slim. When Vasilov brought out bread, a tin of beef, and a large tin of peas, plus a large jug of red wine, Rick realized how hungry he was. Vasilov heated the tins over a gas flame on the little stove, and then dumped the contents onto plates. The men ate hungrily, passing the jug for each to swig.

"So you're Internationals," said one of the men, a fox-face fellow of indeterminate age, a scar splitting the upper lid of his right eye. "We watched your comrades march down the Ramblas a few days ago, the Comintern decided that they had done their share and told them to withdraw. Know why? I'll tell you. They don't want these mensch to carry the truth about the war back to their homelands. The Comintern wants them to return to their origins infected, bloated with their brand of virulence. Stalin is brilliant. He got all the gold in Spain, now he'll strangle his willing hosts, the Fascists will win, and he'll turn to fight the Germans."

"But what of the people in Spain?" Rick asked.

"The Spanish brand of communism will no longer be a threat to the Soviets, so that the only party line will be the word from Moscow. He will assassinate Trotsky, as well as anyone else he perceives to be his enemy, so that dissent will disappear, leaving one party, one message. He's killed virtually all who made the Revolution succeed."

Voznesky broke in, "What news of Isaiah Navarro?"

When Rick told the men of Navarro's fate, Vasilov began chanting the Prayer of the Dead, and the others, including Capa, joined in. Rick was fascinated by the sense of unity, the continuity with those long past. When the chanting stopped, the singularity disappeared as quickly as it started, the men were just the shabby group they had been before, but the fire of the Capala still burned in their eyes. Three thousand years of shaping and burnishing, untold episodes of countless auto-de-fe meant to erase, but serving only to imprint in the arcane genetic message.

Rick stood up and walked slowly to the window, noting the slight jerk of Sergei's automatic pistol. Funny how you don't get over the reflexes of warfare and terrorism.

There was a singular absence of motor vehicles on the Ramblas except for ambulances, which thundered in, around, and occasionally over, the myriad of horse drawn carriages and drays with little Spanish horses straining under their heavy loads. Two large Suizis roared in the direction of the wharves flying POUM banners, mattresses barricading their roofs, apparently pursued by an armored personnel vehicle that could not keep the pace. Rick wondered why they didn't fire. He turned to sit, and found the others looking at him. They had been watching to see if he made an attempt to signal potential hostile comrades, but were satisfied that he had not.

The sun sank red over a city in flames, smoldering shadows oscillated in the changing light,

Abruptly the Jews picked up their weapons and looked towards the door. Rick had heard nothing, but he recognized his own loss of control in this situation. He was a product, waiting to be delivered to the named destination.

Vasily opened the door a crack, the others had moved to different points in the room, points that offered a withering and directed field of fire.

Vasily then threw the door open and let out a low oath and dragged a short, squat older man with a rabbi's beard into the room. Rick felt the name escape his own lungs, "Sasha!" The old Jew had made it! He had escaped to his Barcelona; he could escape with them to Paris! Capa, too, seemed overjoyed. "You must come with us to Paris."

"Rick, your friendship is important but the work here is more so. But thank you my friend" They all embraced and shed some furtive tears.

After the emotions receded, Voznesky described the escape plan. "This will be simple, but dangerous, We will make our way to the wharves, find the French freighter, "L'Etoile Rouge," You will board it with the crew and show your forged seamen's papers to the Captain, then go below and await departure. Once at sea, you'll be safe from everything.

Sergei went to a closet and brought out their seamen's black outfits, rugged, coarse woolen trousers, heavy grease-wool sweaters, and the classic watch cap. Rick tried on his heavy ankle-high deck shoes and laughed, as he was almost able to turn around in them. Capa had smaller feet, as did Sasha, so Rick walked about the room affected a "little tramp" walk. Everyone chuckled as the tension level in the room dropped perceptibly.

An hour after sunset, they left the building in groups of two, Capa accompanying Rick. They followed Voznesky down an alley into an ancient building, then waited for all to arrive. They went down a narrow passageway that stank of urine and the centuries, down a crumbling wooden stairway into a dank, dirt-floored basement. Sergei lit a flashlight and pointed towards the wall. Rick could barely make out a rough stone facade, with one large stone missing. "This is our rat-hole," he said. "He walked to the wall and pulled on one of the stones, opening a faux door large enough for a man to crawl through. "Positively medieval," thought Rick.

Voznesky crawled through first and lit another flashlight. Rick crawled through and stood up with Voznesky in a narrow passageway. The group snaked their way wordlessly for what seemed a half-hour. Voznesky suddenly held up his hand, handed the light to Rick, and began to grope at the wall. Another door opened and they passed through it into a small basement room much like the first one. When all of them were assembled, Sergei explained to Rick, "These passageways were the only way our Jewish ancestors could hold their Sanhedrins and other meetings without attack from their enemies."

Noticing the sand on the floor, Rick asked, "What's the sand all about?"

"It's a reminder of our peoples' 40 years in the desert. And, from a practical point, it muffles sound so the services would not be heard above. We seldom use this area now, but we know we can fall back on it in an emergency. We will now go up and enter the world of today. The streets will be crowded and, if we're lucky, allow us to get to the wharves without suspicion." They climbed the stairs, slipped out the door one at a time, and joined the hoi polloi milling in the streets.

They walked for almost an hour before they reached the port district. There were people everywhere, mostly seamen and stevedores. They passed along wharves, devastated by the bombing. No blackout restrictions were in effect so that they could easily see the half-sunken vessels listing in the harbor.

The wharves and debris-cluttered streets leading to them were also glutted with refugees seeking passage on any kind of vessel. Franco had promised that those who would embrace the "The Anti-Christs" would pay with their lives.

The tumult and turmoil of the crowds made it easier for them to avoid recognition. They found the ship, climbed the gangplank, and waited.

Hours later, Marseilles lay before them, a misted gem rising from the blue of the Mediterranean. Rick marveled at the offshore beauty of this city of international crime, drug smuggling, intrigues of a thousand faces, and now, a haven for the refugees of a shattered Spain. He wondered vaguely how long it would be before the Nazis controlled the Riviera.

Once ashore, it was a simple cab ride to the railroad station, destination Paris.

CHAPTER THIRTY

Paris

The train bearing Capa and Rick entered a Paris still unchanged by the threat of war. Rick gazed out the window at the glowing City of Light, watching as the rising sun changed the slate roofs from blue to gray to gold.

But Rick's thoughts were of Sam. Where would they look, could they find him? As the train huffed into the Gare d' Orsay Rick turned to Capa and voiced his concerns. "Where in hell do we look for Sam?"

Capa shook his head, saying "We'll find him if he's here. Right now we need decent clothes and a place to stay." He gestured down at the shabby clothes he wore. "This is the fashion capitol of the world you know."

Rick said, "My first job is to contact the Banque Credit Suisse and get us some dough." The bank was where Rick's assets were deposited. They agreed that Capa would check out the clothing stores, and then meet Rick at the bank.

The two men rose stiffly as the train came to a jerky stop, and then walked down onto the platform. The hall was an immense gallery with a fenestrated glass dome high above. They walked swiftly to the steps and up the beautiful wrought iron staircase into the main lobby. After the train smoke the smell of strong coffee and fresh baked croissants made him glad that breakfast was waiting. After the shabby Marseilles station he was awed by the beauty of this architecture.

Rick took out his Swiss bankcard and asked Capa where it was. "Oh, that's close to here, on the Rue d'Lille." He gave Rick the directions and then took off for the closest Parisian tailor shop. Rick walked the other way, his first stroll in Paris since his student days. He looked into the windows of the shops, cafes, and patisseries. It was May in Paris and the narrow streets were crowded Small trucks, cars, and pushcarts glutted the cobblestoned streets. The sounds reminded him of New York and the lower east side. He inhaled the smell of baking pastries, the metallic odor of red meats and sausages. His nostrils flared as he passed a poissonerie and its own peculiar odors. He turned left and then saw the Credit Suisse building.

Rick entered the bank, found the administrative section and asked a young, bored looking receptionist for an appointment with one of the bank's officers. She turned in her chair and scanned the ten or so desks lined up behind her. She beckoned to an effete looking young man with a high collar and a morning coat. He wore a delicate pince-nez with a velvet string that disappeared beneath the coat. He tucked his fleshy chin slightly giving him a piscine look, as he peered over the lenses to eye with hauteur the bearded, ill-dressed, haggard young man. Rick strode to the desk where The Fish sat waiting. Rick said, "My name is Richard Blaine and I have an account at this bank." He handed his Credit Suisse ID card to The Fish.

The clerk checked it carefully, looking from the page to Rick and then back to the page. "You've changed very much, Monsieur. How else can you verify your identity?" He looked as if he had just swallowed a bad oyster.

"Don't fool with me, you know damn well I don't need other identification! Take me to your superior. The man stood up, coughed, and then disappeared into a hallway. Rick sat down and looked around the bank. The clerks quickly diverted their eyes as Rick stared back at them.

The Fish returned in a few minutes, suddenly obsequious, and invited Rick to follow him. They entered a room with a large table desk and a tall, fortyish red haired man standing behind it. His face was pale, slimly austere, with a few crow's-feet around the amber eyes. The bank manager said, "I am Monsieur Sagan. The bank is at your disposal." Sagan exuded confidence.

"I want to withdraw 50,000 francs from my account and deposit it in a checking account here. I want immediate access to the money, and I don't want to have to deal with him. He jerked his elbow at the Fish. I also need some personal information from you."

"You are dismissed, Monsieur LaBelle, return to your desk." Sagan turned back to Rick as LaBelle cringed from the office. "Now, Monsieur Blaine, what else can I do for you?"

"I'm looking for a man named Sam Jefferson, a black man, an entertainer, someone who may be an illegal. I need your advice on how to locate such a man."

"Ah, Monsieur Blaine, there are many such people in Paris today. They come from all over Europe and North Africa. A Moor can hide in the black districts for years without being found. May I ask, Monsieur, why do you seek this man?"

"He' an old friend. We had a club in Ethiopia, then I went to Spain and he came here. I'd like to have him play piano and sing at another place I hope to open."

"You were in Spain?" He covered his mouth and coughed nervously. "Ah, what was your business in Spain?"

"I helped lose the war."

"So, you were an International?"

"Yeah, I was with the Lincoln Brigade."

"Monsieur, your request for an account is granted, anything I can do to expedite your plans I will do. And I shall help you find your friend. My brother was an International, but not so lucky as you. He drowned in a river called The Ebro." The man's eyes filled with tears.

"I know it well, I almost bought it there myself. Where do we start?"

"As a banker I have contacts in most arrondissements, and in most police stations," Sagan said. "Such a man as you seek will be known by someone they know. I shall contact the appropriate persons, and when there is information I'll contact you at your hotel. Please leave the name of it with my girl" The two men shook hands and Rick left the office, but not without feeling the murderous stare of Monsieur LaBelle.

Capa was waiting in the lobby. "Rick, I've found a hotel for us but let's buy our clothes first." He led Rick down the Rue d'Lille, turned left then walked to the middle of the block. He turned to Rick and said, "That's our man." Rick saw a sign that announced, 'Habiliment por l'Homme.' The clothier had a fine selection of suits, jackets and trousers, all British or Italian woolens. Rick picked out a navy blue three piece suit, a pair of dark brown trousers, three shirts, several pairs of socks, two pairs of shoes and two ties. Capa bought a dark blue jacket and contrasting slacks. Both bought a pair of black oxfords.

An old Citroen cab rattled up to the curb, looking more like a tin outhouse than a car. As they climbed in, Rick smelled cheap perfume. Capa said, "Hotel Bonaparte." Rick told Capa about Monsieur Sagan's offer of help. Capa said, "That's terrific, Rick. I, too, know something of Paris and I have friends who can join in the search." Rick looked out the window at the narrow streets and the celebration that was the Latin Quarter.

The cab pulled up to the Hotel Bonaparte. Capa paid the driver and the two men walked into a lobby that was old, small and smelled of cooked cabbage. Capa asked the concierge to hold their bags until they returned from a walk.

As they walked down the Rue Bonaparte Rick turned to Capa and said, "Sam is such a sucker for anyone who needs anything, and I just hope he hasn't been taken advantage of by anyone, or had something lousy happen to him."

"Don't be so morbid, Rick, we're bound to find him. Let's have a drink and talk about it." The two confreres walked on through the streets of a sun drenched Paris. They stopped at an outdoor café, its gay sailcloth awning bright against the afternoon light. Capa ordered Pernod and water for both of them. Rick lit a cigarette and thought again of Madrid. Capa looked at his friend pensively, allowing him his private reverie. Finally, Rick drew up his shoulders, snuffed out his butt, and smiled at Capa. "Well pal, we made it out but I can't stop thinking about the ones that didn't make, won't make it, and can't make it. I don't really know if we wasted our time, but I can tell you I'd do it again. Capa stood up and held out his glass, Rick stood to join him. They drained their drinks and walked back to the hotel.

"Bonaparte. Great name for a hotel," thought Rick. "The Spanish, for all the machismo, can laugh at themselves while the French are just pompous. Everything they do seems to put them on the line.

They checked in at the desk where the clerk asked for their passports. Rick waited as Capa talked to the clerk in rapid French. "Give him your passport, Rick."

The clerk said, "Monsieur Blaine?" Rick nodded. "I have a message for you." He thrust a piece of hotel paper at him and strutted away to some greater destiny. Rick unfolded the paper. "Msr. Blaine. La Moulin Blanche might prove interesting to you. The Creole entertainment is excellent. Your servant, Sagan."

Rick was exultant as he showed the message to Capa. "This may be it, Capa!" They hurried to a grilled metal structure labeled "L'ACCENSEUR" and rode the wheezing canary cage to their floor. Their "suite" was papered in a garish floral pattern, with equally garish lampshades. A faux fireplace beckoned uncertainly, fearing any attempt at fire starting in the chimneyless chamber. By paying dearly, they enjoyed their own "cabinet de toilette," with the omnipresent bidet looming white against the jungled wall.

Rick plopped down on a wildly floral sofa and looked through 'Paris-soir' for the nightclub listings. "Here it is, Capa! The Moulin Blanche in the Latin Quarter, Rue de la Huchette. Finest entertainment from America featuring 'Le Jazz' by the men who do it best. What is this, why don't they just say black?"

"Hold on Blaine, they don't have to. Paris is not New York, all blacks are welcome here. Josephine Baker had been the toast of Paris since 1928 but she couldn't get a job in your St. Louis."

Rick nodded sheepishly. "That's right, I'm out of line, I just get sick of pussy-footing around with words. C'mon, let's change, grab a bite, and charge the Quarter."

Capa laughed. "Slow down man, you can't eat 'til nine, and the quarter doesn't light up much before midnight. How about a drink here, a nap, and then dinner when we're ready. If Sam is there, he'll be there. If he isn't, we'll find him somewhere else." He patted Rick on the shoulder and went to the cabinet and pulled out a bottle of Scotch. Rick into the sofa and closed his eyes. Sleep came before Capa could hand him his glass.

Rick awakened to the sound of splashing water, and his mind's eye saw the muddy Ebro surging towards the sea, carrying his dreams away to the sea. Before his image was complete, Capa's voice rang out. "Get up you dreamer! It's time to search for the Blackamoor!" Rick chuckled in spite of himself.

"I'm glad you're going to be clean tonight. If we find

Sam, I want you to make a good impression on him. He thinks in terms of cleanliness and morality. Since I question the latter, we'll concentrate on the clean part."

"You should talk, you've smelled like a Roquefort cave ever since Madrid." Capa was jovial.

"Yes, but you forget that I purposefully rode behind you to be downwind while you were killing the flowers along the roadside. It takes more than one bath when you haven't had one for six months."

"I'm looking forward to you bathing next, Rick. The hot water should be just about gone! Salud! Rick groaned at the thought of an icy tub but the water was still warm and welcoming.

They dressed in their new finery and took the l'ascenseur to the lobby. Rick again checked with the concierge for messages, but there were none. They stepped out into the Parisian twilight and hailed a cab. "Le Moulin Blanche."

The driver responded in French. "Oui Messieurs, but are you going for the show?"

"Oui," answered Capa, "Why do you ask?"

"Sorry to tell you that the show is cancelled tonight, something about the piano player and the police." Capa translated to Rick. "Ask him what happened to the piano player?"

Capa asked the driver and he replied, "Please, I do not know." He's upset with your American manners, and is sorry that Lafayette ever won your revolution for you." Both men laughed, but the spasms in Rick's gut mounted again.

Fifteen minutes later they arrived at the club. The place was half-full, men and women in stylish clothing listening to a Creole woman singing a blues tune. "Small Hotel," Rick remembered. They found the maitre'd and Capa asked him about the piano player. "Oh Monsieur, it is nothing. He often forgets to carry his Cabaret papers with him so the police finally took him to the prefecture for a conversation. You know how these Moors are." He winked at Rick and asked if he wanted a table. Then he asked, "What's his name, your piano player?"

"Sam, ah, Sam Jefferson." relied Capa.

"But this Sam is last-named Blaine." The maitre'd smiled.

"You're joking, you're pulling my leg!" Rick hurried over to a garishly dressed young woman trying to look like Dietrich but not pulling it off. She smiled at him and asked him in English if he wanted to dance.

Rick asked her, "What's the name of the piano player here? Do you know where they took him?"

"But Monsieur I have only come to dance." She turned as if to go but Rick grabbed her arm and thrust a wad of bills into her hand.

"Dance with me then." She tucked the money into her ample bosom and smiled up at him. "You Americans are so good at talking business while you dance."

"Then you do know Sam?"

"Monsieur, anyone who comes to this club knows him. He is the best jazz pianist in the quarter. Do you know this Sam? Have you come to hire him away?" She smiled seductively at Rick and pulled him close.

"Listen sweetheart, I've got more francs if you can remember where the police took him. Is he in jail?"

"The money, Monsieur?" Rick pulled out a smaller wad of bills and showed them to her. "Merci." Her smile was a small, greedy wince. "They have taken him to the central station because the Americans have expressed interest in his case. They say he may be a dangerous criminal!"

Rick walked over to Capa. "Let's go, I think Sam's in real trouble!" They hurried outside and found a cab at the curb. "Prefect of Police on the rue d' St. Jacques, hurry," commanded Capa. As they clattered through the traffic, the driver cursing and shaking his fist at his vehicular and ambulatory adversaries. Additional epithets were directed towards the cobbled roadway. They arrived at the Prefect of Police building without damage, paid the driver and ran up the steps and into the building. Capa asked for information, the uniformed guard shuffled through a sheaf of papers, then looked at his logbook. "Ah, oui, here it is. It is the third floor, room 2189, but you will have to take the stairs, l'ascenseur is temporarily disabled." He looked up at Capa and Rick with curiosity. "Why do you seek the American Moor?"

"Old friends," shouted Capa over his shoulder as they dashed to the marble stairs and up to the third level. They walked onto the third level, looking for 2189. All the doors had metal grates on the outside, with no windows, making the hall ghostly in the dim light. The smell of tobacco was almost overwhelming, even to Rick. They found the room and knocked on the door. "Entre!" came the reply.

Capa opened the door to a small office, an anteroom of sorts. A large florid faced man with a string bow tie, shaven head, and tight fitting suit looked up at them. "Oui?" An insouciant cigarette dangled from his down-turned lips, his eyes were thick-lidded and reptilian. Rick walked to the desk, asking the cop if he spoke English. The man replied, "Oui."

Rick said, "I'm looking for a black man, an American named Sam Jefferson. Can you help?"

"Monsieur, why would I want to help you find anyone?"

Rick held back his anger, and responded, "Because I've asked you for information about a friend of mine, a man whose character I can vouch for."

"Character, Monsieur, is like beauty and the beholder. Your friend is an illegal alien here; furthermore, he is a criminal in your country. Can you vouch for that? Monsieur, I need to know your name, I demand your papers as well as your friend's there, and then we can talk about the Moor Jefferson." He held out his hand as Rick and Capa took out their papers. He looked at them carefully, then at his logbook. "So, you're both back from Spain. Which side were you on, not that it makes any difference here."

"I was in the International Brigades, and Msr. Capa was a non-aligned photographer?

"A photographer? You mean a photojournalist?" He looked again at Capa's papers and passport. "Capa? Not the man who took the picture of the falling soldier?"

"Oui, I am that man."

"Ah, Monsieur Capa, you are an artiste! I have seen all of the photos you have taken in the Paris papers. I am what you would call an amateur, but you have given me much hope for my work. Is this Moor a friend of yours, too?"

"But of course, why else would I be here? This Sam Jefferson is a close friend of Monsieur Blaine's and mine. We want to be sure that his case be handled fairly. Can you help us with that?"

"Mr. Capa, I will do everything I can to help you. We do not really care about what the Americans want with this Moor; sometimes their embassy is a real pain in the ass. The Moor needs papers for France, and if you, a citizen, can vouch for him, we need only to give him a temporary Carte, and he is free."

Rick sighed with relief and disbelief. Imagine a country racked with an overwhelming bureaucracy issuing papers to a stranger on the basis of a few war pictures in `Le Mond.' The detective turned to him. "Monsieur Blaine, we have a few things to settle with you, too. Your embassy also seeks you for `capital crimes.'"

Rick lit a cigarette and looked directly at the detective. "I say it's a crock. They're mad at me for fighting against a fascist dictator because they didn't have the guts to make a choice.

"Be calm, Monsieur Blaine. No one is arresting you. Just let us know if you change hotels, that's all. If you stay in Paris, you have nothing to fear, nothing that is until the Boche get here."

"What makes you believe the Germans are coming?" questioned Capa.

"I firmly believe that the war will come soon to France. Whatever your business, best it be completed before they arrive." With that, he left the room.

Rick remained apprehensive, but Capa was overjoyed. "My God, Capa, you'd think Sam was your friend not mine. How can you be so positive you can trust these guys?"

"Because, Rick, I am French and this is Paris." He looked so prideful that Rick offered no more objections. The door opened, the burly detective emerged, a beatific smile on his face, making him look Buddha-like. Behind him came Sam.

Sam cried out when he saw Rick, rushed up to him and offered his clasped, manacled hands in an almost supplicative motion. Rick grabbed them and said, "Well pal, what the hell have you done now?"

Sam laughed then turned to the French policeman. "Monsieur DuBois, do you have the keys for these?" Rick held his breath. DuBois mumbled something in French and produced a key.

"Jefferson, you a lucky man to have such friends. You will be free as soon as they sign this paper, which makes them responsible for your comportment. You disappear, they pay," DuBois said. "I wouldn't advise that you try it, for if they found you so quickly the first time, they, or we, will find you again."

"I wouldn't think of it, Msr. DuBois," said Sam breathlessly.

"Let me tell you fellows something," offered DuBois. "When and if things in Paris go to hell I don't think the Boche will like your politics. If it comes to this, I would be sure I was out of here. Go to Algiers, Casablanca, or Lisbon. I would get my exit visa now. People like you will be the first to ride the boxcars to the camps." He then shook hands with the three men and handed them the papers to sign. "This may be the last good day I'll have for a long time. He smiled and left the room.

The happy trio left the building and headed for the nearest café for a celebratory drink. The evening was warm and dry, the air festive. They sat at a small table drinking champagne. Rick turned to Sam. "Tell me about your time here."

"When I got to Paris I found a job in the quarter. I started a group called 'The American Jazz Ensemble,' a bunch of American black performers, and we did OK," Sam said. "Lotsa people in the quarter had no papers especially the Algerians." Rick asked him, "Didn't the cops ever show up and check these spots out?"

Sam replied, "Sometimes they would make a quick sweep and close some places for a few days, then allow them to re-open. They was money changed hands plus the club owners kept a few goons around so us illegals would keep our noses clean."

Sam then asked Rick about Spain. He sensed immediately that he had stabbed his tongue into the center of whatever Rick was about.

Rick began. "When we left Ethiopia I felt like a bum. We really did nothing other than give Selassie a few outdated pieces of hardware. We helped Ferrari make a pile of dough on the coin switch and not a penny went to Selaiisse's army. I thought I could help make a difference in Spain. Zero. Nada. The politics took over and that was that. I found some real friends and they died for nothing. I fell in love twice and lost them both. My friend Capa was all I could salvage from this disaster. I'm burned out and burned up. All I want now is for us to start a club and try to forget this other mess. I need a new life."

Sam said. "Let's go back to The Moulin Blanche and check out the fun. Sounds to me like we should talk more about this stuff later." They all stood up and Sam hailed a taxi.

The club was full of revelers; the band was playing a jazz version of "Gaite Parisienne" while a Can-Can troupe flashed their long dark legs into the air. An unctuous maitre'd seated the trio at a premier table where they ordered more champagne. They talked about the coming war clouds and the possibility of a Nazi occupation. The dance troupe left the floor, as the band began to play a soft, lush jazz number. Rick lit a cigarette and thought of Greta, wondering how different his life would be if she were sitting at the table now. He thought of the others he had left behind, Dad, Mother, Gretchen, Jordan, and his former friends in 'The Cell.' How could he ever purge these thoughts from his mind? Did he want to?

Applause interrupted his daydreams as the crowd began clapping and chanting "Sam! Sam! Sam!" Sam stood up and walked directly to the piano. The room became quiet as he sat down to play. His fingers caressed the keys, playing a long ruffle of chords. He smiled into the crowd of faces and began to sing, softly. "You must remember this, a kiss is just a kiss, a sigh is just a sigh, the fundamental things apply as time goes by . . ." As he continued, Rick closed his eyes to the most beautiful love song he had heard in years. He opened them again, and saw a tall, beautiful woman walking languidly towards the piano. Sam looked up and smiled in recognition as he continued his performance. Rick could not take his eyes from this sad faced woman clinging to the piano with both hands as if it was a life raft, her lips moving with the words. He felt a surge of simpatico for this woman and whatever secrets she held in her heart.

Sam finished his song, bowed to the waves of applause, then took the woman's arm and led her to their table. He smiled at her, then at Rick as he said, "Mr. Richard Blaine, may I present Miss Ilsa Lund.

The End